WE LEAVE
TOGETHER

WE LEAVE TOGETHER

A DOGSLAND NOVEL

J. M. McDermott

WORD HORDE
PETALUMA, CA

First Edition

ISBN 978-1-939905-04-8

A Word Horde Book

*For the readers that have stayed with us to
the place where all streets end*

CHAPTER I

We have Jona's truth, taken from his own dead skull, his memories and his knowledge of the night.

You have that. I do not know anything unless you write it down.

I write it down, and that will be enough. Knowledge is enough to stop the city.

The truth hasn't mattered in Dogsland for a long time. You and I have known of Sabachthani's sins for decades. We would have stopped him if we could. That his daughter breaks the city laws is nothing to them, either. The truth doesn't matter here.

The sins are just hidden. They are not on the street, spread out into every corner and the king nearly dead without an heir.

We shall see. Write it all down and we shall see.

***

They called him Dog and he was a man that used to be one of the three street-corner kings of this district. I see him as Jona saw him, and I see him as the rats saw him. I also know what is true in the city, for his life. After the death of Turco, and the long fade of Djoss into the demon weed, Dog remained the last king standing on the street. He slept like an animal in the side room of the ruined brewery. Homeless children slept there with him in heaps of cloth and empty liquor bottles, and he protected them as best he could from the worst of the street that might come after the boys and girls. Rats quick enough to dodge a drunk boy's bottle slipped between the tangled limbs. Rats not quick enough got cooked by whoever caught them. Flies and roaches were small and fast enough to feast in the filth unafraid.

Dog woke up to smoke any ash or resin left in his pipe. His face looked like a cracked pot wrapped in scabbed leather. He mumbled meaningless sounds to the boys huddled against him for warmth. The boys peeled away from the waking giant.

Dog's teeth had rotted out from the pinks. He gummed damp, moldy bread that he kept in a bag tied to a ceiling beam. He stumbled into the light like any of the nameless boys. This crumbling giant's tough body had fallen deeper into street surrender. When the mudskippers' whistles screamed, Dog looked off into the direction of the sound. He did not run after them. He watched the boys darting like small deer to the source of sound, and remained behind.

Boys came to Dog that didn't sleep in the abandoned brewery. They gave him demon weed in pinches, a few bent matches. They gave him scraps of metal. They didn't give him much.

Dog picked at the scrap metal boys had brought for him. He took the scrap to a big can near the water. The side of the can was painted in ash and flecks of sparkling copper: three crowns in a line, like a sentence or a name.

Dog tossed wood and coal into the can. He banged the metal together hard until a few large sparks landed on bits of wood and paper, enough to make them burn. (He wouldn't waste a match on anything but his pipe, unless it was too damp in the air for sparks to catch.)

He fed the fire.

Dog smoked his pipe while he waited for the fire to heat up. He let the pink weed roll into his skin. He stayed close to the heat until the bloody, pink sweat leaked from his pores. Then, Dog shoved the metal into the fire. He used two other strips of iron from a rusted-out crowbar to move the scrap around in the heat. He fed the fire a steady stream of paper and cloth and wood and dried manure pulled directly from the Pens' streets by the ragpickers.

Then, Dog pulled the metal from the fire. He used the ruined blades again to smash the metal into a curve on the ground.

Dog bent the metal into a rough circle the size of a boy's head. When that was done, he used the heat to melt and shape spikes like jagged teeth.

(I do not know if Dog had ever actually seen a crown in his life, but he seemed to make them easily enough to suggest that he had once witnessed a king with a crown. Perhaps he was a deposed king, himself. Perhaps he had been a king, before he came to this city. I can see him now, the victim of labyrinthine machinations that carved away his ears and tongue: a mute prince tossed into a slaver's galley and lost at sea, and at sea until the pink weed filled his head with death, and he fell in step behind the dealer that fed a habit in exchange for cheap muscle. And now, the lost king slept mute among beggar boys and rats spreading crowns in a knighthood of orphans and drugs. Who knows his true history? All we know is his fate among the smoke. All I see is the shape of his path, and never the source of place before the ruin in his life. Rot stench masks all the sweetness of the vine, always.)

After the metal scraps had become a new jagged crown, Dog dropped the hot metal into the canal water with an old crane hook. Some teeth cracked and bent in the sudden cooling. This only made the crown more menacing, like a rusty shark's mouth. Dog handed the crown to the boy that had paid for the prize in demon weed.

Sometimes, the crown fit. If it didn't the boy carried it around, looking for another boy that fit it for a trade of crowns.

And Dog waited there, smoking the demon weed the boys had

brought, measuring the boys' heads with his fingers, and crafting new crowns in his back alley scrap forge, then sleeping like an old monster from a children's story wrapped in lost boys and trash.

This monster of old skin, muscle, and bone looks at the water like he's waiting for us to come and claim his horrible skull, but no one is coming for him.

No one ever comes for him.

***

I have written many things.

As wolves we ran, and as wolves we slipped underground.

We slid up from the sewers, and we stood upon the brink of our destination, where the sewers opened to the empty building of the street, at the edge of our destination.

Aggie knew the way in and out, and so did Jona following Salvatore and Aggie, and so, therefore, did we.

We slipped inside in the dark. We climbed in silence past the rectory kitchen, up the stairs and into the darkness.

Wolves slipped into the rooms, sniffing through them all for the woman who is old enough to be in charge.

We peeled back the wolfskin. We looked at her sleeping. She was an old woman in the dark, with skin empty of sunlight to our dusky brown and golden. She snored gently. She was a thin woman with blue veins like rivers in her wet parchment map of skin. She looked up at us, and pulled the ragged sheets around her body, pulling back.

She reminded me of another woman.

"We are the Walkers of Erin," I said. "We have been hunting the demon stain."

"What are you doing here? This is not the proper channels!"

"The proper channels are too corrupted," I said. "Do you remember Aggie?"

"Of course I do! It was one of the worst things that's ever happened in my life, signing off on her! Where were you? Where was your huntress in the night?"

I placed the papers at the foot of her bed.

"We need your help," I said. I bowed gracefully. "The children of Erin beseech your aid, madame Imamite, against our common enemy."

"And… who is our enemy?"

"Elishta," I said.

"Naturally, but who else? Who has brought you crawling here for my help?"

"We need to see the king," I said. "We need a meeting with him. We need to work together to end the stain in the city streets."

She picked up the papers and shook them. She flipped through them. "Do I even want to know the details?"

I shrugged. "Copies have been made. We want you to make copies, too. Everyone must know the truth. Spread them to every convent, every prayer hall and sanctuary. Tell anyone that listens. This is why we came to you, to be sure you receive the truth directly."

She pushed the paper back to me. "Stay for breakfast. Stay here. No one will know if you remain among the Anchorites a day. There is no contact with the outside world in here. We receive shipments in silence and veiled from one gate. We do not let our girls wander the streets wagging tongues."

I shook my head. "Aggie was not supposed to leave your gates."

"She was a demon child. Who knows what evil magic she used to escape us."

"You should read those. Send your people to us when you're ready to aid us. We need an audience with the king."

She put them on the ground. "I should have you arrested. It is illegal for a man to invade our convent. We are allies in this world but not the next."

"Elishta is our enemy in both. Our faiths are practical enough when it comes to that."

She nodded. She took a deep breath. She picked up the pages. "Go, then. I will make my own decisions about what you have brought to me."

We bowed.

Our next destination was a nobleman whose son was murdered and thrown into the water. We were going to offer him the whole kingdom. All he had to do was be ready to act when the time came to stop Sabachthani, and to make copies.

He would help us. Of course he would help us. He was weeping about his son after we handed him the truth. We told him what happened, and what vengeance he could take. We told him that we had chosen his noble line to support when the king died, and our support came with knowledge of his enemies.

Imam's priests would fall in line with us, and with him.

Our revolution was coming.

***

I see what I see of the city, by the grace of the goddess Erin, who granted me the lost memories of the demon child's skull that I might root out the evil of the world. I do not sleep except that I dream with someone else's memories and wait until they may pass through me like a flood washing away in my mind. Corporal Jona Lord Joni's memories—he is the dead demon child whose skull I carry—pour through me in waves and I am lost in him and his world. My husband is beside me, and he says it will pass soon enough. All these lost dreams will pass.

Give it time, he says. *Just write them down and then you will find yourself again.*

I remember too much. I step away and try to think like he does, and see the city from the angle of his eyes. The nobleman would make the city a series of islands cut open by the canals, where all the people of the street are divided by bridges that can be owned and kept by lords. It was not good that the Chief Engineer was murdered, but his incomplete canal is better unfinished. On an island, the worst would only grow taller, crueler. That is what happened to the Sabachthani on their island, I think, with all the noblemen that repose beside them. They grew too tall on their island. They thought they were more than dogs in this city full of dogs, owned by dogs, that we refuse to name except with the name our wolves have for such a place.

Husband, are you still awake?

My husband has a long, thin body, when he is a man. He rests, now, without the wolfskin on his back. He is like a wet maple leaf with his long, gray hair spread all around across the paper, leaving a rain-damp blur upon the inks. I should wake him, and peel him back from our maps, but we know the city so well, now. One of the remaining demon children is close. Salvatore Fidelio must finally face his death. We will kill him, and fight the stain of demons in this city. We are not executioners. We are healers, now, in a fire and revolution and the reaping of the weeds, to cull the weakness in the streets of men. The streets will burn with fire before we are done here.

—Husband?

The map over our floor, where the city lines and valleys and alleys and corners and the people stay where Sergeant Nicola Calipari's quill placed them, and we find them there as if they were trees that never moved from their roots, and the map has been used so much that we leave it there more from habit than need. We have walked these narrow streets, my husband and I, and we know the city as well as we know the forest hills beyond the city, where we run with the wolf packs, the skin of wolves upon our backs and claws and howls that sing beneath Erin's holy moon.

We sleep, now, upon the rippling paper map, all over the smudged ink of the city, and I touch my husband next to his heartbeat. I feel for it, beating gently like an insect in the dark corner of his chest. I shake him.

Wake up.

He is slow to answer. *Why?*

I have a question to ask you.

Let it wait until daybreak.

Would you die for me, like Jona did for his beloved?

No. You shouldn't die for me, either. Let me sleep.

Liar.

He rolled over with his back to me. I touched his back, where his lungs rose and fell beneath his muscles and bones. I traced his shoulder blades in the dark with my thumb.

Jona burned his life down for the woman he loved.

Rachel and Djoss escaped Dogsland to the north, past the red valley of demons and undeath. They have joined with the dust of the world, living as they have always lived, hiding as they've always hid. They die slowly in their own stains and sins.

Streets shape the people in the streets until none escape where Calipari's ink has marked them down in bleeding black. They cannot make themselves into something new. Humans push between the cobblestones and alleys and tiny doorways, against the walls and boundaries. After all the grinding, a soul might not cling inside the mangled clay and flesh.

Where does the ruin begin, where does it end? An eternal traveler, I have witnessed the crumbled walls of lost cities disintegrate to lines of stones like rotten teeth. I have touched the heads of a thousand children in blessing; some had wealthy families and some only had the clothes on their backs and no one knew exactly where the breach between the generations began. I have watched the noble mayor cry out the first ordinance of his administration, and held my tongue at how this law would slowly wear the buildings down until broken foundation stones alone would remain hidden between tufts of grass. I have watched the virtuous daughter marry the powerful son and a lasting civilization spiraled up like castle spires from their clasped hands in peace.

I have watched men and women fall in and out of love. I have fallen in and out of love. I have watched all creatures fall in and out and in and out of love.

And I, Erin's divine Walker—a woman, sometimes, with the nose of the wolf—I can smell the ruin of this city in the sea breeze. We turn a corner in the streets, and a building stands empty—not burned, not broken, just empty—and the windows have fallen away with tile roof and wood like leaves in autumn. Witness it. The ruin is already here. It will grow. There is a king of the day and a king of the night. There is a push between the ruin and the building of things, and the daylight has already lost. The night king rules the streets. The ruin is already here.

We remain in the city, my husband and I.

I can see more. Every day I see more. Jona's mind and memory unravels around me, through me, in memories and feelings like what people think they mean when they talk about their soul. I smell beyond his sins and sorrows. I smell and I see and I feel a lost world. What matter is truth to memory? The feeling of truth is all that remains. Sabachthani would melt the truth away, why not I, too?

I write it down, even in this darkness while my husband sleeps, upon the backs of the paper of the maps.

My quill crawls. I do not know what to tell you anymore of the city that haunts my memory. Dogsland is the same city she has been for all these pages—the Pens District the same horrible place they've always been. The smell in the air grows stronger in the long heat, without rain to sweep the rotting meat into the sewers.

Shall I speak of the cobblestones like buried turtle eggs all fossilized and crumbled under layers of silt? Shall I speak of the creaking buildings hunched into each other's shoulders, all these sick and drunk buildings leaning against other sick and drunk buildings to keep their shoulders up? Nothing changes. For more than two decades Jona lived here, and nothing changed for anyone except that everything was worse.

Jona Lord Joni did not see his world that way, but I do. Jona sees a world full of people and memories and feelings, not things. He does not know the horror of his home, for it is the only home he knew.

I know him, and his home, because of the skull we found below a bluff, far from the city he called home. Hunting demon children brought my husband and me to this city, by Erin's will.

***

Jona saw this old woman sometimes in Rachel's building. This old woman wore putrid bandages wrapped over her arms and legs where the rats chewed her rotting flesh.

The rats tell me that the woman's arms tasted like rotten meat, and it is a soft and supple meat and easy to digest for rats. She swung at the rats with rags and trash that didn't hurt the rats much. Sometimes she just lay back and wailed as if she were making love to a paramour shaped like a pack of rats.

She had rats because her little room was filthy all the time. She was too old and tired to clean it. She wrapped her arms in dirty bandages. She walked the halls and stared beautifully, terribly at the young men there. No one helped her, there.

Once upon a time, young men would have killed each other to follow her into her little room.

Now, there were rats.

Jona passed this old woman's open door. She sat on her dirty floor, looking up at him. He looked long enough to avert his eyes. He kept walking to Rachel's door. His boots were in his hand so he wouldn't stomp her awake with his footsteps. He didn't know if Rachel was home or not. He picked her door open with a knife. He peered inside, at the demon's child sleeping there, half in shadow and half in the sun of the open window. All thoughts of the hideous woman of the rats faded, for the horror of the rats was a mundane thing, and the beauty of his beloved resting there was the unspeakable beauty that had no place to him, in this city.

Another memory rises, then.

Outside, standing on the corner, a girl waited for her lover to return from the abbatoir. She smeared her skin in white chalk, like dusting herself in corpse lime. She did it to make her skin beautiful white, and to quiet her body's smells. Her hair, all braided and smeared in greenish-hues from the lime, hung like vines from her ceramic face. Her dress was sewn like a quilt from scraps, but it fit her well.

She was a dirty thing, wearing mud like it was her true skin and all that lime on top of it. She looked up into Jona's eyes with no artifice to hide her contempt for him.

And, she was a pretty thing.

Someday the street-sweepers would come, the engineers with golden hammers, and the king's men, and rat bite death and they'd scrape away all the things that made the girl beautiful.

Until then, Jona walked past her. She was the queen of the corner and sitting in the only place she'd ever know.

Her lover waved to her somewhere behind Jona. She left to kiss that man on the horizon, waving to him. She ran off past Jona's eyes, into the crowd behind him, after her lover.

Pup smacked Jona's arm. "You hear something?"

Jona's attention returned to his job. His ear caught a sound bouncing around the narrow brick walls of alleys and small streets and crowded places. He gestured to the other King's Man on that walkabout.

Around a corner and around another corner and then one more, and all the bodies in the mud were swinging fists like monkeys in the animal Pits. A local stevedore gang fought kids in crowns. Grown men with hands like bags of meat swung at kids that had never had a real meal they hadn't stolen. The kids climbed up and down the big brutes like apes climbing moving trees. They got thrown off. Little ones sat and cried. They clutched at their heads and twisted limbs.

Pup reached for his bells.

Jona stayed Pup's hand with a touch. "We ring the bells over a turf war, they're just going to fight somewhere else," said Jona. "Just watch. Anybody gets killed, we roll the killer when they're done." Jona shouted at the crowd of men. "You hear me! You can fight with your fists, but I see anybody swinging bats or teeth, I'll roll you now and save ourselves the paperwork!"

Pup had his bat up and out. "We just let 'em fight?"

A man peeled a boy off his back, and threw the boy into a wall. The boy made this sound like dice rattling in a cup. His broken ribs showed through the holes in his shirt, like kindling wood in a skin bag. He sat there, clutching at his chest, trying not to cry. He would not survive this wound, but he would survive long enough it wouldn't count to Jona.

Pup's hand went for the bell in his pocket again.

Jona snorted. "I'm no scrivener, Pup. You the one to scribe it for Calipari and me both."

That stopped Pup.

Jona saw a shimmer of metal in the corner of his eye. A boy tugged the crown from his head, and raised the jagged teeth of the thing up like a lamprey's jaw. He swung down once, not strong enough to draw blood. He pulled it up again, poised to strike harder with both hands.

Jona jumped over broken boys in the battlefield. Jona plucked the crown like plucking fruit. "I said no teeth!" shouted Jona, "That means these crowns of yours, too! These're all teeth!" Jona leaped back over the broken boys to Pup.

Jona handed the crown to his fellow. "What do you think?"

Pup had a flask in one hand and the crown in the other. He paid more attention to the flask. "I think the big fellows are winning this day," he said. He pointed at the boys that had fallen with the flask.

Jona spat. "You a pup and you ain't pulling for your own? I'll put three on the little ones," he said. "Lots of them."

"I'll take your money, Lord Joni."

Jona shouted into the crowd. "You're taking forever! Hurry up!"

One of the Pluckies chuckled through a bloody nose. "You want in on this?" he said, to Jona.

"If I come in there, I'm fighting with the kids on account of it ending faster that way, plus I got money on them. Too many of them kids with crowns. Lots of swings of the bat. You and your fellows'd go down like broken eggs and I don't break a sweat."

A stevedore collapsed under the weight of the boys on his back. He crawled a bit and tried to roll. Kids jumped on his head with bare feet.

"Don't just jump on him!" shouted Jona. "Get the next one down!"

The kids listened. The new weight on the back of the nearest stevedore wore the weary fighter to his knees. Kids kicked at his face with their bare feet. They pounded on him hard.

Pup handed Jona the flask. "Put this in your mouth and maybe you don't help any more. You know those kids are going to be in for the real trouble if they take anything pink. They got crowns to mark 'em, too. Don't help them. You're rolling them into the canal, and what they ever do to you?"

Jona took the flask, but didn't drink. "You care about the mud-skippers, now? Where'd those crowns come from, anyhow? I don't know anything about crowns."

Another giant tumbled down under the weight of children.

Pup watched with wide eyes. The children jumped on top of the fallen fighter's body, grinding their heels like making meat.

Jona shouted at them. "That's enough on that one!"

Some of the kids listened. Some didn't.

"Pup," he said. Jona whipped his bat from his belt fast, and swung it backhand in the same motion. Two kids tumbled off like broken crates.

The one they saved was the stevedore with the bloody nose who had spoken earlier. "Bunch of dirty rats!" he snarled.

Jona handed the man the flask. "Drink up," said Jona, laughing, "You'll need your strength to live with the shame. I know I'm telling this one to everyone I know about you going down to a couple kids in crowns. I've seen 'em around, but I never saw them all together like this. Looks like something we should know about, don't it?"

"These kids, they think they're something now." He took the flask slowly with a battered hand. He drank. He gave the flask back to Jona. "You tell Calipari anything goes missing, it'll be on his head what gets done about it. Lucky we weren't carrying anything pink. They thought we were. Mudskippers need to learn their place. There's more of us than them, once we get all together. And you know we will."

Blood was smeared all over the brass of the flask. He took another drink, then handed it back.

The kids didn't linger to drink with the King's Men. They gathered the wounded, adjusted their crowns. Jona tried to stop one or two and ask them about the crowns, but none stuck around to chat. Jona didn't really care to fight kids about a question like that. Where they got the crowns was not as important as them having the crowns, and fighting smugglers with them on their heads. Calipari would want to know about that. New gangs meant fighting over turf, bodies dropping into the canal. Both the king of the day and the king of the night preferred an orderly street for the business at hand.

"We should have grabbed one of them," said Pup. "Right by the ear and take him in. Little mice got no business fighting dogs."

***

Later, much later, Jona slipped away, telling the King's men stories about a birdie singing a song about the kids with crowns, maybe, and no one believed him. King's men laughed too loud about this bird's particular tailfeather and about this bird's song that sounded like moaning. Jona muttered at them and wandered off to Rachel's building.

(He walked past the old woman in the rat-infested room. He averted his eyes.)

He broke into Rachel's room quietly. He had his boots off and in his hands so he wouldn't wake her stomping across the floor. He stripped his uniform quietly. He spread it on the empty bed near hers, against the adjacent wall.

He slid beside Rachel slowly to try not to wake her. She woke up, anyway. She adjusted herself in the bed to let him lie down with her.

Rachel was warm in Jona's arms. Damp sweat seeped out from the places where skin touched skin. Before her eyelids dropped again, he coaxed her voice from the dreaming.

"What do you dream about when you dream about me?" he whispered.

She answered quietly. "When it is a good dream, I dream of your breath moving in and out of your chest and my ear pressed against your chest, and the breath flowing in and out of both of us, and it is the same breath. Blood flows out of our skin, and into the other's skin."

"Sounds like us doing this," he said. "It's good. I mean... I like this. I could do this more if you want."

"I think you are cursed, Jona, to live without dreams. I think it's a horrible thing," she yawned and her next word stretched like crying, "*hooow*... the demon stain has touched your life. It's always horrible, but for you, you are truly cursed to live without dreams. Better to just have wings on your back instead of scars."

"I don't think I've ever heard you say that before."

"I have watched your life's flower grow a while. Don't speak again, Jona. Let me have my dreams. I have to work tonight. You should be at work."

"Work can wait. I get paid wherever I go. I'm on walkabout. I go anywhere, and do what I think is the king's business."

"Please, Jona don't be like this."

"I'll be gone when you wake up. I just want to hold you a while."

"What will you do when my brother and I travel on?"

"Don't."

"It's not a choice we make for ourselves. Leave, Jona. Don't come back. We're going to have to leave soon, he and I."

"Don't joke about this. We're it for each other. There's no one else like us. There's no one else. I really like you. I feel… I don't know what I feel. I feel like I'm better with you. I feel like I'm not so…"

She said nothing. She looked at him with tired eyes. She wasn't really listening.

He stood up from bed. He looked down at her. She stretched her arms over her head and rolled away from him. She placed them over her head and held very still, like sleeping.

He put his boots on in the hall, and walked away. The sound of his boots on the wood was the loudest sound he had ever heard in his life.

***

I thought we talked about this, Jona. I thought you wouldn't come back. What if my brother shows up again?

I'll hide under the blanket until he passes out. I don't want you to leave. Don't leave. You're safe here because I can protect you.

I know that, Jona, but… Djoss could come back in the middle of the day. I honestly don't know where he is. I don't know what he's doing. I'm frightened for him.

When's your next night off? We can go see a play. There's a new play and it isn't so serious. In fact, Geek said it wasn't any good. Maybe you'll like it.

I won't. There are only beautiful people or ugly people on the stage.

There are never any people like us.

They're like you. You're beautiful.

Stage beautiful is different. I don't want to see a play, Jona. You're not listening to me. I wish you would listen to me. I have to leave the city soon.

Want me to find him for you?

You leave him alone.

If I see him, I'll tell him you're looking for him and see if he wants to leave the weed behind for you.

I said, leave him alone.

I'm just saying that maybe your brother is caught in the pinks, and maybe you'll spend the rest of your life dragging him out of it until his head is gone or maybe you spend it with me, instead, and we have a good life together.

And what, then? What if we have a child?

We won't have a child.

What if we do? We can't keep it.

We could. My parents kept me.

No, we couldn't. Jona, stay if you... I don't want to argue about this. Just let me sleep. I'm so tired, Jona. I'm so tired. I wish you could just close your eyes and be still.

***

My husband tells me what he learned from Calipari's birds. I combine this with what I know from the ragpickers that used to be kids wearing crowns and with what we know from the push of the demon weed hookah on a brain. Djoss left the three crowns in a row and the whistling boys after Turco was killed. He walked where the weed took him.

The pinks seeped into his blood. His skin began to thin like the hard users get. Eyes seeped water day and night. Clots of sleep dust needed to be brushed away all the time. They were pink clots, because they were tiny flecks of clotting blood.

Djoss felt the emptiness of his pockets when his head was clear.

Whistles in the streets from the ragpickers in crowns went ignored. Djoss walked past the boys with scrap metal crowns, and past the boys with none. Djoss went east of the Pens, then north into a cluster of nicer houses. He walked through the yards of craftsmen's homes to the larger houses.

The children here played the same games as the ones in the Pens, but here the children had clean shirts, and they didn't curse when they lost a round of dice.

Djoss saw a door hanging open with no one in sight. He stood still, looking slowly all around him.

Up the street…

Down the street…

Around the yards…

The door was still there, hanging open, and not a soul watched this one ragged man in the street.

The pink emptiness behind his eyes pushed his feet towards the door.

An old woman appeared in the yard from the open door, carrying baskets of laundry. Another woman swept the dust of the house out the open door.

Djoss walked away. His hands shook. He didn't know if this was excitement or unrequited addiction or both. He shoved them in his pockets to keep them still.

A pink emptiness spread behind Djoss' eyes like a butterfly.

CHAPTER 2

In the night, the streetlamps masked the stars with lamp light. Men in stilts walked the darkness with casks of oil on their back, to refill the lamps under the king's command. In morning twilight, the lamps all burned down to nothing below the brightening sky.

Flying insects flew into the lamps and died with screams that only my husband and I could hear.

The king's men on the night shift stumbled back to the station, bleary-eyed and pale. The day crew was there, bleary-eyed and tan. Sergeant Calipari called all the boys together before roll call, both day and night.

Calipari raised his hands so people would stop jabbering and listen. "We all been hearing those bloody whistles," said the sergeant, "We seen them running like little king's men to their little bells. They're wearing crowns from who knows where, now. Birdies're telling me these ragpickers are getting in deep. Dumb little ragpickers don't know the way of things in the Pens. There's dozens of them. More than dozens. Too many. Gonna make trouble before they know what trouble they're in."

The king's men nodded. The night shift swayed their weight from one boot to the other. The day shift fidgeted with clubs.

"Thing is, I don't want to walk about clubbing kids. Do you?"

"Better to club than hook them dead into the sewers," said the night sergeant.

"That's right. It's better to try something first." said Calipari, "First, I want to set a mouse trap and catch all we can, and ship 'em out to sea for the king."

Geek snorted. "You know someplace they all go and you not telling us?"

Calipari looked at the other sergeant once, hard. The other sergeant coughed and looked at his hands.

Calipari continued. "The gang's wearing crowns, right? These kids're dumb as pigeons. I figure we got ourselves a king making crowns, hiding somewhere. Who's running the show? Who's making the crowns? We catch one of them, sit 'em down and talk, and maybe there's a center one and set mousetraps where we land, and we impress every one that shows their faces into the king's navy instead of prison until the gang's back breaks. I'm calling a hold on the clubs until we can find the maker. Any kid you catch with a crown, drag him in and he leaves that day for the navy."

Moaning, all around. The night sergeant shook his head. "Nicola, I wish you had talked to me on this first. That's a lot of work for boys on walkabout. No purse cutters, no smugglers, no breaking up the fights? Just kids with crowns and shuffling them off to the king's navy?"

"Now," said Calipari, "I don't doubt that the might of the king's men in the Pens District can come down like Elishta's howling demons on those little mudskippers, bat in hand. But, if we club these boys out of the district, they're just going to get clubbed out again and again until they fall in bad somewhere else. Then, these brats grow sour until they're old enough to hang." The sergeant paused here. He took a deep breath, like he was waiting for someone to say something. Nobody said anything. Calipari darted his eyes around the room. "Maybe, instead, we do a little looking around first," he said. "Maybe we turn these kids' lives into something better than doomed for hanging."

Jaime nodded with the rest of the boys. He popped his bat in his hands. He looked like he was listening a little too close, like he disagreed but he wasn't saying anything. He had a mean squint in his eyes.

The night sergeant grimaced. "You got it, Nic," he said, "but one week's all I'm willing to give on this. I already had my boys looking for kids to club out."

"You find any?" said Nicola.

The night sergeant shrugged. "I don't know," he said, "Ask the boys. Boys?"

Mumbles and denials from the tired night crew. They hadn't been looking and the night sergeant had said this to cover himself about something was going on in his district that he didn't know about. Jona was dead certain of that, and so am I.

Sergeant Calipari nodded at the king's men. "That's all, boys. Night crew's dismissed and day crew better be out and about. You got your assignment. Get the new songs from your birdies on these little kings. Until then, no neglecting the usuals. Any cutters or foreign thieves about, roll 'em on up my way like any walkabout."

The corporals all gave their best military *yessir,* but these men were no phalanx. They had the slouch like a street gang. They had the mussed up uniforms like a street gang.

Like dogs, not wolves, these men were more scavenger than hunter, sniffing through trash heaps for easy kills.

Dogs are scavengers, not hunters. They root in filth for roots and larva and bits of rotting meat.

These men, they would walkabout, but the king's navy would have few young recruits.

***

The hazy dread was too much to bear. Jona couldn't help but feel followed. He hadn't been told to kill anyone in a while, and he was glad, but he couldn't help but feel like he was being followed. Nicola was buying, and Jona wasn't drinking. The boys were gone drunk, tired and falling asleep at the table. Jona never slept. The demon stain in his blood kept him always awake, always thinking about being watched.

Jona looked over his shoulder at shadows. No one was there.

Live a life like this, in fear. Surrender to it. Become a slave to the shadows.

Demons abide such misery in the bonds of Elishta, below the ground. Children of men do not live in fear, but must fight back. It was the human in him that snapped.

The long night, when the bar gets quiet, and there is no dancing and the bells have stopped ringing and almost everyone is going home, the daylight crew had gathered what was left of their weekly pay to settle in for a long, hard, angry drink. Jona was more sober than the rest. He touched Calipari's arm and leaned in close. When we started talking, Nicola felt himself sobering quickly.

"Nicola, I don't know about you," said Jona, "but I'm sick of the pink weed running these streets that ought to be the king's and used to be my father's land. I'm sick of the hold they have. I'm sick of wondering who is what and where and knowing it's there, in front of my face, and not a thing to do about it. We ought to stop it. We ought to drive back to the source and roll all the bastards without a trial."

"There's battles we don't got the manpower to win," he said. "Leastways looking the other way now and then, we can take a little coin for ourselves and our families."

"We're trying to mousetrap children who skim off the top of the real trouble, we ought to be chasing down the pinks where they are."

"You go after that, you'll probably get a coffin in the water, and a bunch of your brothers-in-arms floating beside you."

"We got real trouble and we're not doing anything."

"We're containing it, Corporal. We're keeping it separated from the street, so people that don't go looking for it don't find it. They know that we only look away when it's kept off the street, out of sight, and away from the good people of this city."

"It's a lie."

"It's a way to let the people of the city live without knowing how bad it is, or feeling it in their skin and hands. Because if they knew…? If anyone really knew?"

"You going to stop me?"

"No," he said. "Get yourself killed. I won't stop you."

"I want someone to follow this guy. I know he's running a show."

"How do you know that?"

"He bribed me, Nic. I've done jobs for him, too."

Nicola took a sip of piss gin. He darted his eyes around. The other boys were deep in the cups, not listening. Nicola was almost completely sober just from the fear.

"You can't trust Pup," he said, softly. "I know that for sure, so keep him out of it, far away. Jaime's rotten to the core. You can trust Geek as long as you can buy him off or trade a favor. I'd have assumed you were crooked as sin, what I heard about you. You're awful rowdy in the dark. Lots of bad things happen when you're around. When do you sleep?"

"My hands aren't clean. Are yours? I know your heart is right. Who's got clean enough hands, here? Who has the heart for it? I'm done with that, now, and I mean it. There's you and me. Maybe there's Geek? That's why you want him as sergeant, right?"

"Geek would keep his boys alive, is all, fighting battles they can win," said Nicola. "He plays a lot of cards. He's got a lot of girls he sees for free. I don't know if he's in too deep otherwise, but he doesn't seem as bad as other options. The last thing we need is someone coming in here trying to be everything good in this world. He'll get killed and take a lot of good boys with him. Better Geek than someone doesn't know the Pens."

Jona nodded.

"Can you get my guy tailed?"

"Maybe, yeah," said Nicola.

"There's a carpenter. He's got a front a few blocks from here. He's high up. I followed him back a few times, and you know where he went in the night? Where you don't go if you aren't high up. The Island."

Nicola nodded. "You took his money, so he'll see you a mile away, right? He could have been leading you anywhere."

"I don't think he cared that I was following him, and I've spent my time on the Island and know what it means. I've crashed parties there. I was dirt under his fingernails, and he wanted me to know it. They all did."

"Never turn down the money, and pass along anything you find out. Let them think you're still their boy, and let me know what you do. See if you don't come to your senses in the morning, too, and stop telling me a thing."

"I'll show his shop to you. Where does his stuff come from and where does it go? Tail him and let me know. I'll go poke around where he ends up, and I'll find something we can really use. If we do it fast enough…"

Calipari nodded.

"I've got another thing I got to go run down on this. I know the two are connected, but I can't say how."

Nicola lifted his glass to Jona, and toasted him. Jona looked down at his. The glass was filthy. There was mud floating in it. It left grit in his teeth to drink it. He handed the glass to Nicola, and stepped out into the night.

Boys with crowns running in the dark, and evil men walking the streets, and children of demons stalking prey. It was hard for Jona to see three women walking together, smiling and singing. There were working men walking home from the canal boats. There were working men that had nothing to do with anything but their own life drinking in the streetlamp glow and candlelight, calling out to the girls selling hot food in carts walking past.

Jona wanted to run, but he couldn't run. Not here. Dogsland was awake in the night, singing and laughing, and it wasn't anything like all he was afraid of.

The city did not share Jona's fear.

The messages came from time to time, from all the places these messages come. Jona's hand reached into a pocket and discovered a scrap of paper signed with a stamped code. A man stepped from an alley with a feather in his hand. He handed the red feather to Jona, and the man said the message and ran away. A woman in a tavern leaned over Jona from behind and whispered her sultry words into his ears.

A hot-apple girl stopped and saw Jona. She laughed because she thought it was some kind of love letter or something. She had been paid to hand this message to Jona, and she thought it was the funniest thing. She held out her hand. She was smiling, and had said his name, and he had said "What?"

"I was paid to give you this," she said. "Your girl is an ugly one, king's man. I wouldn't marry her if I were you."

"Thanks," said Jona.

It was a note, from the night itself. *Leave Salvatore alone. Be a good boy until we call again.*

He crumpled it up and threw it away into the mud.

***

Geek tapped Jona's arm and pointed. The two king's men quickly ducked back against a wall. One of the street rats that called himself Mudskipper was hard at work.

This dropper pretended like he had found this box with someone's address on it.

The kid wouldn't give up the box without a reward, and the victim would be thinking about a reward, too. Usually the boxes had dead rats or rocks in them. The addresses were only occasionally real.

This mudskipper had a normal left arm, but a right arm twisted up and small, like fruit withered on the vine. He smiled with only a couple yellow teeth sticking out at weird angles from his mouth. He walked up to a carriage.

"Hey," he shouted, "You going anywhere near this box I found?" He held the box up with his one good hand. The address pointed up at the carriage driver. He averted his eyes.

The mudskipper pulled the box back into his body. He walked down to the next dogcart. The driver bit his thumb at the boy.

Normally no one cared about a little dropper. If you're dumb enough to fall for the scam, you deserve the trash inside of it. This mudskipper was wearing a crown on his head of bent metal.

Geek asked Jona if he was interested in the contents of the box. Jona nodded. Geek went around the corner with a quick step. Jona watched until he saw Geek on the other side of the boy, poking around from an alley in front of the body.

Then Jona walked towards the boy fast. He wanted the boy to see the king's man coming for him. The mudskipper jumped to run for it, but Geek snagged the boy by the hair below the crown and pulled.

The box fell and the boy was screaming.

Jona snatched the box.

Inside was a dead rat, half-eaten and rancid.

"That ain't yours, king's man!" shouted the mudskipper.

"Right, you are, Mudskipper," said Jona, "This here rat belongs to… My goodness, Corporal, did you know that the name on this box does not exist in this city?"

"It do!" shouted the boy.

Pup pushed the boy against a wall and tied the boy's hand to one of his ankles behind his back. The deformed hand bounced in the air.

"It do! I found the box."

Jona rolled his eyes. "You're dropping. That's your grind. Don't act like you weren't."

"I wasn't dropping."

"Nobody cares that you were dropping. Where'd you get that sharp-looking crown, kid? Someone give that to you?"

"I'm not your birdy, king's man!" the boy spit.

Jona smacked him across the face. Geek had a good grip on him, with both hands. Jona pulled the crown off and looked hard at it.

"Lots of you runts running around with crowns," said Geek. "You think you're a street gang? You forming up some kind of operation?"

The boy spit again, and got hit again.

Geek hefted the boy up off the ground and over a shoulder. "I'll run him in and question him," said Geek. "He might not survive if you run the interrogation."

Jona grunted assent, holding the crown.

Jona watched Geek with the boy on his shoulders. He stood in the street, alone. He stepped into an alley, and watched the street. He sat on a barrel. He pulled a flask from his jacket. He drank until it was empty. He turned the crown over and over in his hand.

He hadn't seen Rachel for three days. He had been looking for her.

Corporal Jona Lord Joni was not the kind to swallow his own anger like a rotten fruit. His mind reached out for someone to dwell upon—someone to push.

Jona curled his fist and punched his palm. He wanted to kill someone. A name emerged from his lips, and he knew he couldn't kill the fellow, but he could hurt him. He could hurt him, bad.

"Salvatore Fidelio," said Jona.

There was a darkness in him and Jona recognized it. He thought of it as the black demon in his chest. He felt it there, pumping acid in his veins in darkness. It was an evil feeling. It made him want to crawl into a black corner of the basement, where his father used to stand in chains in the night, and sit in the dark alone a long time.

CHAPTER 3

L ike a flock of ravens flying low to the ground—layer upon layer of fluttering black cloth—the form of a man ran in the gaps of the black clothes. Jona stood between two buildings on the dark side of the street, where the moon was blocked by a long eave. Jona peeked around the corner at the man he had followed through the night.

Jona shadowed the edge of crowds. He moved from alley to alley in the dark over sleeping men and wet rags and shit and broken crates.

Then, out of the Pens, and down into a sewer and up again and into a shadow and Jona watched Salvatore Fidelio scurry over the yards. These street alleys were walled by fences that held small gardens back from cobblestones. In the alleys here, Jona had to hunch low to stay in a shadow and he was mostly alone among strays and trash.

Salvatore didn't try to hide anymore. He walked down the middle of the street like a resident, dressed in fine clothes for the location. Tonight he was going to a ball, uninvited, to steal the costume jewelry that crashers wore and then lost to the thieves. The thieves would sell them to the fence where the crashers would buy their own costume jewelry again. As long as none of the true guests were robbed, no one would stop him.

And a young woman was awake right now, leaning out of her

window. Her red hair was a purple ribbon in the streetlamp glow. Her skin mirrored moonlight.

She and Salvatore kissed. She crept from her window in a chiffon dress. She had to hold the edges up to keep the weeds of the yard from dirtying her hem. In the street, she held his hand and skipped like a child. Salvatore tried to calm her down, and be less conspicuous.

Jona waited. He knew where they were going, and felt no need to go to Lady Sabachthani's garden gathering of thieves and noblemen and those who aspired to both ranks uninvited. Two more lovers in fine clothes ran away from a house in the dark, smiling like fools—like Aggie had smiled. Jona waited until he couldn't hear the soles of their boots on the cobblestone. Then, Jona listened for any new noises in the night. He heard wind. He heard—he listened hard—snoring from the house at his back.

He stepped into the street. He kept his head high and his pace calm, as if he was supposed to be walking here in the dark. He didn't jump the fence. He walked behind the house, to the servants' gate. Jona picked the lock and crossed the shadows in the little yard.

Jona peered into the girl's open window. On the white corner of a bed, a man's naked leg stuck out across a patch of moonlight.

Jona pulled out his knife.

He watched that man's leg for movement.

Jona dug his knife along the top of the windowsill. He carved a single letter, slowly. With the cheap knife on this hard wood, he had to dig hard. He had to be careful not to make scratching noises. He needed to apply pressure, and indent the wood.

This wood was not from the rotting Pens.

Jona's hand hurt halfway through the first line of the first letter of Aggie's name. He listened while he shook his tired hand. He glanced at the man's naked leg, unmoved on the bed. Jona touched the line he had carved. The thought of rolling the next letter on that hard wood with a sleeping man a few feet away, and thought about getting some mud or ship's pitch, instead—or anything.

Jona looked around the yard for an idea. Jona saw a long, thin, low-hanging branch on a tree. Jona used his knife in his rested hand and wrestled the branch off. He took it back out the open servants' gate. He stripped away his overshirt and then peeled off his ragged undershirt, exposing his scars and skin to the darkness. He put his overshirt back on. He wrapped the ragged undershirt around the edge of the stick to make a torch. He reached up to the top of the fence near the gate. He hooked the blunt butt of the stick into the streetlamp's latch, and put the cloth end into the fire. It sparked like a match from the demon stain in the ruined cloth. Jona leaned into the bedroom with the burning stick like a torch in front of him. He looked around. A nude man was asleep on the bed, his mouth hanging open. He didn't look up at the light beyond his eyelids.

Jona placed the burning branch onto the edge of the bed, beside the sleeping man's leg. He ran.

He didn't want to listen for the screams of the man, waking up to the fire on his bed, or the sound of the booming bells of the fire captains.

When he reached his little corner of the night, and safety, a thought came to Jona: Perhaps the girl had drugged the man.

He thought maybe he had killed someone. Maybe he had killed because he was angry at Salvatore. This only made his disgust with his fellow demon child grow like a rotten fruit swelling on the vine.

***

I see him now in the shadow of a dream of memory lost and found and maybe it never was real but I can see it.

Salvatore, the look in his face was this: He dreamed of cities across the world that had never known his face and king's men weren't hounding him day and night. These cities, their young women were lovely, lonely, and bored. He could escape there, with help from his friends. He knew that. He never quite knew exactly why they helped him.

Salvatore watched Jona's back and thought about leaving Dogsland forever, and all the industry and all the city's petty intrigues could fall into the fog of the immortal bloodstain.

Even Jona dies someday, whether Salvatore kills him or not.

He's in a hammock. He's in a cave, and doesn't remember how he got there. He's in the city again, and he doesn't remember how he got there.

He knows that he cares about someone, out there. That's all he knows. He only remembers what he can love.

***

Jona listened for the reports and rumors for the fire he had set in the bedroom, and heard nothing. He watched Calipari's hands moving over the different papers of crimes, like cards scanned for signs of cheating. No search for an arsonist came through the messenger boys. Jona thought to peer into the paper and seek it out, but if there was no report, then there was no report and looking for one would only be conspicuous.

After dark, Jona watched for Salvatore, and saw the girl as bright as sun in the dark, dancing with her criminal.

Jona went back to the house, a few nights later, expecting it to be damaged. He didn't want to go to Sabachthani's latest ridiculous party, where the two were inevitably going.

Jona walked down through the houses in the dark, looking for any sign of what had happened.

The house stood fine, with no sign of fire, and not even a singe at the windowsill.

Jona stopped at the tree he had cut, and saw where his knife had plucked the branch. He reached over the fence to touch the wounded stem.

It could've been just a gardener's blade.

Jona climbed up the fence enough to look inside the window, and he saw the same thing he had seen last time. Moonlight spilled on a bed. A man's naked leg glistened on the white sheets.

Jona walked away.

He felt like punching Salvatore for this, as if Salvatore had done something to stop the fire that had burned out all by itself. He felt angrier and angrier until he wanted to grab Salvatore and shake him and hold his head in a fire even while Jona's hands felt the burn. He should have felt relieved.

***

Mishaela was smiling when they met. Then Salvatore said something to her. She placed her hands over her face like she was playing peek-a-boo. Her shoulders shook. Jona wondered, for a moment, whether she was laughing or crying. She had been smiling. She covered her eyes like playing peek-a-boo. Then, her hand reached out, and touched Salvatore's shirt. Half her face was crying, the other half was still hidden.

Under that hand she could have been laughing. Jona had a vision in his mind of a drama mask, and Mishaela laughing under the hidden hand because this was all an act. A single tear flickered like a burning flame in the lamplight down the side of her face.

Jona watched Mishaela crying. Salvatore stood up, and the girl's hand reached out to his black shirt that turned away and away and then was lost into the night shadows. Then, Mishaela was alone, and crying.

In the street, outside the tavern, Salvatore shoved his hands in his pockets. He slouched with his hat low against his head.

Jona strolled up behind him. "Only a matter of time before you tossed her off, anyway."

"That wasn't about you," said Salvatore, "It never is. You don't know anything about me."

Jona snarled. He spit at Salvatore's feet. "I don't know what you're talking about," said Jona.

Salvatore spit back at Jona's feet.

"I've been told to leave you alone" said Jona, "I just thought you should know that I'm done with you."

"Toss off, then. I hope I never see you again."

Salvatore turned his back to Jona. Salvatore strutted away like he was untouchable.

And Jona couldn't touch him.

Jona walked behind Salvatore a while. They crossed the same bridge to the same lonely street. The same drizzle misted their shoulders from the same cloud.

Salvatore turned a corner to his own home.

Jona stayed on the street until he found Rachel's apartment over the butcher shop. He looked up through the streetlamp glow. He saw her pulling her brother's clothes in from the line at her window. She was home right then. He waved up at her. He called out her name. She waved back. She looked inside, and shook her head. *My brother's here,* she mouthed silently. She held her hands up and mimicked sleeping.

Jona shrugged. He blew her a kiss. He walked on, to the station house.

***

Are you drunk? Have another drink and then you will be.

I want to believe we're good, you know.

We are good. Jona, I'm tired, and I want to go home and sleep. You have to go back to work. You should stop coming to see me. We need to stop before we fall in love.

Don't say that. We're it for each other, so don't tell me not to love you. Listen, I want to know it in my heart that all of us—all the people like us—that we're really good. That if we do something bad, it isn't because we are something bad.

What did you do?

Nothing. I broke this girl's heart.

It wasn't mine.

It was over this fellow I know.

This fellow you know. Name?

Salvatore Fidelio. You remember him, right? That burned girl? I threw him in the lake.

Did you break his heart, too?

If he has one, I did. He had another girl, already, and she loved him. I don't know what happened, but I think I had something to do with it.

You didn't do anything.

I set a fire in her house. I might have scared her.

Is she pretty?

She wasn't as pretty as little Aggie from the Anchorites that got burned dead for Salvatore's sake.

If Salvatore is as bad as you say he is, the best thing is to back away, and walk away, and let him find his own death.

Right. I wish I could talk to you all night.

I couldn't stay awake that long. I have to go. I have to work tomorrow night.

Can I come?

Don't be foolish. Give me a kiss good-bye.

When can I see you again?

Not this week.

Want me to help you with your brother?

No, Jona.

I can help, you know.

I said no.

CHAPTER 4

We do not know the fact of Djoss, for he was not held in any demon's skull. I can only piece together what the rats tell us about the pinkers, and what their nature tells us, and what Calipari's flock of birds tell us and what the stories of the street tell us.

Is this Djoss? Is it a lost vision of a dream of another man?

I do not know.

Still, the story fits into the puzzle that I piece together from the demon skulls. I shall include it here, so all will know who to seek when they seek out Rachel Nolander.

***

Djoss paid a fellow all he had to acquire this little wooden tile with a number on it. Djoss took the slab to the bartender. The bartender tied the tile around Djoss' neck with a string. He led Djoss behind the bar, into the back rooms. Bottles of alcohol in crates were stacked between giant casks of piss whiskey and ale. The door was built into the side of a cask. The back half of the cask swung inward. A fat stairwell led down past an old woman, and into a room smothered in pillows.

The old woman's clothes were too fine for this place. Her red and blue silk dress matched the fan she used to blow the pink away from her face.

She waved Djoss down to the basement with her fan.

Djoss slipped a coin into her hand. "Let me stay a bit, eh?"

She took the money and waved Djoss inside. Four men lingered on dirty pillows, their mouths plugged into the hookah's long stems. The four men didn't look up.

The hookah was an upside down glass squid, as tall as a man, with many lithe tentacles. The pipe bubbled gently with a low flame. Four curled limbs reached up from the ground, out from the hooks at the top and out into the mouths of the fallen figures lingering the flickering haze. Djoss couldn't see through the dark where he could find a place.

The old woman touched Djoss' arm with her fan.

"In or out," she said, softly. "Hurry up, now."

Djoss stepped inside. He grabbed one of the open limbs coiled at the top of the hookah. He sat down on an empty mound of pillows. He bit down gently onto the hookah's tip like sucking a new thumb. The first wave of joy poured through him, and he was swimming.

When Djoss emerged, he heard a voice on the horizon: the old woman. "Nobody wants to hear about your family," she said, to someone.

Djoss pulled himself up to sitting. Djoss sat up too fast. His head spun, and he fell back to the filthy pillows. The spout of the hookah slipped from his fingers and jumped away with the coiled tube. Djoss reached around for his among the pillows. His fingers found the rear end of a rat. The rat hissed and scurried off. The rat had been eating vomit. Djoss ran his hands over the powdery dried vomit, looking for his piece of the hookah.

"You hear me, king's man?" said the old woman, "If you start screaming, I'm throwing you out."

Djoss pulled up onto his elbows, and this time he managed to stay there. He looked up at the man at the door.

Jaime, in his king's man uniform, sneered at the fan held between him and the hookah. "Don't be like you, lady," said Jaime, "I'll ring the bells for you here. I'll call the others. I will."

The old woman gestured with her fan. Jaime stepped into the room. The only empty spot was next to Djoss. Jaime picked up Djoss' lost hookah limb and sat down where it had been hiding among the pillows. He took one long drink of smoke, and collapsed to kneeling.

"King's man," said Djoss. He sat up and reached out for the lost pink smoke. "Hey!" he said.

Jaime didn't hear him.

Djoss touched his back.

Jaime smacked Djoss' hand away.

"Hey, that's mine!" said Djoss, "Hey!" Djoss waved at the old woman.

A woman shoved her fan over her face and stepped into the little room. She kicked Jaime in the head. Jaime looked at her like he was afraid of this old woman.

The old woman snatched a new limb from the hookah off the floor, and shoved it at Jaime. Jaime took that one, and shoved them both into his mouth.

The old woman pointed at Djoss.

Jaime's eyes were closed. She had to reach into Jaime's limp hands for the end of the lost hookah limb. She placed it between Djoss' lips.

Djoss swallowed joy hard one last time before he drowned too deep to swim ashore.

He woke up in an alley. Jaime was there, next to Djoss, deeper than Djoss had been. Jaime hadn't been smoking as long.

Djoss reached out his hand to the prone guard. Djoss fingered the king's man's uniform.

If Djoss had been stronger, he'd have stripped the uniform from the sleeping man's limbs. Djoss was still too weak.

Djoss felt his stomach rolling. He pulled himself up to the

king's man's face. Djoss curled his lip. "The king's loyal dogs piss-ing and drooling themselves," he said. Djoss opened his mouth and tried his best to smell all the filth of the alley, all the smells rising up from the pink king's man.

The king's man opened his eyes.

Djoss closed his mouth. "Hey, dead dog," said Djoss.

The king's man's eyes tried to focus.

Djoss slapped Jaime's face lightly. "Look at me, dreaming hound."

The king's man focused.

"Hey," said Djoss.

"What do you want?" said Jaime.

Djoss looked up and down the uniform of the man below him. "You a king's man?" said Djoss.

"Corporal Jaime," he said. The king's man's stomach convulsed. Djoss rolled off the king's man fast. Pink bile leaked from Jaime's lips without much substance, like smoke congealed into flecks of watery vomit.

Jaime choked on it. His arms reached out to the walls. He rolled himself onto his side.

Djoss pulled himself up to his boots. "You ain't so tough, now," he said. Djoss lifted a boot up and let it fall upon the king's man's back. "You're the guy with my sister, aren't you? I saw you naked, with her. I heard your name. She called you Jaime."

Jaime took another boot between his shoulders. His stomach was still rolling over everything inside, and it was all pink.

Djoss dropped his boot again upon the king's man's back. Djoss leaned against the wall to walk away from the man on the ground. On the main avenue, he grabbed the first person he saw.

"Hey," he said.

A shopgirl took one look at Djoss' bloodshot eyes and pink sweat. She jumped away and walked fast down the sidewalk.

"Wait!" said Djoss, "There's a king's man over here pink as El-ishta! You can walk right up to him and kick him like nothing!"

People kept walking.

Djoss stumbled down the street to the closest fountain.

He puked at the base of the fountain. He splashed water over his head. He rinsed his mouth out. He waited there for his limbs to recover their strength in the fading afterglow. He watched people come and go. Young women, ignoring him, brought buckets to the fountain to carry back to their apartments and homes. Young apprentices brought water back to their businesses and horses. They stepped around Djoss like he didn't exist.

Eventually, Jaime stumbled up next to Djoss. Jaime splashed water on his own face, and rinsed out his mouth. Jaime stripped to the waist and shoved his uniform shirt into the water. Jaime had to get the smell out of his clothes as best he could before muster.

Jaime squinted at Djoss. "You kick me, tosser?"

Djoss balled up his fists. He snarled. "Kick nothing," said Djoss, "I don't know about any kicked king's man. You stay away from my sister or I'll know nothing about a tooth in a king's man belly, either."

"What time is it?" said Jaime. He wasn't listening to the muttered threats. "Where're the cryers? Where're the bells?"

Djoss turned and walked away. The lingering fog in his limbs slowly diminished. The boots walked with certainty. The eyes squinted less and less in the streetlamps.

He made his way back to the small side street in the Pens. He climbed up the stairs, opened his door, peeled his shirt from his back, and fell into his bed.

He didn't notice it, but he had just fallen asleep on Jona's uniform.

Jona and Rachel, wide-eyed, held their breath in her bed on the other side of the room.

Rachel pushed herself away from Jona. She grabbed her Senta leathers from off the floor. She stepped lightly across the room. Her talons clacked on the old wood without socks or boots to still them.

Djoss didn't seem to notice the sound.

Rachel grabbed the edge of Jona's clothes and nudged them out from beneath Djoss, one item at a time.

Djoss didn't even groan.

Jona took his clothes from Rachel. He pointed at Djoss, and gestured with his hands like smoking a pipe.

Rachel touched Jona's cheek. She nodded, knowingly. She pushed Jona towards the door.

Jona pulled his clothes around his body, haphazardly. He picked his boots up from the floor. He tiptoed into the hall. He waved good-bye to Rachel from the stair. She waved, and closed the door.

In the hall, he sat down on the stairs, and pulled his boots over his feet.

He sat there, in the black hallway.

Outside, the sun rose. The city groaned awake in a hum of boots and birds and carriages and wandering shopgirls. In the apartments, doors opened and splashes of light filled the dark hall. The people said hello to each other, but they ignored Jona. They crawled past him, saying nothing to him in his uniform sitting on the stair.

Good men and women were on their way to work.

***

Jaime didn't show up for morning muster. Calipari shrugged. "He's been running late now and then since his wife," said Geek, "He'll show."

Calipari stood up. He put down his quill. "Hey, Geek," he said, "Take the desk today and keep an eye on the scriveners and anything that turns up."

Geek coughed. "Sir?" he said. He looked at the desk like it was an ugly woman with a fire in her eyes.

Sergeant Calipari snapped his finger at Private Kessleri. "Private, you're coming with me. Grab a bat and a good pike. We're going somewhere deep, you and me. How long you been a private, Kessleri?"

"Two years, Sergeant." Kessleri stood up, and handed his quill to another scrivener. Kessleri smiled, but his hands trembled.

Calipari nodded. "Long enough to see this, then."

Geek looked Kessleri up and down. "What's going on Sergeant?" said Geek.

Calipari rested his knuckles on the desk. He looked down at the papers in front of him. "I hope nothing," he said. "Stinks in here," he said, "Too many of you. Walkabout, boys. Geek, if Jaime shows up, make him work with the scriveners until I get back."

Jona and Corporal Kelper stepped into the street, and immediately turned a corner to an alley. Kelper pulled a coin out. He flipped it in the air, and caught it. He slammed the coin on the back of his hand, keeping it covered. "Call," said Kelper.

"Castle side," said Jona.

Kelper revealed the coin face side up. The king scowled at Jona for choosing wrong side of the coin.

Kelper patted Jona's cheek. He placed the coin in Jona's breast pocket. "The face is mine, then. Good boy," said Kelper, "Have a good walkabout." Kelper peeled off his uniform jacket, and handed it to Jona. He only had his white undershirt on now, like a sweat-stained white flag.

"You'll stand out more like that," said Jona.

Kelper shrugged. "Nic will see me no matter what. This way he can pretend like I ain't what I am, if he wants." Kelper peeked his head around the corner. He saw Calipari and Kessleri far down the street.

"Nic's acting like bloody Elishta's going on. You think Jaime's into something deep?" said Jona.

Kelper snorted. "I don't think nothing 'til I see it with these eyes, Jona. Best not to speak bad of a fellow we don't know where he is. He's still our boy. Mayhap we find him in the street dead drunk." Kelper looked into the sunrise. "Mayhap dead."

Jona said nothing else. He didn't walkabout right then. He watched Kelper's dirty white undershirt slipping in and out of the crowd. After the white shirt was gone a long time, Jona leaned against a wall and thought about finding a powerful drink, strong enough to blind him and turn his stomach and make him hungover before he even wakes up. A good hangover is like being swallowed up in darkness, and there's no room for thinking inside of it.

***

Djoss woke up in the room, next to Rachel. She had been sitting next to the bed, waiting for Djoss to wake up. Rachel touched his arm. "Rent's due tomorrow," she said, "but you don't have any money, do you?"

Djoss shook his head.

"I don't want to leave Dogsland over you," said Rachel, "I like it here. I have a friend, here. I've never had one before now."

Djoss nodded. "We should've left after Sparrow's kids cut down to your scales. I like it here, too."

"Stay here a few days," said Rachel, "Don't go out. I'll bring you food. I'll make rent."

"How much money do you have?"

"I'm not telling you that, Djoss." Rachel ran a hand through Djoss' hair. She touched his face. She touched his lips. "You need a bath. You want it hot?"

· "No," said Djoss, "I'll take one later. Did you already get the water?"

"I did," she said. She pointed at the bathtub on the other side of the room. She shrugged.

Rachel saw a snowfall hidden in the room. Unsaid words coagulated into ice and descended to the ground like cold, white ash.

Rachel closed her eyes. "I don't know what to do with you," she said, sadly. "I don't know what to do, Djoss."

Djoss rolled towards the wall. He shoved his face into his pillow.

"Tell me what to do," she said.

Djoss moved his head out of the pillow. He stared at the wall. He spoke to the wall. "You could go see Dog. He's still got some things going, and if you tell him I sent you, he might have something. He might know someone."

"Where's Turco?"

"Turco's dead, Rachel," said Djoss, "He's been dead weeks now. A king's man rolled him into the river. They're asking around for Turco now, and he's already... Well. Dog's living in an empty brewery with a bunch of the mudskippers we hired, but there's nothing anymore without Turco knowing who. I think some of the older kids might be running the stuff on their own. I kept out after Turco got rolled. The kids aren't smart about it, you know?"

"No one was smart about it," she said. These words spilled like snow from her lips, and spilled all around the room. Ice everywhere, so cold. "I'm running out of clothes again. I'm going to need you to get me something I can wear, Djoss. Can you do that?"

Djoss said nothing back.

Rachel reached her mind into the air between them, full of fire and ice and cool winds and throbbing with the energies of the Unity and this ashen snow of unspeaking. The room was just a normal room, like every too-small, stinking room jammed into the corners of the too-big buildings in the huge city, but in here it was snowing.

"You do that without money. Bring me clothes. Make that happen for me. I can't give you any coin for it right now. We need it all to make rent. Got it? You always got clothes for me, Djoss."

He nodded. He didn't look like he meant it.

Disgusted, Rachel left her brother without another word. She walked outside. She felt into the Unity for all the energy hidden in the air, where people live and love and the threads of life swell into one pattern.

In every room—every single room—her breaking heart was not alone.

A thousand upon a thousand snowfalls, and all the city weeps in the dark, alone.

***

In the Docks south of the Pens, crates ascended up and out from the ship's hold by a crane that placed the crates in leaking heaps on the docks. A dozen stevedores hauled on the crane ropes to muscle the crates off the ship. Once upon the ground, the stevedores unhooked the crane, and cracked open the crates on the spot. They pulled sacks of ore out of the crate, and threw them one by one onto a flat river ship in a messy heap. A merchant sweatier than the stevedores counted the sacks.

The sacks seeped ore across the mud. The yellow-white ore splashed all over the naked chests and backs of the porters. It filled their hair and clumped in the sweat down their leggings. Tonight, the men'd find the ore's flecks behind them in the chamber pot. They'd dream of ore. They'd taste ore in their lovers' skins, if they had one to taste. Most did not.

Rachel sat down on a porch stoop across from the stevedores. She waited until she saw one wearing a wedding band around his neck on a chain, where it wouldn't catch on the hook in his hand, or any of the ropes and pulleys. He had a neck the size of a small tree. His hair was burned-off along one side, and he laughed with a sound like coughing smoke.

She caught the man's eye. She walked towards him, slowly.

He sneered. "Get back, Senta."

"I have a warning for you, friend," said Rachel.

"I ain't your friend."

"Your wife knows," said Rachel. She placed her hands on her hips and shook her head. She tsk-ed at him.

The man looked sideways at Rachel. "My wife?" he said, "What's she know, then?"

Rachel looked around at the stalled stevedores, waiting for their fellow to get back to work. She winked at the married foreign man. "I'd tell you if we were friends." Rachel turned to walk away.

One of the other stevedores smacked the dock worker on the back. "Hey! Pay the Senta lest she curse you for it! She done you a favor!" They shouted at him, and they urged him on.

The stevedore with the burned head and the wedding band threw off the hands of his fellow superstitious stevedores. He jogged after Rachel.

The merchant shouted about how he wasn't paying for foolish trips to the Senta.

The stevedore shoved a hand into his pocket for a few coins, and jammed them into Rachel's palm.

"Thanks, I guess," said the stevedore, "Don't curse me, Senta. I paid you fair."

Rachel nodded. She walked away.

She needed more money than this, and soon. She asked a shop-girl about an old brewery. She pointed to the edge of the pens, on a three-edged corner between the Warehouse District, the Pens, and the maw of a canal.

When she finally found the decrepit building, she saw Dog pounding away at some lump of malformed metal near the water's edge. A street boy, with only one good arm and the other twisted and limp like a chicken wing jutting out of his shoulder, dangled his feet in the canal.

Dog lifted the lump of metal in the air. He threw it to the boy.

Rachel saw the shape of the metal: a crown.

The boy couldn't hang onto the hot metal in just his one hand. He dropped the thing into the canal. Then, he cursed at Dog for throwing the crown into the water.

Dog ignored the boy. He shoved a pipe into his mouth and sat down with his back against the brewery.

Rachel frowned at what she had seen. She turned back into the Pens District and walked away.

She only knew one person near the Pens that cared enough about her to give her money.

The sun was still high. Rachel knew Jona's mother wouldn't be at home. She didn't know if he was off today or not. He wasn't. The house was empty and dark. Her boots echoed on the old wood and tiles.

(Jona never knew how Rachel managed to get into his house when she did. He never thought to ask. It was a large house where the absence of anything worth stealing protected it from thieves more than a lock, and more than a king's man living there.)

She walked up to his room through dark halls. She peeled her boots off. She stretched her lizard-like toes. She fell face first into the bed. She wrapped her arms around his pillows, pulling them into her face until she had trouble breathing.

She felt like crying, but she knew she'd destroy his bed with her tears. She held them inside. She told herself to be strong.

The more she said it to herself, the more it sounded like a lie.

When he showed up, she knew that she couldn't touch him because if she touched him she'd burst, and her body's water burned things. If she kept the water inside her, the water only burned her heart. He grabbed her, and smelled the ore all over her. He didn't care. They stripped each other of clothes with a need neither cared to discuss.

***

Jona stared down at her nude body in his bed. She was curled into him. Her foot moved up and down Jona's leg and he didn't say anything to her but the scales scraped his skin and hurt a bit and might have drawn a line of blood and the blood might burn the sheets. He figured she'd fall asleep soon, and he wouldn't have to worry about any little cuts burning out.

"Thanks for that, Jona. I needed it."

"I wish you were here all the time and we could do this when I came home all the time," he said, "I wish you didn't leave."

"Please, Jona."

"Please, what?"

Her leg stops moving. She's staring at her own hands running across Jona's chest.

"I need money, Jona."

"So do I. You find some, you let me know."

"Djoss lost the rent."

"Pinkers do that. Gets worse. He'll fence anything he can carry. Then, he'll go too far one day, and he'll be cheese-for-brains. You'll have to dump him at a temple or something."

"Don't say that. He's my brother, Jona. He's more than that. That's awful. He'll quit. I'd never dump him at a temple. I'd never do that."

"Better for you if you did. He won't quit, Rachel. They never quit for long when they're sucking on the hookahs."

"He's not like those people."

"I hope not, for your sake. Lots of strong men go cheese-for-brains and don't get better."

"Did you ever try it?"

"Yeah, but I was just an eater now and then when I was a dumb kid no different than red roots or hardmint leaves, and only now and then since I couldn't really afford it too often. Eating's different from smoking the hookahs. It passes through you like a strong drink, and I guess I'm demon child so demon weed doesn't do much to me. Eating doesn't hang in your head in a cloud, though, or eat away all your skin. Anyway, that was before I knew what it really was. I went out to the woods for guard training, and I cleared my head. I never touched it again. It wasn't really a big thing to me, before, anyhow, and mostly I cleared my head. Anyhow, when I was scrivening, I kept reading about all the stuff about the demon weed—the real stuff, what it does to everyone, and all the crimes hurting people. Anyway, if you need money, I don't have any. Maybe you turn birdy on a big something and you can get some money. If you got any dirt about a street gang name of Three Kings, maybe Sergeant Calipari'll pay for that. Can't you just go read fortunes somewhere?"

"I can. I don't like to."

"Why not?"

"Because people want you to tell them something happy. People cling to it. And nothing's happy. Nothing is ever happy. Everyone is going to lose someone they love, and then they're going to die and face their goddess alone."

"About your brother. You told me once that you can see the patterns in people's lives, right?"

"Don't start playing Senta. You're wrong about him."

"You'd say it to me."

"No I wouldn't, Jona. Not even if you paid me for a fortune and I hated you. I love Djoss. He'll get right."

"I guess you know him better then I do. But, if you need money, I don't got enough to split it three ways when I'm already here with Ma. The only things Calipari wants right now are some real scary stuff that I wouldn't even touch myself with ten hard boys behind me and a street gang full of kids running around with crowns. They're into the pinks a bit. Sergeant wants to find the top men. You find out who they are, and where they are, and he might pay you for it."

"Do you have any money right now?"

"I do."

"Can I have that, too, and I'll pay you back later, when I find out about the kids?"

"Yes." Jona reached into the pants at the foot of the bed and pulled his purse from his belt. He had a little extra money under his pillow and he pulled that out, too. While he did this, he thought about how loud skin sounded moving across blankets, and how much he hated how long it took him to dig up all the money. He thought about this pit in his throat from doing this and he didn't know why. He held the money out to her and he listened to the sound of her naked body moving against the sheets and against his skin and everything in the world was wrong when she held out her hands.

She had this look on her face like she was about to cry.

"Do you love me, Rachel Nolander?"

"What?"

"Do you love me?"

"I wish we had a different life, Jona. I wish we were two peasants in the woods, tending sheep and sleeping beneath the stars, and all human, and all in love."

"Do you love me, Rachel?"

"I don't want to say it when your money's in my hand!" She said it again, in a whisper, "I don't want to say it. Do you?"

"I do," he said, "You're the woman I love."

"Even monsters can love, then. I hope it's not the demon in me that you love. I don't know who I am, right now. This street gang you were talking about. You're looking for a guy named Turco?"

"We are. He's a Dunnlander and he's dressed like it. I heard he was doing something pink with the ragmen, but we don't know exactly what. What do you know?"

"Turco's dead. He started the Three Kings. It was just a bunch of ragpickers with whistles. Turco's been dead a while. He was friends with my brother, and he's the one who got Djoss on that awful stuff. My brother's been out of the work since Turco died. This other fellow named Dog is probably running things now, in his way. Dog's hiding out in the empty brewery at the edge of the Pens. You know the one, right?"

"I know it."

"Dog has no tongue, and no ears. Anyway, that's probably it, yeah?"

"Yeah. I'll tell Sergeant Calipari. Why didn't you tell me right away about it when I asked you?"

"I want you to help me because you love me. I don't want to tell you about Turco and Dog, Jona. I hate what you do."

"What? Why?"

"I've been hiding from city guards my whole life. No matter what there's going to be street gangs and people getting killed, and the king doesn't care and the nobles don't care and the good citizens don't care, so why don't they just leave the rest of us alone? We can take care of ourselves. It's the only thing we know how to do, because it's all we do our whole lives."

Jona pulled away from her. He pulled his feet around and planted them on the floor like he thought about standing up and getting dressed and talking to her with his uniform on.

"If we don't stop these kids now," said Jona, naked, and on the edge of the bed, "not a one will take care of themselves because the real power in the Pens is going to wake up and roll them hard and all at once. If we don't get those kids off the trouble they're in, the big smugglers are going to take them out. I think Calipari's been working his contacts and begging for time."

"How come you go after the kids instead of the smugglers?"

"We go after them, too. I'm working on that one hard, but I can't move, yet. They're better so they're harder to catch."

"They're probably just richer and stronger."

"That, too, and they buy their share of king's men. Bought me for a while, too, but I'm past that now. We ain't all good, but we ain't all bad either. And you can hate me for what I do, but I've been better since we met. I mean, I'm not as bad as I was before, and I can't really explain that, but I promise I'm better than I was. And it's because I love you."

"You know that thing about the patterns, and how there's no escaping them?"

"What patterns you mean this time?"

"I mean nothing. I think I'm in love with you, too. And I'm

too angry to tell you the right way about how I love you. So, we're going to have to do this later. And, I have to get my brother out of the city before he… You know. I can't stay here. I've been telling you that. Djoss and I could never stay forever. We have to move on."

"Can I see you again tomorrow?"

"I don't know. We have to go. Aren't you listening to me? *We… have… to… leave.*"

"I love you, Rachel Nolander."

"Not tomorrow. Not ever again. I'm sorry."

"Please."

She got dressed. He watched her getting dressed. He held still. He held his breath. He felt a pain in his chest like his heart was winding up in a coil, like a spring breaking. He watched her, and she pretended she wasn't being watched. She bent over and kissed his cheek.

"Please, don't go," he whispered.

She shook her head, and she left Jona there, with his money in her hand.

***

Rachel paid the butcher the rent in his shop between two customers. The butcher didn't deal in fine meats. He sold sawdust sausage, and lots of it. He sold cuts of meat that nobles wouldn't feed their dogs. He made most of his money renting the rooms over his head, and ran the shop so he could feel like a butcher instead of a slumlord.

The butcher asked Rachel if she needed any meat. She shook her head. "You got all my money in your hand," she said.

The butcher nodded. He wrapped two handfuls of scraps in cheap paper and gave them to her. She thanked him, and asked him how much it cost.

He told her they were dog scraps, and he didn't want anything for them, but they'd do her fine in a little rice.

She probably considered putting the scraps back on the counter—everyone has their pride—but instead, she nodded at him. She got this sad look in her eyes like she had become a beggar again out of nowhere. Then, she thanked the man, and went back to her room.

The butcher told us all of this when we met him—a polite enough man who spoke like he was cutting meat with his tongue and didn't know the difference between Erin and Imam. He described Rachel as a pretty bird with weird clothes and the brother as just another street thug beating his life down to dead with bats hacked from paving stones. Such a pretty, strange thing hanging to him for nothing good but that's how it always is around the Pens.

***

"Hey, Djoss, are you still here?"

"I'm here."

"Good. I made rent. Don't ask me how, okay?"

"You never ask me. How did you do it?"

"Just don't ask."

"Was it bad?"

"It was the best thing ever happened in my life, I think, and the worst. I'll never see him again. And I feel awful about it. Anyway, you're going to stay away from the hookah, okay? You can't go anywhere near it anymore."

"It's everywhere."

"Not for you. Did you get any clothes for me? I'm running threadbare, Djoss. I'm feeling the breeze where I don't want to be feeling anything at all."

"I'll try, Rachel. I'll do what I can."

"That's the best you can give me? That's it?"

"I promise I'll do my best."

"Please, Djoss," she said, "Please."

"It's hard," he said. "You don't know how bloody Elishta much I want it all the time. It's so bloody hard."

"Please," she said. "We can leave any day, okay? We can leave right now. Please, can we just go?"

"I like it here," he said. He rolled over. I think this was the last time he had the bed before he sold that. Maybe he had already sold it. Inside the shape of things, making the best gestures I can from what I can see and smell and remember and know. Had he sold the bed? Was he on the floor? Did any of this happen like it did?

I could ask the butcher if he had already sold the bed to smoke the hookahs. The butcher would know.

My husband can sense my indecision.

It doesn't matter if it feels true to the Rachel he knew. Write it down, move on, and we will find her.

How far gone was her brother? Had he sold the bed?

It's not important.

If he sold the bed, he was much farther than even Jona knew. How could he go north?

I don't know. It's not important. What Jona knows is what you know. What Erin wills for us to know from these things we learn, we know. And, what we think is true is close enough for the hunt. Trust your instincts. Write it down. What do you feel, beloved?

Maybe it doesn't matter. Maybe that's what I'm feeling about the bed.

None of it matters, for Rachel is gone. She and her brother ran north across the red valley when Jona died.

CHAPTER 5

J ona believed Rachel, but he had been doing the job too long to take any bird's words at their face value. As soon as she left, he got dressed and left, too. It was something he could do. His chest felt like Geek was sitting on it, but he didn't know what to do about that. He had to do something. He had to get out and be out and act. Checking her word was something to do. Checking her honesty seemed important, to him, as well, in a way he couldn't describe. He had to know if she was just taking his money for its sake, or if she was really being honest to him. Jona did not have the experience in love to understand these things. He pulled his clothes on and stormed into the street. He scowled all the way to the abandoned brewery he thought she meant.

A light rain rolled through. Generations of fish had hatched from their eggs in the season of rainstorms, feeding on the filth and silt and trash that filled their seaweed sanctuary.

The fish grew up big on trash, until a fisherman's net pulled them from the water, and a fisherman doused the fish in salty brine.

And Jona stopped a shopgirl with salted halibut in a bucket. He ate while he walked. He tossed the bones and tail into the street where it would be washed in the rain to sea, his demon-stained spittle seeping into the natural cycles of the city's discarded things.

He arrived at the empty brewery, seeing nothing, and sat among the folks waiting for a ferry like he was supposed to keep an eye on them today. He yawned. He looked around like he was watching for droppers and cutters and pickpockets.

And where he stood he watched the corners of his eye for rag-pickers. He listened for the clanging of a scrap forge.

When the crowds got bad, he ambled around like he was just keeping the order. He watched for anyone with a crown. He peeked into the alleys running beside the building to the water.

He saw the three copper crowns on the side of a metal tub. He saw the ashy lips where many scrap metals burned off their impurities.

If he set foot in the ruined brewery alone in his uniform, he probably wouldn't get too far in the dark, where he didn't know what trouble was inside except that it preferred not to be disturbed. He sat down within earshot. He waited to hear the clanging of the craftsman. That didn't take too long.

Jona peeked around the corner. He saw the boys beside the giant man and the faint whiff of demon weed beneath a trash fire.

He saw the crowns being forged for demon weed, and handed out like treasure to boys that were not a gang anymore, just boys—wild mudskippers running through the streets and begging and stealing and eating anything they found like little wild dogs.

***

"Nic, we gotta talk."

"Talk nothing," said Calipari. He didn't look up from his reports. "You're on walkabout today, Jona."

Jona sat down on the edge of a scrivener's desk. The scrivener leaned back in his chair and cursed at Jona for sitting on the scrivening. Jona ignored the private. "I got a birdie singing a song on the Three Kings, Nic. I put together two and two. I paid 'em for their trouble on account of it being true, and I'll need to be reimbursed for it. I found the scrap forge where they're making crowns. Whatever they were, they're nothing now. Their leaders are already dead. It's just boys buying crowns. Nothing more."

Calipari put down his quill. "Nevermind walkabouts," he said. He stood up. "Call the boys back, Corporal. Hey, scriveners, go call the boys back!" Calipari looked Jona in the face. "This the center?"

Jona sighed. "Yeah, but like I said…"

Calipari clapped his hands. "So, we mousetrap it, and the king's navy for all of them we catch," he said. "Where is it?"

Jona wasn't as happy as Calipari. Jona's shoulders sagged. His face begged forgiveness. His voice was calm and slow. "Mousetrap won't work," he said.

"Mousetraps work," said Calipari, "Show me, and I'll set it and you'll see. Every mousetrap's a bit off."

"I'll show you, but the leaders are already gone. It's just a bunch of kids with crowns and whistles. I don't think they're even running pinks anymore, on account of their source got rolled," said Jona. "You know our boy Bially?"

"What about him?" said Calipari. He folded his arms.

"Bially was running his pinks to Turco," said Jona. Jona moved a finger in the air like connecting all the dots. "Turco was running the pinks to all the mudskipper boys. The mudskippers call themselves Three Kings and they start marking turf because they're dumb kids and they start blowing whistles and smacking folks around, acting tough."

Calipari cocked his head. "You found Turco, then?"

"Turco's rolled," said Jona, "Turco's been dead weeks. Heard it from my best, he's dead and rolled, and I believe her. Turco was too pink to hide this good, and you know it. He's rolled. The other fellow running is out, too, on account of the kids getting stupid. Anyway, he's so pink he's cheese-for-brains any day now if we just wait him out. The only one left is probably cheese-for-brains, too, but he's still down with the ragpickers. He makes the scrap crowns for the kids and they keep his pipe full, and he's nothing to nobody, and not a mudskipper knows up from down anymore. This last king got no tongue, no ears, no nose. Everybody calls him Dog."

"Dog?" said Calipari, "I know a fellow name of Dog. Heard about him, anyhow. Big fellow, and a real rowdy tough. Been working muscle at the red doors since before I was a scrivener."

Jona lowered his voice. He leaned forward. "There's nothing anymore, but a bunch of ragpickers, Nic," he said, "We're busting it trying for these kids and there's nothing. We can mousetrap 'em, but the only ones that come back to the center want a crown. The ones that got crowns don't come back to the center, so we can't mousetrap anybody worth taking."

Nicola hadn't uncrossed his arms. "Show me," he said.

Jona stood up. He brushed off the salt that had gotten on his uniform from the scrivener's desk. "Tell your fellows that there's nothing there," he said, "Give 'em Dog. Maybe they ease off, and give the kids time to fade."

Nicola reached behind his desk to put away his quill. He reached for weaponry. "Jona, show me," he said, "Let's go." Calipari pointed at the scrivener whose desk Jona had been sitting on. "Hey new kid, you too. Grab a bat. You know how to swing a bat, new kid? They teach you that where you come from?"

***

Jona led Calipari around the side of the brewery to the scrap forge where one metal tub was marked with ash and flecks of bronze. Dirty smoke crept out of the tub into the skyline.

Nicola told the new kid to touch the side.

The new kid—Jona didn't remember the kid's name—had a thin black moustache and small eyes set deep in his skull. He probably couldn't grow a full beard, yet. He looked foolish with the moustache. He reached out a glove to the side of the metal can.

He pulled his finger away, and shook it. "It's hot, Sergeant," he said.

Nicola laughed. "Of course it's hot," he said, "Didn't you see the smoke? Don't be an idiot. If I tell you to do something stupid, don't do it. You're no soldier anymore. I need all my boys to stay alive. There's no medals in the Pens. There's king's work, there's funerals, and there's fun in between and there's nothing else."

Jona snorted. "He was a soldier?"

Nicola shrugged. "See how he ain't answering your question because you directed it at me and we're both higher rank? The kid's got lots to learn about the Pens before he can walkabout with you tossers."

Jona thumbed at the door. "Maybe the soldier'll be rough with a bat like a rolling pin. Our boy Dog's in there."

"You ever talk to Dog?" said Nicola.

Jona squinted. "I don't think so."

"You think he's dumb?"

Jona shrugged. "If he was smart, he wouldn't have lost his tongue, and that was before he was a pinker. I don't know how dumb he is now."

Inside the brewery, Calipari and Jona and the new private looked in the slanting light that slipped through the cracks in the ruined walls. A boy cooked a rat over a small fire. Dog was asleep, like a pile of rotten meat and mud that breathed. He looked like death. He looked like misery. He looked like the trash and the boys huddled against the giant had all become one, stinking entity of filth. Dog's face smiled in his sleep. He was dreaming of something that made his nightmare face smile.

A boy apart from the sleepers, cooking his supper, didn't look up from his rat. "I ain't sharing with you, king's man," he said, "I caught it. Catch your own rat."

"We're looking for the Three Kings," said Calipari, "You running with the Three Kings?"

"You're in the wrong place, king's man."

Jona leaned against the wall. "You don't mind if we sit here," said Jona, "and see who shows up?"

The boy looked at his rat like nothing else in the room was real. "Dog won't like to wake up with you here unless you bring him something. I won't share my rat."

Nicola crossed his legs and sat down on the ground, next to that boy. "I ain't here about rats," said Nicola, "I'm looking for kings. Let's say I wanted to get me a crown like you tough boys around the Pens."

The boy chortled with a deep voice, like a man. "You want a crown, king's man?" he said, a boy again, "You're lying."

"I'm not lying," said Nicola, "this lady I been on with has herself a son. He's growing up tough, like you mudskippers out here in the Pens. He wants a crown. How do I get one?"

"You're a king's man," said the boy. "Take one. That's what you king's men do. If I could stop you, I wouldn't have let you in."

Calipari laughed. "How else?" he said.

The boy with the rat looked over at Dog. "He makes 'em if you bring him something."

"What?"

"He won't make anything unless you give him something. You rolling him for it?"

"No," said Nicola.

The boy pulled his dead rat off the fire with two scraps of wood. He picked at it with his bare hands like a hairy chicken wing.

"Where you from, mudskipper?" said Nicola, to the boy.

He shrugged. "Ma said we were from a farm, once."

"Where's your ma?"

"I don't know," he said.

"Just you, then?"

"I got two brothers. I don't know where they are, but they're around."

"You know a fellow name of Turco?"

The boy smiled. "I knew the fellow. He's been gone a while."

"We know," said Nicola. "We were looking for him."

The boy snorted. "You check the water, king's man? You check the bay?"

Jona nodded at Calipari. Calipari got thoughtful. He looked at the sleeping heap of a man on the floor.

Nicola, deep in thought, snapped his hand at the soldier in the Pens.

"Sir?"

"Go get me some demon weed, soldier."

"Sir?"

Jona rolled his eyes. "You heard the sergeant. You need me to come along and hold your little hand? If we're going to be waking this Dog, we're going to need to feed his appetites or we're in for a tustle, and you ain't ready for a tustle in this pit. You don't even know what else is hiding around here in the dark, and neither do I, and I don't want to find out."

The new kid looked away from Jona with no hate in his eyes. "Why?" he said.

Nicola took a deep breath and spoke slowly, calmly. "We're going to need him to make as many crowns as he can," said Calipari, "This kid's eating rats and talking about his missing ma, and if we don't do something, kids like this roll into the river. So we need more crowns. As many as we can get."

The kid swallowed a chunk of his rat. "What're you talking about, king's man? I don't need a thing from a thing, and I don't need a thing from you."

"Never you mind, mudskipper," said Calipari, "How's that rat?"

"Good," said the boy, "You bring me one I'll cook it for you. Don't charge for it, either, on account of us being friends." He spit out a bone in the general direction of Calipari.

Nicola smiled at the kid. "I'll keep that in mind," he said.

***

When Dog rolled awake and peeled the clumps of mud off his skin and gummed his pipe like it was full and lit, Sergeant Nicola Calipari was there, with the weed. Calipari said, "Just because you can't speak, don't mean you're dumb. We got this problem, and we need to talk about it. You understand?"

Dog nodded.

Calipari told Dog that the smugglers were going to come down on the boys with crowns if the boys didn't stop wearing them, or otherwise if the smugglers figured the boys weren't really a gang at all and the crowns were just a thing everybody's wearing these days.

Dog shrugged.

Calipari asked Dog if he could stop the boys from wearing crowns.

Dog shrugged, again.

Calipari asked Dog if he could make lots of crowns.

Dog held up his pipe.

"You'll get paid for your time," said Calipari, "But we need you clear enough in the head to make lots of crowns. Lots of them. I want you to show my boy here," Calipari pointed up at the new private, "how you make them, so he can make them, too, when your head is all demon weed cheese."

Dog shoved his pipe between his gums. He didn't have any matches. He didn't seem to notice that he didn't have matches for his pipe. He grabbed a burnt-out husk of a splinter and flicked it like it was a new match. He held it up to the edge of his pipe. He breathed in like he was going to smoke weed that wasn't burning, because it wasn't a match, and he didn't seem to notice or be in a pantomime. He really didn't realize what he was doing. He looked at Calipari—straight at Calipari—like Dog was looking beyond Calipari, and beyond the old brewery and beyond the mess of buildings and ships. Dog was staring off into the sunset of his life in a windowless room.

Calipari held a new match out for Dog. Dog didn't notice it.

The boy that had cooked the rat jumped up to snatch the match from the air. The boy pocketed it like a coin. Calipari tossed the boy a box of matches. Calipari snapped his fingers at Jona. Jona produced a fresh match for the blacksmith's pipe.

***

Crowns rolled out into the Pens from the scrap forge. Jona peeled off his uniform and scrambled with the mudskippers for scrap metal in just his white undershirt. They brought it back to Dog and the new private at the forge. The new private had stripped to the waist. Dog started crowns, but he couldn't finish them. He took a few whacks, then he took a few puffs of his pipe, and then he forgot why he was holding the hammer and the tongs.

Then, Dog sat with his feet in the river. He smoked until he ran out of weed in his pipe. He stood up long enough to start a new crown that he couldn't finish, because new demon weed found its way into his pipe.

Calipari distributed crowns to mudskippers. He told them to get everyone they knew, and anyone they didn't know to wear a crown all over the Pens. He gave them notes, too. He had carried quills and ink in his pockets in cases, and he had a metal cases full of paper and writing salts. He wrote out all his favors in ink on the scrap paper. He told the kids where to go with the paper, and who to give it to, with crowns for everyone.

Calipari paid the kids for their time. When he ran out of money in his pocket, Jona paid them. When Jona ran out, Calipari sent for Geek and Kessleri and Kessleri came and took over the forge for the sweaty new private. Jona and Geek sat with Calipari, reading over the sergeant's shoulder and handing out Geek's coins to the kids that carried crowns and paper.

The new private disappeared, and Jona thought that was a good sign that he'd work out fine in the Pens on account of how fast the new private was learning how to disappear when he was sick of being the lowest rank around.

Geek didn't spare a single thought to the new private. He thumbed at the mudskippers. "How we going to impress them all into the navy, now? They still growing up wrong."

Calipari shrugged. "When they roll, they won't all be just kids," he said. "Maybe a couple get honest somewhere, or get a soldier's pay to get out of the city."

Geek snorted. "You been in this too long, Nic. When's the last day?"

"I got some time left. I'll stick here until they replace me with a real sergeant ready for the job. You got your stripes, yet, Corporal?"

"Nope."

"Then what do you care?"

"I'll get them, soon as I can, Sergeant."

"You do that. Who knows what kind of soldier they send down here if you don't. You got any good leads on your stripes?"

"This."

"Jona got this one while you weren't looking."

Jona shrugged. "Sorry, Geek. Want to write it up like it was yours?"

"No," said Geek, "You're after that fleur more than I'm after stripes."

Geek pulled out a flask from his pocket and took a long drink of whatever was inside. He handed the flask to Calipari. Calipari drank and handed it to Jona.

Jona drank, and almost spit it out in disgust. It was well water, once-boiled and it tasted like runny, rotten eggs. He poured it out in the street and handed the flask back to Geek empty. "Nic, you got anything better than piss water?" said Jona.

Calipari handed Jona a flask of piss gin. Jona drank it all, fast and to the bottom, and the other king's men were howling about it.

Jona didn't want anyone to drink after him, even if it made him look greedy. He didn't want anyone to get sick.

***

Three days for the three kings, and everyone wore their crowns, king's man, stevedore, baker, mudskipper, and even beggars of skin and bones.

For three days, this was a king's land, not the dog-infested Pens.

Then, the crowns were gone like they had never been there, at all. The fashion turned faster than any noblewoman's dresses at the balls.

***

The season's heat had not fallen asleep when the rains began to come. The heat lingered like a bad guest. The heat drank deep of the swampy, damp city and had no sunlight to burn off the humidity in the dark. A hot fog filled the night with all the heavy stinks that had been hiding in the mud. It was like walking in an oven. There would be no great capers that night. There would only be waiting and cool drinks and few bothered to leave their shelter for the night.

Mishaela had bound her red curls up above her head to keep her hair off her shoulders and neck. She loosened her dress down scandalously to get more air flowing over her skin. This didn't help much, and it wasn't the sort of tavern where the scandal drew attention when the district was so bloated with prostitution.

The tavern keeper put a fire on in his hearth, and lit candles up across that half of the room. He led his patrons away from the fires, to the darker side among long shadows. He wanted the fires to dry the room out, which would cool it off a little compared to the street. His few patrons let their eyes wander to the scarlet-haired girl in a loosened dress sweating with the kind of sweet smell that could drown a man in drink, because they were pretty sure she wasn't a prostitute.

Salvatore and Mishaela had one long table to themselves. They sat across from each other, sideways at the table, each with one leg down a bench. Their backs curled against a brick wall at the dark edge of the tavern because the stones were cool to the touch.

She reached a hand out to him, to take his sweaty palm in her own. He squeezed her tiny, little hand. He marveled at the smallness of her hand. He placed her hand on her own cup of tepid tea.

He didn't want to touch Mishaela tonight, because the skin contact would be too hot.

He sipped his tepid tea. He asked her what she thought about the men in the room, if any of them might have anything worth taking.

"My mother," replied Mishaela, "back when she lived in the Pens and my da a stevedore here, she'd see men like that and tell me never to talk to those men. Never have anything to do with them."

"Why?"

"I don't know why. I never did. Then, I married one of them because he had his own room by himself when an uncle died. I don't know why I did that, either."

"Did you love him?"

"No," she said. She touched his hand again. She looked into his eyes. "I wanted to be by myself somewhere, and marrying got me out of my mother's house for good, and I was alone all day long in an empty house and I didn't have to take care of my brothers and sisters. I didn't have to sleep with all of them around all the time. I just wanted to be by myself for a while. Then, he got sick and died, and I married his boss because I wanted a garden and a place that smelled clean. Not like this."

Jona, just another man at the bar, drank his cool ale. In the heat, he had stripped his uniform jacket off and thrown it over a chair. With his back to Salvatore, and his uniform jacket off, he was just another body in a dark room, a figment haunting a forgetful man.

Salvatore, deep in his immortal soul, knew that Mishaela loved her husband once, and would love him again someday. In his wisdom, he didn't tell her these things he felt in her.

Jona looked over at Salvatore from time to time. He listened for their conversation in the quiet room. He drank slowly. He allowed his anger to smolder.

Next to him, Nicola Calipari drank slow, too. He clutched his cup delicately like an egg. He sipped it. He stared into the liquid.

"Hey, Lord Joni," he said, "You ever think there's a better way?"

"No," said Jona.

"I think there's a better way."

"There isn't a better way."

"There's got to be a better way," said Calipari. His voice trailed off into a long silence. The room filled with this silence. The heavy air sank deeper into the lungs with the silence. The wet heat pushed into the silence like wind pushed chimes into song.

"Nic," said Jona, "You'll get up in the morning, and you'll feel like yourself, again." Jona slapped Calipari's back. "We'll find someone to push until he breaks and you'll feel like yourself. Happens to me all the time."

Nic made a sound in his throat, low and brusque, like the beginning of a word held down too long that came out all mangled and wrong. He took a languorous gulp of his ale. He rolled the liquid around his mouth by rolling his head around his shoulders. He swallowed slowly with his head straight up, his open eyes staring at the ceiling. Nicola put the half-empty cup down. "I'm going home," he said. He stood up carefully, like his knees might not hold his weight but his thighs and feet could.

"Go home, then," said Jona, "Write a letter to Mishaela."

"Yeah," said Calipari, "Wait… who?"

"Franka, I mean," said Jona, "Write a letter to Franka. I said Franka."

"I wondered what that Senta's name was," said Calipari, "You'd best go home to your mother."

Jona lingered in the chair. The empty night opened up like a bottomless ocean. He looked over at Salvatore with Mishaela.

Jona thought about choking the girl in some far, dark place, while Salvatore ran on ahead. Salvatore'd be thinking about joy and glee, and he wouldn't know what happened to Mishaela until he turned his head. And Jona would leave a note pinned to the dead girl's dress, for Salvatore to read every morning, or else, to keep Salvatore away from all girls. It wouldn't work. He was a creature of habits.

Jona strained his ears to hear Salvatore on the other side of the room. He heard almost nothing. The man and woman sat in a sweltering tavern on a sweltering night, and said almost nothing to each other. It was too hot to form words in the thick air, and push them out with heavy tongues.

Jona stood up. He paid for his drinks. He stepped into the insect hum and gauzy lamplight. He walked home through a sweltering fog like walking through smoke that wept.

CHAPTER 6

With the aborted construction of the new canal, carts had to meander around the ditch that would become a river. Between the mounds of upturned dirt and rocks and the housefronts and storefronts, pedestrians struggled to push past each other.

Stray dogs swerved through the legs of the pedestrians to get to the mounds of fresh tossed dirt. The dogs sniffed through the slowly drying muck for any grubs or trash.

The sweaty faces of workmen slipped in and out of the piles of dirt and dogs through the shopgirls wandering with hot corn, and fresh fruits that weren't really fresh by now.

Rachel had to push through the crowd to get to work on time. She worked at another inn near the Pens that wasn't technically a whorehouse, but whores and pimps worked their trade in the tavern and rented rooms by the hour from the innkeeper who was smart enough to look the other way unless a tax assessor was pushing him about it, and then he'd probably turn them all over. Rachel stripped sheets and refilled peter pots the same as if she were at a whorehouse. (The innkeeper was an eater of weed, and he spent every night falling down. He didn't worry what happened in his home, and as soon as he fell to smoking at the pipes and hookahs, he'd probably sell his establishment to a better pimp and all the formalities would finally fade.)

The chamberpots and waste baskets splashed on the tops of people's parasols. Rachel had no parasol. She had one eye towards the windows and one to the ground. She didn't want to step in anything, and she didn't want anything to fall on her hair.

Jona, with Pup next to him, caught sight of Rachel on the other side of the emerging canal. He jumped up to catch a better look. He saw her profile walking away.

"What is it?" said Pup.

Jona waved his hand at Pup. "Nothing," he said, "Just someone I know. I think we should split up. We won't catch any trouble if we both stand around looking like king's men. We have to move around a bit, and see if we can catch them between us. Trap 'em between us, you know."

"Right," said Pup, rolling his eyes, "Who you following? Some birdie with a nice tailfeather?"

"You ain't been out of the scrivening that long, Pup, so don't talk like you some kind of something."

Jona jumped and ducked his way through the mess of bodies on this side of the road. Jona and Rachel weren't far from the tip of progress. Jona pushed through the funnel of bodies. He lost track of Rachel's back in the crowd. He moved faster, seeking the lines of her motion in the crowded street.

She was nowhere.

Then, Pup's finger touched Jona's shoulder.

"Hey," said Pup.

Jona turned. He raised his hand like he was going to hit Pup, but Pup didn't flinch. Jona lowered his hand. "What?" he said.

"Who're you looking for, anyway?" said Pup.

"I'm watching for cutters, just like the sergeant says."

"Calipari says you got some girl around here."

"So?"

"So, none of the boys met her around with you. I heard she was a Senta."

"Yeah, so?"

"So, I saw a Senta with a face only half as ugly as you'd think. It's who you're looking for, right?"

"I ain't looking for her."

"She went over that way," said Pup, pointing down one of the smaller cross streets that led to the heart and soul of the district: the labyrinth of animal pens beside the massive abattoir. "If you were looking for her, that is."

Jona smacked Pup behind his head. "Don't be yourself," snarled Jona. Jona dashed to the cross street after Rachel. Jona reached a new block at the edge of the Pens.

Pup laughed and called out his best wishes to his walkabout partner's back.

Rachel didn't notice the king's man watching her through the crowd. She walked to work with a serious face. Already, her eyes glazed over into the grind of stripping sheets, mopping floors, and dumping chamber pots into the sewer grates behind the building.

Jona leaned against the wall where he stood. He watched the door close behind her.

Pup showed up next to Jona. "She work there?" asked Pup.

"Guess so," said Jona.

"She's not... You know what I mean..."

"She's a maid."

"Still..."

Jona hit Pup hard upside his head. Jona sneered at the new corporal like Jona was about to shove a knife in the boy's gut.

Pup laughed. He stood up straight. He pointed into an alley. "Hey, Jona," he said, "If you're looking for cutters, they're on the other side of the street."

Jona kicked Pup in the gut, hard. Pup doubled over, trying not to laugh as much as he was hurting with the muddy boot print on his stomach. Jona turned back to the whorehouse. Jona watched at the windows for the woman he loved in the windows.

"Want me to let you go for the day?"

"Not a thing to a thing between you and me and you're starting something you can't finish."

"Oh, poor Lord Joni, lovesick and all that nonsense! Poor you!"

Jona smacked him across the face, but Pup kept laughing even as Jona kicked the air where Pup dodged and ran away.

When night got close, Jona was still there. Jona scribbled a note on a scrap of paper from his pocket. He flagged down a shopgirl, and paid the girl a few coins to take the note to Calipari.

The note said something quite nearly true. Jona had a lead on a birdy, and he wanted to see it out, and he should be checked out with Pup in the records.

Jona waited. In every tavern in town the six o'clock bell rang. In the Pens, the butchers and cutters and drovers and porters walked from the killing floors in one stinking clump. Jona hopped into the crowd. He pushed his way across, shouting at the men walking that he needed to get across the street.

Jona slipped in the inn along with the stinking workmen.

His uniform pushed the crowd back. His uniform attracted every eye in the room. The innkeeper stood up from his stool. He had trouble focusing his eyes. A half-chewed weed dangled from his lips like a wet, black noodle. He pulled the plant out, and threw it down behind the counter.

"Hey, king's man!" shouted a butcher. He sat down at a table with a woman. He already had a pipe in his hand. It trembled a little. He clutched the pipe too strong, his hand giving away the fear his face refused to show. "You tossing us all in?" shouted the butcher.

The girls at the table giggled.

Jona shook his head. Jona pushed the butcher's hand with the pipe under the table. "Don't let me see any pinks, and I won't," said Jona, "No raid tonight. You fellows work hard all day, and you're trying to relax. I'm just looking for the same. Foreman don't mind you, then I don't."

The butcher nodded. "I am the foreman," he said. He kept his shaking hand under the table.

Jona turned to the innkeeper. He nodded at the man. "You own this place?"

The innkeeper nodded. He tried to speak, but he coughed instead. A pimp reached over the counter to pound the man on the back.

Jona smiled. He put his hands up. "Nothing to it," he said, "I didn't come here official or anything. Even king's men want to piss at the end of the day, right?"

The innkeeper kept coughing. Finally a ball of phlegm emerged from his throat. He stumbled over to a pisspot and hacked out a black ball of weed, blood, and snot. The innkeeper hobbled back to his stool behind the counter.

Jona gestured to the pisspot. "You sell that to the fullers?"

The innkeeper shrugged. "Sometimes," he said.

"They won't take it with all the eater's weed in it. Gets into the cloth."

"I won't sell 'em that one."

"How much for a room?" said Jona.

"What you need a room for, king's man?"

"I told you I ain't here on official business. I need a room, is all. How much?"

"How long you need it?"

"What're you charging."

The pimp next to Jona was no dandy. A rusty spike was strapped to each leg and one empty eyesocket was un-patched like the man was gazing through old gore. He placed one bent finger on the counter. "You should charge him triple," the pimp said.

Jona rolled his eyes. "Treating me different from any other paying customer on account of my clothes is undignified. I could've come in here with all my boys ringing bells and rolling everyone into the tanks, but I come in here respectful and alone with money to spend like any working man at the end of the day."

The innkeeper looked over at the pimp and shook his head. The innkeeper shrugged at Jona. "I'm sorry king's man, but I think we're full up right now."

"Full up?" said Jona.

The pimp cackled.

"That's right," said the innkeeper, "Looks like we're all full up."

"Full up, it is," said Jona, "I'll just be heading out." Jona pointed at the foreman hiding his pipe under the table. "Why look at that pipe!" said Jona, "You wouldn't be a demon weed smuggler, would you?" Jona pulled the hidden pipe back out from under the table.

The foreman closed his eyes. He dropped the pipe on the table. Little bits of ash spilled out.

Jona licked his finger and touched the ash. He brought it up to his nose and sniffed. "That's demon weed, butcher."

"Is it?" he said.

Jona picked up the pipe and slipped it into a pocket. He took the man by the arm. The foreman came quietly.

The girls at his table waved with big, glassy smiles. The pimps looked at each other sideways, but nobody did anything. They weren't here to protect customers, after all, just the girls. No point fighting a king's man who could ring down the bells over a customer.

Jona looked over his shoulder at the innkeeper, sourly.

Jona walked with one hand on the foreman's shoulder into the night street. He walked beside the man. "You know where the station house is, butcher?"

The foreman took a deep breath. "I do," he said. Out in the street, he wasn't a large man. Animal blood had dried in his hair. Little flecks of skin and hair lined the shoulders above where his apron covered his clothes. Beneath where an apron would be, he was sweaty and muddy, like anybody around here. The stink of the Pens was stronger than the sweat-stink of man, though.

"What d'you do in those Pens?" said Jona.

The man scoffed. "I won't be a thing to a thing, soon."

"They ain't big on hiring the birdies to carve the meat are they?"

"No," said the butcher.

"I wouldn't have pulled you at all except for the innkeeper being how he was. We'll sit down and talk a minute about your pipe, and then you'll go home and get some sleep and be at work in the morning like nothing happened."

"I don't want to talk about the pipe," said the butcher.

"Of course not," said Jona, "so maybe while we're walking you tell me what I want to know, and then you make a break for it and I pretend to chase you, but you get away free and clear and nobody thinks for a minute you're my birdy."

"Sounds like a trap."

"It's your best shot, though, and I'm an honest man, a king's man."

"What do you want to know?" said the foreman. "You ask, and I'll think about it."

"Where do you get your stuff?"

"Asking for my neck."

"I could break your fingers now, or we could wait until we get to the station house. Your call. Hard to work in the abattoir with broken fingers, and plenty of men to take up where you leave off. Where do you get your stuff?"

"I get it off the top of some stuff that someone else brings in. It's just a big crate. It's full of the stuff, and stinks."

"Who brings it in?"

"I don't know."

"They know you're skimming?"

"That's how I get paid. It comes in a crate with these sheep. Sheep come in on a sheep ship, and they all got their ankles cut already, so they can't run around. My crew goes on board, and slits their throats. Then we carry them from the ship to the floor. In with the sheep there's a big crate. When it's quiet, after all the sheep are off the ship, I open it. I take my cut. I move the rest to this porter I know on the other side of the floor. Sometimes the crate's full, and sometimes it ain't. It stinks the same either way.

The crate goes back on the same ship it came from. Sometimes it ain't and I do it myself."

"Who got you started on this stuff?"

"Foreman before me ran it, so I do, too."

"I'm not after you little fellows," said Jona, "I want to make that clear to you and yours. I want to know who's on top. I want the paperwork, not the people. What's this porter's name who takes the stuff off you?"

"New Nima."

"New Nima? How new is he?"

"He been there longer than me, but everyone calls him 'New Nima'."

"Who runs the sheep?"

"The only sheep ship every single day on my watch and no one else's sheep comes here. You run the books, and find it for yourself."

"Good enough for now, foreman," said Jona, "but I want you to say hello to me when you see me. And if you don't give me your real name, I'll ring down the Pens to find you. Don't test me on that."

"I'm Havala Veriki."

"I'm Corporal Jona Lord Joni. If one of my other boys starts pushing you too hard, you tell them you're with me, and we won't forget a good bird. Don't test me lightly, Veriki. I don't like my time abused for nothing."

"Right," said the foreman, "so I got to keep singing when you want and I got to take my punches, too."

"But not too many. That's how this deal works," said Jona, "You'll like it. You got a friend. Before, all of us were enemies, right?"

"What you are now is trouble, king's man," said the butcher, "So, I make a break for it now?"

"Go on, Havala Veriki. I'll remember you real good."

The foreman took a deep breath and took to the street like a galloping mule. He wasn't fast. Jona reached out to him, but let one of his boots catch on the ground. He stumbled a bit, caught himself, and kicked his boot at the air behind the runaway.

Jona turned, and walked back towards Rachel's inn. He staked out the place from the outside. He watched her rolling sheets out on the lines from the top floor. He watched her carrying buckets of water.

He wanted to go over to her and ease her burden. He didn't. He watched her in the dark.

He wanted to help her with her brother. He wanted to be good to him, and help him, so she'd see. It wouldn't work, though. He was mature enough to know that, at least.

Rachel left halfway between midnight and morning with a large bucket of water in her hand. Jona followed her down the street, to the edge of the Pens.

The fence between the street and this edge of the cattle pens was twice as tall as a man. The wide wooden slats ran sideways for twenty feet to keep the casual rustlers from banging a few nails loose at the bottom and slipping smaller animals between the gaps.

Rachel halted against the fence. She jammed an ear against the tiny slits in the wood. She placed the bucket of water next to a fence. She looked as best as she could between the slats, but with the lamp light behind her and the darkness before her, and the slats so small, she couldn't see anything but darkness. She whispered her brother's name through the fence.

Piles of clothes that stank of pink smoke staggered in an alley near the fence. One of them came over to Jona and begged for coins. Jona didn't look long at the man. Jona punched him in the throat to shut him up and shoved him off.

The man choked, took three steps, and then fell over.

Jona realized he had just punched someone he knew. He bent over and touched the man's leg. "Hey, Jaime," he said, "That you? You get yourself tossed that bad?"

Jaime rolled over onto his back. He coughed. He looked up at Jona with big, spinning eyes and sweat that left a pink trail of dots everywhere it touched.

Jona's eyebrows bunched up. His lips tightened. "I ought to roll you for this," said Jona, softly, "At least you left your uniform at home. I can pretend I don't know you."

"It's not what you think," he said, "I'm investigating. I need some money to go back in and talk to this fellow."

"Yeah?" Jona dropped a single coin on Jaime's body. "What's this fellow's name?"

"Please, Jona," he said, "please, I'll need more than that."

"His name?"

"Please, Jona..."

"Your head's all cheese. You're thinking straight, you wouldn't lie to me. We all got our sins, but we stay out of the sinners' dens that go for the demon weed. We keep clean of that Calipari and captain and king's command. Your head's so gone you trying to toss me for a coin and I see through you so easy I'm embarrassed for you. Let me explain your situation, Jaime. I am not giving you one more coin to cheese your head with, and I had better see that report you write about your birdy in the morning," whispered Jona. "You hear me? I better sit with him in the room when you bring in the birdy in the morning. Calipari was looking for you the other day. You're lucky he didn't find you here. How you get the coin for this, huh? You can only call in so many favors to the night before they start calling favors from you. You know that, right?"

"What are you doing out here?" said Jaime. He rubbed at his throat, coughed again, "Elishta, but what'd you throat me for?"

"I'm surprised you can feel anything like you are," whispered Jona. Jona pointed at Rachel.

Rachel hadn't noticed the king's men in the shadows. She called out for her brother against the fence.

Jaime managed to find his feet below him like a new foal: all awkward angles and knees. Jaime leaned into the wall. He looked over at the Senta with the bucket of water against a fence.

"I've seen her," said Jaime, "I have seen her."

Jona punched Jaime's arm. "Hush up," he whispered.

Rachel walked around the fence, with her bucket, calling out to her brother. Her voice had reached panic pitch. A couple stragglers dressed like gangers with the same dirty red shirts—just drunk street fighters, not too dangerous—ambling down the street stopped to laugh. They mimicked her cries for her brother in high-pitched voices.

Rachel turned and snapped her fingers. A line of fire shot up to the two men's faces. They ran off, cackling like drunken crows.

Rachel turned back to the fence. She pounded one of the slats with her palm. She threw the bucket over the top.

The bucket splashed water all over the other side of the fence. The bucket itself landed on something soft.

A human voice moaned.

Rachel leaned against the fence. "Djoss, is that you?" she said.

A man's voice called out to her by name.

"Djoss, I brought the bucket so you could get over the fence," she said. She gestured with her hands as if he could see her. "Just put the bucket upside-down and get on top. Then, stand on it and climb over."

Djoss' voice reached over the fence. "Rachel, how in Elishta'd you find me here?"

"I saw the shape of things, just now. Djoss, I saw you here, like it's where you might never leave. Someone came and told me you. How in Elishta'd you end up in there, anyhow?"

"I jumped over."

"Why?"

"You don't want to know," he said, laughter in his voice. "Thanks for finding me."

Rachel frowned at him, but he couldn't see it. He was still on the other side of the fence. "Why are you laughing?" She crossed her arms. "You're sleeping in cow shit and you're laughing about it?"

His fingers appeared at the top of the high fence. His grip slipped, and he fell back into the pen.

He laughed again. He tried to speak to her, and explain himself. She didn't listen. She told him to go home. She said it like she was angry and sad and begging and commanding all at once. "Go home," she said. Her arms stayed crossed while she walked away, alone. Djoss still hadn't made it over the fence.

Jona saw Djoss' hand on the top of the fence again, pulling hard.

Two night shift king's men strolled around a corner, and saw the hands and heard the grunts of the man pulling himself over the top.

Jona stepped out of the alley. He waved the two king's men over to him. With his hands, he urged them to ignore Djoss. Jona pulled the king's men into a dark alley, beside the hidden hookahhouse.

The night shift king's men asked Jona if he knew what the fellow throwing himself over the wall was about. Jona said the fellow got thrown there by a bouncer, and he was nothing to nobody, and just trying to get back to the hookah.

The night shift king's men asked what Jona was doing there. Jona pointed at the house. He told them that Corporal Jaime of Calipari's crew was inside, in plain clothes, and cheese-for-brains at a hookah after his wife and child had died. "Somebody should do something about it, yeah?" Jona had said. "He's gone to the other side forever if he's at the hookahs. The king will never get him back from this."

The three king's men nodded all around. Their faces were grim like blood monkeys. This unanimous decision came to them all at the same time.

People sucking on hookahs never came back. Every king's man knew that. Eaters could come back. Pipers might make it if they were forced to it and strong. The people at the hookahs were walking dead, paying every coin for the privilege.

The three king's men braced the back and side doors closed with crates and trash jammed into doorknobs and hinges. Jona and one of the night shifters took a corner in the back so they could watch for men jumping out alley windows.

One of the night shift king's men tugged his bell out of the lapel pocket in his jacket. His partner stepped into the front door, pulling at the pocket with the bell. Jona tugged his bell out, too. They waited until they were all ready and holding a bat in their hands, or a long, sharp tooth. Their man was inside, and everyone inside was rolling tonight to get him off the street.

Jona swung his bell first. It clanged like a cow's, but with a harder edge to the sound, like the bell might crack a skull in a pinch. Then, the other king's men rang their bells.

The king's men all over the district and beyond it heard and rang bells, all running to the center of the clanging sound.

Bodies banged into doors, but they were all braced shut from the outside. Some men tried for windows, but Jona and the other king's man knocked them back with bats or the blunt edge of swords before anyone got out.

Every king's man in earshot came in minutes swinging bats and swords and bells that called every other king's man in a wider ear shot and every man, woman, and child in that building got surrounded and then the king's men went inside and pulled every soul to the station houses.

And Jaime was in there, laughing when they pulled him out, unable to speak.

***

The night sergeant clomped Jona on the back. "You must be stamped, Corporal—rolling hard since daylight and now morning's back again."

Jona pretended to yawn. He shrugged. "Send me to Elishta,

Sergeant. All the same to me. Work is work."

The sergeant scribbled a note to Calipari about all that had transpired. "Take the morning off. Get some sleep, and come in for lunch shift. I'll make two of my scriveners work the morning to cover for you and Jaime a while. We're too short right now to give you all day, and we got too much paperwork after that little thing we did tonight to send too many scriveners walking about."

Jona saluted. "I never needed much sleep, sir," he said, "I'll make it in early so your boy is back tomorrow night."

"I bet Calipari'll want to know exactly what happened, from your mouth," said the sergeant.

"What happened is what happened."

"Wish it hadn't on my watch," said the night sergeant. "I knew they were looking for Jaime the other day out in the tombs below the temple, with his kids resting and he can't afford a decent funeral for them out on the bay. He crossed over, took money for something he shouldn't have and spent bad coin on bad. He should've spent it sending his kids to the water. Maybe could've looked away from him on that one a little while if his reasons were right."

"We didn't know they were looking for Jaime," said Jona, "We knew they were looking for somebody, but we didn't know it was Jaime."

The night sergeant nodded. "Right," he said, "and you find him at a hookah in the middle of the night even though you didn't know we were looking for him, and you rang down the bells clear in the head and not a drop of drink in you?"

"Something like that," said Jona.

"You want to be sergeant when Calipari's through, or you still after that lieutenant's fleur?"

"I hadn't been thinking about any of that stuff in a while. Just been doing the job, walking about and staying on the king's business."

"You think about it, Corporal. I know you want the fleur, but no reason not to be a sergeant a while first. Geek's not sneaky like you are. We hear things about you always turning up. We hear rumblings in the room that the worst people in the city are scared of you turning up to rumble, and we all hear about it. You know your way around, day or night. It's useful is what that is."

"I think Calipari wants Geek, and I think Calipari's right. Geek's better with the privates." Jona pointed at the scriveners. "Geek's a good boy. He's cleaner. My hands get dirty, Sergeant."

"Geek is no cleaner than any of us," said the night sergeant. "Calipari's been at this longer than I have. Longer than anybody I know. If anyone has good judgment it's him. I'm just saying about how us on the night crew like our boys sneaky, and clean never kept order on the street. Day shift is probably different. We like to know the trouble only comes to folks like Jaime that go looking for it, and the good people who don't want trouble get none. Sneaky's good for that."

Jona said nothing to that. He stood there until he thought he was probably dismissed. The night sergeant had already fallen back into the paperwork in the candlelight. Night shift scriveners always had bad eyes. Night shift desk sergeants had bad eyes, too. Jona didn't want to ruin his eyes like that.

***

I worry when you don't make it home.

Ma, I'm fine. Worry when you hear something bad.

What were you doing?

I was working, Ma. Sometimes I have to work to the long hours.

You should've sent a note, at least. You should've sent a boy with a note.

Ma, I'm fine.

You come home like you've been rolling in the mud without a coin in your pocket and bruises on your neck and you want to tell me that?

If I'm on a fellow hard like I was, I'm not stopping to write a note.

I might as well stop to shout my name and what I'm doing to the whole wide...

I hate...

Ma, I know. This is how it is. If I can send a note, I will. That's all I can do.

Did you catch anyone bad tonight?

Yes, we did. We caught a king's man in a hookah pit more cheese than alive. We ran the whole place down. Did you hear the riot bells from here? That was us. That was us bringing down one of our own who went as bad as it gets. That was me hunting him and finding him, and he was on my crew.

Oh. Did you know him well?

I did, Ma. Been running with him since I don't know when. I rang the riot bells, and now he's walking to the noose. His head's going to be on the wall and I was the one sent him to it. I knew him since I was just starting out. I knew him so long, Ma, and I was the one finding him and ringing the bells.

I'm sorry.

I'm sorry, too, Ma. I'm sorry I didn't send a note. I know you worry about me.

CHAPTER 7

Bricks and rotting wood and the oily dandruff of the paint that had bubbled and cracked and fell like tiny, dirty snow from the wet heat.

Rachel ran her fingers along the edge of her own room.

She couldn't sleep. Every time she closed her eyes she dreamed of Djoss grabbing a good man in the dark, throwing the good man against a wall and shoving a knife into the good man's stomach. She dreamed of Djoss snatching ragpickers by their ankles and lifting them upside down to shake out all their coins. She dreamed of Djoss slipping his hand into an open window and grabbing anything he could fence. She dreamed his hand found a neck and he squeezed off the skull to sell with his big hands.

She dreamed of Djoss in a pink pit, his eyes glazed over like he was dreaming of Rachel dreaming of him dreaming of Rachel dreaming of him dreaming of Rachel dreaming of him dreaming of Rachel dreaming of him...

Where did the dreamcasting end, and the dreams begin?

He came home, when he came home, with no food. He opened the cupboards looking for food. He ate what he found, raw. He slept with his back to Rachel if he stayed long enough to sleep.

They had stopped talking to each other.

Silence is a word, too. Silence is a terrible word. Silence is the sound of bridges crumbling in the dark, of flowers wilting, of dead tongues.

***

Once he knew where to look, it was so simple. Jona took Geek with him into the Pens. They passed the feedlot where animals were droved into pens marked with their owners. They came in on ships, and overland, and sometimes they were just pulled in one at a time from someone who had an animal on his own and wanted to sell it. All the killing happened here. Animals were pushed and prodded into narrow stalls, smashed with hammers or cut across the throat to bleed out. The House of Sabachthani owned the building, and pushed the law through that made all butchers licensed, all meat passing through these walls. And, Jona knew where to look.

"I see it there, Geek," said Jona. He pointed at Havala Veriki, prodding at a large wagon crate with a prybar. It was the kind of crate that came on galleons, big enough it was too big to move overland, too big for carts and wheels. It would come up from the bowels of a ship on a crane, land there, and stay there. Havala Veriki was the man at the gate with the crowbar, waiting for them. As soon as Jona and Geek came in, he knew. He didn't pretend he didn't. He saw from across the room. He grabbed a crowbar and stepped up to the right crate. Havala Veriki was resigned, pale.

"It's a sheep shipment from a boat. It sits around a few days. Pull the numbers off the lot and go get the paperwork. I want to know who owns the shipment. Move fast. We got to move fast before anyone knows what we're doing."

"You sure this is a good idea?"

"It's a terrible idea, but do it anyway, Geek. If it's good enough, you can take the bars for it in the write-up. Move fast."

Havala Veriki was there, and said nothing to Jona. Havala wouldn't even look up.

"Go on, then," said Jona. "Go to the business, man."

Havala pressed his ear against the door. "I don't think it's ready," he said.

"Crack it, or give me the crowbar. Doesn't matter to me."

Havala looked down at the crowbar and thought about it. He pushed it into the wood and half-heartedly worked it.

"The sheep come in, and we don't open it," he said. "Comes off the Island and we never open it until it's quiet."

He worked at it a little harder.

"You're going to get us both killed," he said.

"Don't got any guts in these Pens with all these hard boys?" said Jona. "This is on me, not you."

Jona looked around, seeing how many men there were watching from the corners of their eyes. There were hammers that killed cows, here, and men who carved meat with knives all day. Jona was alone on the floor, with Havala hesitating and play-acting.

Jona shoved him aside. He pressed his ear against the wood, and heard the baying and shuffling and scratching. He cursed and slammed the crowbar into the slats, pushing hard. It cracked, and the smell hit, nearly blowing Jona over. It was a smell like rancid blood and flowers in bloom.

Havala stood sheepishly beside it, willing himself not to look.

The shipment of sheep was not of sheep at all. The animals bayed and keened, and some were as big as sheep, but the weed was in them, growing pink and flowering from inside of their guts and shoulders and necks. It was a vine that wrapped around them. Without tongues to truly howl their pain, they could only grunt and wheeze and occasionally bay a bit, with muted voices.

Dogs, carrying the weed that grew into their very skin. The foreman refused to look. "Ain't supposed to open this cart for another week at least. Ain't supposed to even open it."

"It's open now," said Jona. "Look at them. Do you see?"

The foreman was afraid.

"Do you see this?" said Jona. "Do you know how to make a dog grow a weed like that? Do you know what kind of plant that is?"

The weed was sick and purple-veined, feeding on blood and soul not light. The flower bulbs were open, redder than blood and stinking of dead meat. Jona knew the smell too well. It smelled like his own blood. The demon weed came from demons, somehow. It was a demon, or a product of one. He curled his nose.

"Why won't you look at what you do?" he said, to the foreman.

"I'm paid not to look," he said.

Jona grabbed him hard at the back of the neck and arm. Jona wrenched him into the wall, furious. Then, Jona threw him into the crate to look and fall into the stench of dying dogs and living weed. He slammed the door. The foreman didn't scream. He whimpered a little, then began to cry. It was a quiet thing, barely as loud as the tongueless dogs that died inside the crate.

The abattoir was bustling, but once the crate was opened, all men had backed away and fallen still. All the men stood or worked around the far side, away from the crate. Dead animals were splayed open, gutted, hacked. Living animals keened and moaned in fear beyond the walls. The men here were silent. They wouldn't even look up. They just pretended to be working somewhere far away from the crate.

Jona grunted at them. These men, who refused to see, refused to fight. It's no wonder Salvatore had lived so long here, and Jona's father and grandfather, too. No one wanted to look at what was right in front of them. They were afraid to look. These tall, strong, hard men who carried knives to work and muscled down cows and horses with their bare hands and iron hammers were afraid to open a crate.

Geek was in the main office digging through papers with a note sheet ready.

"Hey, Geek," said Jona. "We don't need to worry about that stuff."

"Why'd you send me over here, then? Bloody hell, Jona, you know I didn't want to stick a finger in the hornet's nest."

"I know where the ship came from. I saw what was on it, and

I know where that came from, too. I know, Geek. I know everything. Frankly, now that I know, I think it's better no one else does. If I can stop it, I will, but… I won't. I can't. The ship came from the Island. I know where it came from. I know who."

He crumpled up the sheet of paper and threw it on the floor. "Calipari told you that, didn't he, back when you started poking into this business? Anyone could've told you that. Bloody hell, Jona. Might as well be digging a hole to Elishta itself."

Jona nodded. Back at the station house, he wrote a report and handed it to Calipari. The old sergeant folded it in half. "Do you want me to read this?"

"Sure," said Jona. "Not a lick of it is true. Read whatever you want."

"Can I send it up to processing? Can I send it to the captain?"

"Yeah. I have to go," he said. "Sorry I'm not walking about, but if I don't get ahead of that report, my ma and me don't survive the night."

"Are you leaving town?"

"No," said Jona. "I won't leave town, and I won't tell you where I'm going. Should be all right, though. Hey, how long have you known?"

"I make a point of not knowing, Lord Joni. I do everything I can not to know because long live the king and all that. You can be a fool if you want, but I'm sending Geek to ground with enough coin to pay for his hiding hole. I wish you hadn't dragged him into your folly."

"Right," he said. "I'm going to go see someone I know and let him know it was all a mistake, and I'm hushing it up. I got a copy of the report I'm sending up the chain. Any heat comes down to me. Geek will be fine, I think."

"I'm almost done. I'll have land out there, where me and Franka can raise a family and work the land. I got a letter from her just the other day. Watch your step, Lord Joni. I hope you get your officer's fleur and marry a nice merchant's widow and get out of this mess with your skin and your teeth on the same bones."

Jona nodded. He stood a long time, looking at Nicola, and Nicola looking back. Both men looked so tired.

Then, they both went back to work.

CHAPTER 8

The first real, hard rain of the turning seasons came. The clouds blew in from the ocean when the city slept, and by morning, the oppressive weight of the air gave warning of what was to come. By mid-morning, the air was so fat with water, it could no longer hold. The rain fell. This was a rain to melt old roof tiles and flood new sewers and old sewers alike and to wash all the city raw. There were no people anymore, just parasols and high boots and cloaks. Everyone that could found shelter from the storms. In the Pens district, in every house and working building, empty pots filled up with water to be dumped out windows. In the empty rooms, water filled up the floors to rot them out. It was the season when squatters were tolerated who would be willing to handle the flood. It was the season when every doorway became shelter from the storms for dogs and people who might as well have been dogs.

Mishle Leva's final canal wasn't finished. Water would have to erode the final stretch with mud spilling over the malformed shoreline, cutting its own pools and runnels down the seven or eight blocks to the edge of the docks. A pinker talked about how nothing ever worked right down here, and about how the people had all melted away, and that's why no workers were left to finish the canal.

This pinker, I'll call him by his true name for there was someone observing him. Djoss was his name and his listener didn't know it—leaned over to the fellow next to him in the bar and explained these mysteries. Salvatore heard Djoss' story. Salvatore leaned over to the woman he was with, Mishaela—her of the luxurious red hair and the lonely heart.

She, Mishaela, leaned over to Djoss. "Tell me, fellow," she said, "How long have you been sucking on the hookahs?"

Djoss mumbled something about a red parasol, staring at his own hands.

Mishaela touched Djoss' arm. "You want some money?" she said, "You can head down a bit if you get some of that. You bring me some jewelry and I'll give you some coin for it. Go get me some jewelry and I'll buy it off of you."

Djoss pushed her hand off. He stood up. He turned from the bar. He walked into the rain, no parasol and no hat and no cloak to keep the hard rain from falling on his skin like warm needles.

Salvatore kissed Mishaela's neck. "That got him moving. You up for a kick?"

Mishaela took Salvatore's hand. "Poor fellow can't tell a lady from a parasol."

"Maybe he did," said Salvatore. He pulled Mishaela up to her feet. "You need any redroots? They got 'em here."

"I can sleep all day if I want as long as dinner's on time. I told you that."

"Oh, sorry."

"He's nothing but trouble, but I'm bored. Think he might be carrying anything?"

"Probably not."

"I'm bored, Salvatore. I've lived here my whole life and I don't care about the rains."

The storm embraced Salvatore and Mishaela harder than they embraced each other. It shattered on Salvatore's big, black hat. It slid over the lip of Mishaela's parasol like a walking waterfall.

***

Djoss stumbled down the street under the full weight of the rain, unaware of his audience. The lighters didn't walk around in this. The streetlights lasted as long as the kerosene inside of them. In and out of the flickering light, Mishaela couldn't follow Djoss with her eyes. Salvatore, with his ancient eyes, could.

Salvatore followed Djoss. Djoss' cheap, dirty linen shirt clung to his skin like water-proof mud.

Salvatore pointed at Djoss' back down the street.

A strong gust blew rain up into Salvatore's face. His hat blew back. Mishaela angled her parasol to protect Salvatore's face. Their capes caught the wind but didn't fly out far with the sheets of rain falling hard.

Djoss stopped to gawk at every shop window, and all of them were closed.

Dogs stumbled in and out of the alleys, watching the scrap trash rinsed away into the rivers that flowed to the sewers, and all the smells of the city merged into one mud smell and all the boots of the people—where dogs saw them—were caked in mud and all the dogs were caked in mud, too. All the daylight rivalries found a truce in the rising mud. Dogs huddled together to stay warm in the covered places out of the blustering rain beside cats and rats and large birds.

When Djoss staggered like he was going to fall, Salvatore held his breath. "He could drown on his back with his mouth open like he is. We're counting on our fellow to lead us to coin, not drown."

Djoss turned down an alley that still had plenty of streetlight. A red line of paint—gambling—hid in a corner between a boarded up basement and a large fence. On the other side of the fence, boar pigs tried their best to sleep. The muted grunting snores from the animals were not as powerful as the smell.

Salvatore gestured with his neck. Mishaela didn't see it. Salvatore pointed at the door. "Red door. Card game," he said.

Mishaela nodded. She squinted into the rain. She saw nothing but rain.

Djoss pounded on the door. It opened into blinding light. A black shadow filled the entryway with a club over one shoulder.

"You up, wet bear? This is a five table. Five gets you in the door." The man chortled after he spoke. Djoss looked like exactly what he was: a pinker desperate for more coins to fall into the hookahs.

Djoss tried to push into the room.

The man pushed Djoss back with his free hand, and adjusted the club on his shoulder.

"I need to know you can stand the table. Got any coins?"

Djoss scowled. One leg dropped back and his back hand curled into a fist.

"Didn't think so, pinker."

The man turned to close the door.

Djoss' pendulous fist cut through the rain. Mishaela heard the thump of knuckle on the back of the bouncer's head, where the neck and the skull connect. Djoss was still strong. No one expects pinkers to be strong.

The bouncer fell into the table. Furniture crumpled inside the room.

Djoss went in with his fists up.

Salvatore told Mishaela to wait for him. Salvatore jumped down the alley. Mishaela didn't wait. She jumped after Salvatore, and slipped a kitchen knife from her sleeve.

Salvatore unfolded his blackjack from his pocket.

A king's man—I'll call him by his nickname: Geek—pulled Djoss out from the room with Djoss' arm pulled up behind the back.

"Calm yourself, killer," said Geek. "You got some rowdy stuff in you doing like that when your head is all cheesed. You just want some coins so you can suck on some hookah somewhere, right?"

Geek pushed Djoss off into the rain. Geek pulled a few coins from his belt and threw them at Djoss' feet.

"Get out of here," said Geek.

The bouncer who had been struck in the head had not, in fact, been holding a club. He had the steel weapon in his hand now, and the thick wooden sheathe in the other. The steel flashed and flickered where it wasn't dusted by rust.

Djoss bent over to collect the coins. Geek turned around to go back to the game. Geek saw the bouncer with the rusty sword out, cutting at the rain. The bouncer had that angry sneer on his face that meant only one thing from a red door bouncer with a sword in his hands.

Geek held up his empty palms. He shouted for the bouncer to cool.

The bouncer lunged.

Geek shouted, "No!" He jumped in front of the bouncer, and grabbed at the man's sword arm. The two giant men crashed like ramming ships, then crumpled into a heap of breaking masts and shattered hulls.

The bouncer ended on top. He stood up. He didn't have the sword in his hands.

Geek didn't get up. In the crash, the sword blade was angled down his back, and he had fallen on it. And he made soft gurgling noises in his throat, but the rain drowned him out.

He looked up into the storm clouds. He looked up into the rain that ate tiles and nibbled at foundations like rats and filled the sewers up until everything spilled over into the canals. The rain seemed to be everything gray in the world, gray water falling from gray clouds and his eyes were gray now, too. The rain washed Geek's blood away, washed his skin away, washed him away forever.

Djoss ran stumblingly away, carrying coins to the hookah pipes.

The bouncer had this look on his face like he had just accidentally killed a friend, which I imagine is precisely what he had done. More importantly, he had killed a king's man.

Salvatore called out to the bouncer. "It was an accident," he said, "I saw it with these eyes. But you think for a minute the king's men are going to care if a plug ugly animal like you rolled their fellow for real, or not?"

The bouncer turned. He reached into his empty scabbard for a sword, but there was no sword there. His hand clenched on air twice. Then, the bouncer lifted the club-like scabbard up.

"Easy," said Salvatore, "I don't even want a name. I want the uniform, and I don't care about this fellow who's dead. I don't know a thing from a thing about that king's man or you. Give me his uniform, and dump your mistake into the swollen river and consider it lesson learned. Never be flashing a tooth when a blackjack'll do you fine."

Salvatore swung his little weapon in the air. Mishaela remained in the shadows.

The bouncer kicked Geek's body in the stomach. "Take whatever you want," he said. The bouncer's hands shook. His face was paler than Salvatore's. His eyes were scared. He walked back to the door with the red stripe on it. The bouncer didn't think to recover his sword.

Salvatore went to work on the body, fast. He pulled the bloody sword out from the back, and tossed it into the canal. He stripped the body nude.

Mishaela stepped carefully from the shadows.

"This is horrible," she said. She was pale.

"I know people pay good money for bloody uniforms," said Salvatore.

"Who?"

"King's men. We dump the body, and sell the bloody uniform back to the king, and he figures out which fellow won't be back for muster so the families find out, you know? Do a good deed for this fellow, and make a bit for ourselves, too."

"Right," said Mishaela, "What about the bouncer?"

"It was an accident," said Salvatore, "Didn't you see it?"

"I could barely see it through the rain."

"I saw it fine. I was closer. No one's fault, really. Just an accident. King's man got in the way of the bouncer and they both fell. King's man fell on the sword."

Geek's mute corpse kept looking up into the rain. His mouth was full of pinkish rain that spilled out of the sides of his mouth like the water was coming from inside of him instead of from the sky.

Salvatore finished stripping the uniform. He folded it up small and shoved it into his deepest cloak pockets. He rolled the naked corpse into the water, and watched it float away until the rain shrouded the white skin in darkness.

(Jona had seen very little through the rain. He had seen only enough to know that someone was knocked down. He hadn't seen the uniform well enough in the dark. He hadn't seen anything real. He had been trying to decide if he should follow Djoss, or stay with Salvatore, or just go home and hide. He knew someone died, and Salvatore was taking their clothes. I can see what he cannot, because I can smell the rain on the uniform when it turns up again, and the rust from the blade's edge. Still, I am not completely certain. Memories are only as good as the mind that carries them. Blessed Erin has shown me this vision in the night. I show it here.

Know that neither Salvatore nor Jona did anything to help the dead man. For this sin, alone, they deserve their fate.)

Jona stood in the dark, watching the rain fall, and wondering what exactly had happened up ahead, where he could barely see through the torrential rains.

It was so thick in the air, and he was so tired of following Salvatore and of living someone else's life, when anger boiled up cooled into a simmer until it didn't matter that he was angry. He was tired, and wanted to go somewhere warm and dry.

He went home.

Salvatore didn't seem to recognize him, anyway.

***

Clouds curled into themselves like gray hair in water. The old woman of the winter storms wiped away the sun's summer rage with her mop of thick, gray hair.

The rain was far worse than the summer heat for the Pens District. Salvatore's building flooded out, and water devoured the limestone foundation. Half the building crumbled into rubble. Salvatore was asleep in his hammock. He woke to the groaning in the walls where the bricks worked loose from mortar. Then, the crash and the screams.

Salvatore's room, on his half of the building, hadn't collapsed, yet.

Salvatore rushed out of his room, and down the hall and to the stairwell and on one hand he had sturdy brick walls and on the other open air and rainfall where wall used to be and a dozen screams fighting up through the fallen bricks and some of the people of the street had thrown aside their parasols and hats to tug at the bricks and some of them kept walking like this catastrophe was just another street trick to sucker them.

Survivors piled furniture on carts, covered them with blankets and bed sheets that didn't keep the rain out.

Two little kids—for laughs—were beating on the dead with sticks. They were cursing this mangled body for the crimes it had committed in life, and these kids were laughing.

Salvatore shuddered at that.

I'm convinced he shuddered at that. It's the sort of thing that would happen there, and it's the sort of thing that would make him shudder. He is a wicked thing, but he does not believe in his own wickedness, and he can not love wickedness in others.

CHAPTER 9

"Wake up, Djoss," whispered a voice. "Djoss!"

Djoss groaned.

"Djoss!" shouted the voice. It was Rachel. He felt fingers on his arms. Fingers wrapped around his wrists, and pulled at him. They were Rachel's fingers.

"I'm awake," he said. He opened his eyes. His legs and arms still weren't working right. In his hand, he still held the long stem of the hookah.

Djoss smiled. "I had a horrible dream." Djoss looked around the room. A low haze of purple smoke hovered in the air. Soft pillows stank of vomit and pink smoke and spread along the filthy cellar floor.

"I was looking for you all night!" shouted Rachel. "I didn't know where you went!"

Djoss laughed. "I'm sorry," he said.

"You spent all of our money, didn't you?"

"No," he said. His body slowly discovered solid ground below him.

"How much did you waste this time?"

"Not all of it," he said.

Two mostly nude men with the tans and hats of foreign sailors watched listlessly as the siblings fought. From upstairs, a bouncer peered down into the cellar. The light and the noise of the tavern spilled in from the open door. He shouted, "Take it outside!"

"I had to pay just to come down here and find him!" she shouted.

"I don't care!" shouted the bouncer, "Keep it down!"

Djoss nodded. "We'll go," he said, "Will you help me outside?"

"No," she said. She let go of his hands. She had been holding his hands. He sank back down to the pillows. She snarled, and grabbed his hands again. She dragged him to the stairs.

He struggled to work his legs. He couldn't quite make them work.

"Hey, you!" shouted Rachel to the bouncer. "Hey! I'll pay you to throw him outside!"

The bouncer shrugged. "I'll do it for free just to be rid of you."

Djoss dropped asleep when the bouncer picked him up. Djoss dreamed of flying. He woke up lying in an alley behind the tavern, his face covered in mud. He looked up to see his sister's frowning face. He grimaced. "Rachel," he said, "Have you been here long?"

"Yes," she said.

"Have I been here long?" he asked. He tasted the rising bile on his tongue.

"Yes." She folded her arms. "How much did you spend?"

He threw up into the mud.

***

The siblings sat on his bed below the window. Djoss stared at a cup of tea she had made for him. He didn't feel well enough to drink it. He held the teacup in his palm like an egg.

Rachel sat across from him, and stared at his tea. She didn't want to look at him.

She leaned back, calmly. "Aren't you going to tell me you're sorry?"

"Probably not," he said.

"Are you sorry?" She looked at his face, desperate to see remorse in the crevices.

He thought about his answer. He looked down into her eyes. "Yes," he said.

The tea's waves of steam faded into tepid nothing. Time passed in silence.

"Drink your tea," she said.

"I'm not ready, yet."

She sniffed. "Drink it anyway." She was calm.

He nodded. He held his breath, and swallowed as fast as he could. It burned down his sore throat. When it landed in his stomach, it sunk like lead weights.

"Feel better?" she said, bitterly.

"No."

"Good," she said. "What are we going to do with you, Djoss?"

"I don't know," he replied.

"We have to leave the city," she said, into her hands, "I would rather spend the rest of my life sleeping under a tree than watch you do this to yourself. We have to leave any city that has that awful stuff."

"Where will we go?"

"Do we have any money left?"

"I have a bit in my pocket. I think I won it gambling." He looked down at his hands. Geek's coins looked up at him, winking in the light like thieves. "I hope I won it."

She coughed. She shook her head. "That's what will happen if you keep this up. You'll spend the rest of your life staring at the ceiling and drooling. You won't remember a thing. You'll do terrible things, and you won't even remember, and you won't be doing them for the right reasons."

"I know."

She clenched her fist, and pounded the wall. The tea trembled. "If you know…!" She hit the wall even harder. The plaster dented. She heaved her teacup out the open window.

"I don't know why I do it, Rachel," he said. Djoss' bottom lip trembled. He closed his eyes.

"We have some money left, however you got it. We'll sell everything. We'll sign on with a merchant in need of haulers and pack handlers, if we can. We'll walk through the woods if we have to. We have to get out of the city. We'll find somewhere new, somewhere far away. We'll start over, new."

"I'm sorry," he said, "I guess it's all me this time. First time it's ever been me, huh?"

She held the rest of her words inside of her. They burned like acid.

***

Rachel carried a small sack on her back full of the pots and cracked crockery they had been using. They would sell all of it at whatever fence would offer any money for stuff that was almost worthless. Djoss searched around for the teacup, but already the street had swallowed the cracked, white clay egg. Djoss carried nothing at all. He was still too weak and uncoordinated.

The landlord's wife came out from the butcher shop and asked if they were leaving. Rachel told the landlord's wife that she and Djoss were going to buy new furniture soon.

The butcher's wife snorted. "Tell me when you're done. You paid up and you can stay until the end of the week, but you get nothing back from us. Don't even ask."

Rachel didn't repeat her lie about new furniture. She didn't say anything at all. The two women looked at each other in the street, both of them gauging the other.

"Will you wait until we're done moving out?" said Rachel. "We'll be done today. We've already sold everything of value. Nothing is left worth stealing.""We'll wait until sunset," said the butcher's wife. "Once the Pens empty out, people come asking."

Djoss coughed. He rubbed his hands together like they were cold. "We'll be out by then," he said, "Just give us a chance to finish and don't show anybody the room until we're done clearing it."

"I'll do what I want with my room," said the butcher's wife.

Djoss popped his fist into his palm. "I'll do what I have to do about our stuff. We need the money more than some thief."

The woman looked Djoss up and down with empty eyes. She smiled, wanly. She spoke to Rachel. "You picked a hard boy, but I can see the pink in his face. I've seen it from the start. I'll give you to sunset, woman, and I hope you pick a better man when this one smokes his head to cheese. If you was a real Senta... Well, you ought to see his fate easy. Everyone else does."

Rachel sneered and snapped a flame in and out of the air where she could feel the combustion in the koan of the spaces between. "Maybe I'm the only one who does see his fate," she said. "You don't know anything about us, or my brother."

"Maybe you're right," said the butcher's wife, but she clearly didn't believe it. "I won't put the sign out until sunset."

Rachel and Djoss were done within the hour. After nothing was left. Rachel gazed at the empty room. She smelled the bittersweet manure and meat rot of the butcher shop and the salty smell of more sea rain to wash away more of the animal smells that seeped in from the porous wooden and brick walls.

Rachel leaned out the window. She turned around to look up at the swirling clouds overhead. She turned around again to see the narrow street and all the people there that didn't know her name. She sighed. Djoss said nothing. He waited quietly in the hall for his sister to close the door behind her.

***

A sidewalk café cut into the warehouses for the porters. Djoss and Rachel sipped berry tea even though they hated berries in tea. The berry tea was the cheapest thing to drink, and they could get lots of it with all the rainy weather spoiling the berries that hadn't ripened yet.

Djoss and Rachel ate wheat bread and stew because it was the heaviest thing on the menu. They couldn't afford to eat twice that day.

They spent one more night in a trashy inn. She tied him down to the bed with ropes she borrowed from the innkeeper's stable. He didn't argue with her about the ropes. She showed Djoss what she had gotten, without consulting him about it. She told Djoss where to place his hands. He complied.

She slept sitting in a chair with all of the money under the cushion below her.

He didn't fight her.

That night must have been so long. I can only imagine the howls that must have emerged from that room, like a beast was chained down and dying. Rachel never told Jona about that night.

I have heard the men deprived of the demon weed wailing like banshees caught between the real and the damned. I imagine she watched the contortions of her brother's face, and saw her father there, writhing in a demon agony inside of the ear. She saw the dying poplars where she says he fell, how the trees puckered to ash like paintbrushes drying up, and all the bloody puke flowing from her brother's mouth was like a river of death that washed him clean.

I imagine she pulled ice from the air, and wrapped it around his head to cool the burning fevers. I imagine she called forth the wind and the fire of the Senta to burn away the stink of his sick body, and blow it all out the window, if she was clear-headed enough to think of it.

He could barely walk the next day. They spent all day wandering the streets slowly, looking for a hiring caravan. Men looked at the man who could barely walk, and did not hire him. Rachel and Djoss knocked on the doors of warehouses and asked whoever opened the door if they had a caravan leaving the city. Djoss was in no condition to walk, much less work.

A sea of faces, all of them hard and bedraggled and tired, with one rough dog voice barked the two away back into the street.

***

Jona was across the street looking out a window with a scrivener from the guard. Jona sipped a beer slowly and waited for Rachel and Djoss to step out from the barred doorway where they slept out of the rain.

He waited a long time. He sipped only the one beer.

Next to him, the scrivener won round after round of drinks in a card game with a couple lowlife smugglers that had gone birdie for a drink. Jona had bribed the gangers to keep the scrivener drunk and happy. A week of Jona's wages slowly traveled from Jona's pocket to a street thug to the scrivener.

Jona's mind did not hold that scrivener's name, or his face, or anything about him at all except for this: when he was drunk his cheeks reddened and his smile was very wide and the more he drank the redder his cheeks became and the wider the smile and the Pluckies found the kid's joy infectious and they cheered the boy on letting him win every round, and the scrivener was king for a day of all the Pens and all the fates. Jona drank so slow. What more was there to know about the truth. He had always known. The pieces he had put together were there for anyone to find that cared to look. The Night King's power was so great, that she did not even have to hide for people were too afraid to look. What was the point of writing any of it up?

He had gone to the man that ruled his night, a carpenter to the street. He had left a single note, with a single line. *Now that I've seen it, I know who I'm working for, and that's fine.* He watched the woman he loved leave an alley where she had been sleeping with her brother, and he felt dead inside. He felt like even suicide was pointless.

***

Djoss rested his elbows on his knees and stared at his fists against the cloudy night sky. His sister watched him from the other side of the alley. Read his lips if you can, Jona. She doesn't even see you to get closer.

"I took care of you," he said, into his hands, "I took care of that monster that made you. I took care of you after our mother got taken. I always took the best care of you. You were never evil. You were supposed to be evil, but you're not. I don't think you even feel the bad stuff in you because of me. I raised you, Rachel. I raised you good."

She said nothing.

"I hid you when they burned ma," he said, "I've escaped with you in every city. I can get us some money. I'll go get us some money. Untie me, and let me get us some money. I always find a way to take care of us."

"Please, Djoss…" she said. That's all she said. It rained on and off all night. The mud was all over their cloaks and clothes. No one could tell Rachel was a Senta from her clothes because the red X she had sewn on Lady Joni's cheap dress, getting leather over the cloth that would wear through, was smothered in thick, black mud. She was just another body sleeping in the street.

Before the sunlight returned, they both fell asleep in the mud. When they woke they felt the wet stink of it pressing into their skin through their clothes.

Rachel left Djoss there in the morning. When he woke up,

bound and alone, he assumed that was going to be it for them, and he'd never see her again.

And, he was glad for her, even if he wanted to die because of it.

CHAPTER 10

As wolves we ran, and as wolves we slipped underground.
We are hunters.
We hunt.

We slid up from the sewers, and we stood upon the brink of our destination, where the sewers opened to the empty building of the street, at the edge of our destination.

Aggie knew the way in and out, and so did Jona following Salvatore and Aggie, and so, therefore, did we.

We slipped inside in the dark. We climb in silence past the rectory kitchen, up the stairs and into the darkness.

Wolves slipped into the rooms, sniffing through them all for the woman who is old enough to be in charge.

We peeled back the wolfskin. We looked at her sleeping. She snored gently. She was a thin woman with blue veins like rivers in her wet parchment map of skin. She looked up at us, and pulled the ragged sheets around her body, pulling back.

She reminded me of another woman.

"We are the Walkers of Erin," I said. "We have been hunting the demon stain."

"What are you doing here? This is not the proper channels!"

"The proper channels are too corrupted," I said. "Do you remember Aggie?"

"Of course I do! It was one of the worst things that's ever happened in my life, signing off on her! Where were you? Where was your huntress in the night?"

I placed the papers at the foot of her bed.

"We need your help," I said. I bowed gracefully. "The children of Erin beseech your aid, madame Imamite, against our common enemy."

"And… who is our enemy?"

"Elishta," I said.

"Naturally, but who else? Who has brought you crawling here for my help saying proper channels are corrupted?"

"We need to see the king," I said.

She picked up the papers and shook them. She flipped through them. "Do I even want to know the details?"

I shrugged. "Copies have been made. We want you to make copies, too. Everyone must know the truth. Spread them to every convent, every prayer hall and sanctuary. Tell anyone that listens. This is why we came to you, to be sure you receive the truth directly. Read it from every street corner. Send it to every library, every scholar, every speaker."

She pushed the paper back to me. "Stay for breakfast. Stay here. No one will know if you remain among the Anchorites a day. There is no contact with the outside world in here. We receive shipments in silence and veiled from one gate. We do not let our girls wander the streets wagging tongues."

I shook my head. "Aggie was not supposed to leave your gates, either."

"She was a demon child. Who knows what evil magic she used to escape us."

"You should read those," said my husband. "Send your people to us when you're ready to aid us. We need an audience with the king."

She put them on the ground. "I should have you arrested. It is illegal for a man to invade our convent. We are allies in this world but not the next."

"Elishta is our enemy in both," said my husband. "Our faiths are practical enough when it comes to that." He pulled the wolf skin back over his back, and stretched, menacingly flashing fangs. He was ready to leave. So was I.

The Anchorite nodded. She took a deep breath. She picked up the pages. "Go, then. I will make my own decisions about what you have brought to me."

We bowed.

Our next destination was a nobleman whose son was murdered and thrown into the water. We were going to offer him the whole kingdom. All he had to do was be ready to act when the time came to stop Sabachthani.

He would help us. Of course he would help us. He was weeping about his son when we handed him the truth. We told him what happened, and what vengeance he could take. We told him that we had chosen his noble line to support when the king died, and our support came with knowledge of his enemies.

Imam's priests would fall in line with us, and with him.

Everyone will know. Everything hidden comes to the light. This is the revolution: No one can pretend they do not know. The Sabachthani hold on this city will crumble at the word of truth. There are faithful in this city who would fight back. There are men and women who would relish the chance to pull the Sabachthani down.

We spread these words to every street corner, every one in the city. We got the idea from Calipari and the crowns. He did it to put out the fire. We did it to start one.

***

Jona leaned against the door. "You've been gone," he said.

She pushed him hard. He didn't expect that at all. He fell back, stumbled a little, and collapsed onto a small table against the foyer wall.

Rachel was smothered in black mud. Only her green eyes gleamed through to reveal her face. Rachel raised balls of ice in her hand like she was going to throw them. Fire popped in the air like exploding fireflies.

Jona smirked. "Rachel, I've been worried," said Jona. "What in bloody Elishta are you doing?"

Rachel stopped. Her throat clenched with crying. The ice dropped. "I wanted to rob you."

Jona snatched her wrists from the air. He pulled the filthy things to his lips. He kissed first the left wrist, then the right. He wiped his dirty lips off on his sleeve.

"I'm trying to rob you, Jona," she said. She kicked at his shins.

He grabbed her by the waist and pulled her in close. "You could just ask for help," he said.

"Please, Jona!" said Rachel. She was crying now. "I don't want this!"

"Calmly, Rachel," he said. He wrapped his arms around her. She collapsed into him. He held her up, and the mud everywhere was a gritty, hard thing to hold, worse than jagged scales.

She pushed him off. "Jona, please."

She looked away from him. He pressed his lips into the mud across her cheek. "I won't let him go. I won't."

"Djoss?" Jona tried to go for the other side.

She let him kiss her there, too, and kept looking away from him.

She was disgusted and impatient. "He's my whole life. I won't let him go, Jona."

Jona leaned back. He tried to get eye contact. "Your brother fell into the pinks," he said, "I told you about that." He let his forehead fall into hers. She had no choice. She had to look into his eyes. "Come on, you can take a bath and get some food. My mother went to work already. She won't be back until sunset."

"Are you on duty today?"

"No. I'm off today. It's Adventday soon. It's off day today so

I can work Adventday. I should be at temple, if I went to such things."

"Jona…"

He pressed his lips into her. "I missed you," he whispered, "Why'd you leave me? Where will you go? Why leave?"

Rachel pushed him off. She leaned against the door.

"Jona, I have nowhere else to go right now, and I don't know what to do, so will you stop talking about it, please? I don't want to talk about this."

"I missed you. Your brother is full of something terrible."

"I won't give up on him. Why are you trying to force me to do something I can't, Jona?"

"You did it to me, first," he said.

They stood still there, in the entryway. They couldn't look each other in the face. Jona's eyes wandered from the muddy clothes, to his hand, to her boots. "You're filthy," he said, "Go take a bath." He placed a hand on her muddy cheek. He looked up into her eyes. He kissed her gently. They looked in each other's eyes. "Tell me where Djoss is, and I'll go get him."

Rachel's face broke. Her lip trembled. Her eyes shut. She fell into Jona. He saw it coming in time to catch. He ran his hands over her hair. She lost three wracking sobs. Then, she swallowed her tears, and she stepped back, acid steaming off the mud at the corners of her eyes. She took a deep breath. She looked up with her face back. "Thank you, Jona," she said. She took another deep breath. "Thank you."

***

Djoss was awake when Jona arrived. Djoss squatted half-naked in the mud, tied up with his own shirt. He didn't move. He didn't look Jona in the face.

Djoss looked at Jona's uniform. He nodded.

"You look like a tosser with lady troubles."

Djoss shrugged. "I got no trouble with you, king's man."

"Me? I got trouble with you. I got lady troubles deep." Jona laughed at Djoss' hard eyes. "Your sister sent me."

"What?" he said, "When I woke up alone…"

"She did and she didn't. She left to get help."

"Oh," said Djoss. Djoss processed this statement in his head like a mathematical equation and deduced no solution. He squinted. He looked up at Jona. "I remember you."

Jona scratched at his scalp. "Like I said, I got lady troubles."

Djoss stood up slow. He walked slow, too. His eyes never left the ground at his feet. Jona walked beside him. In his mind, he was trying to figure how gone the pinker was.

Djoss' hands began to shake. Jona wondered if the trembling hand was frustration, rage, or pinks. He decided it was pinks, because frustration and rage would only make Djoss want more false bliss.

At the house, Jona led Djoss in through the kitchen. There wasn't anything worth stealing in the kitchen but old clay dishes. Jona handed Djoss some cheese and bread. Djoss ate as slowly as he had walked. He didn't look up from the table.

Jona leaned against the cupboard. Jona watched Djoss nibbling. Djoss looked back, shifting in his seat.

"Where's Rachel?" said Djoss.

"She's upstairs, I think. I can hear someone moving about up there, taking a bath. You'll be having one of those soon, too, so my mother won't know you're here. Mess like that everywhere, there's no hiding a thing."

Jona watched the stranger in his kitchen eating. Around the edges of the eyes, Jona saw the man beneath the shame: strong, proud, and dumb.

Djoss stared at his hands.

***

Rachel plucked out the darkest dress with the longest hem and the highest collar and tried to figure how to sew what was left of her Senta leathers over it to get a red X across the chest. She poured the bathwater down a drain in the floor, and she pumped for more water from the wall. Then, she scrubbed at the basin.

The Joni house was huge and larger in its sparse furnishing, full of bright white paint and dark woods. Her bare feet echoed in the upstairs hall. Her scales clicked quietly in the air. She walked naked, poking her head into the different rooms she found. Most of them were just naked walls, where furniture had been sold off and not even drapes covered the windows. When Rachel found Jona's mother's room, she dug through the drawers to find something that covered her scales and boots. She dressed. She wandered through the house again, searching for signs of life. She found her way to the kitchen.

Djoss looked up at her, in her ill-fitting new clothes too thin in the hips and too loose in the stomach.

Jona placed more cheese on the table.

Djoss stood up.

"Hello, Djoss," she said. She sat down at the table and tried to act natural. She didn't feel natural. She was clean and he was dirty. She was in Jona's kitchen with nowhere else to go. And Jona watched them both, a scowl locked in his eyes.

"Djoss," said Rachel, "you could use a bath."

"I could," he said, "have you eaten?"

"I have," she said.

This was all that was said. Djoss ate more cheese and none of three people said a word. At first, Rachel felt like standing up and moving and walking around a little, but she didn't want to be the first to move.

Jona pierced the veil of still. "What's your plan?"

Rachel looked up. "We'll leave together." She pointed at her brother, then herself. "Him and me."

Djoss nodded.

"How?" asked Jona.

"I don't know," answered Rachel.

Jona placed a hand on his chin, thinking deeply. "Right," said Jona, "that is certainly a thing to think on. I figure you got no money or you wouldn't come to me." He scratched his head. He shook his head. He stood up, "Come with me, Djoss. I'll get you in a bath and get you some clean clothes while we all think about this."

Djoss followed Jona up the stairs and down the hall. He was careful not to tramp too much mud in his wake. He couldn't help it. He didn't have Rachel's fires to burn it away on his boots.

Djoss said, well out of Rachel's hearing, "What's to think about?" said Djoss, "We have to steal it. Enough money, I mean." He looked at his hands. "She can't do it. Not with her blood like it is. I do what I have to for her, to keep her good. Only I can do it. I have to steal the money, somehow."

"Never occurs to anyone to get a job, does it?" said Jona, "You know I'm a king's man. I can arrest you just for saying it."

"Arrest me, then," said Djoss, "Set her free of me. I know you're a child of a demon, like her. She told me."

Jona took a deep breath. Instead, he led Djoss to the bathtub and gave him some of Jona's old clothes. "Don't rob anybody without warning me first," he said, "And I will be counting the silver 'fore you leave. You got any teeth?"

"Me?" said Djoss, "No. Rachel ran off with my cutlery. We sold it all."

"Right," said Jona, darkly. "Tell me that again. Show me those teeth, like a rowdy dog."

Djoss pulled a long dagger from his boot and tossed it at Jona's feet.

Jona nodded. "I'll give it to you when you leave. I'm no thief, and this is for your own good."

Jona took everything sharp from the room. Djoss watched from the middle of the floor. The shaving razors and the toothpicks and the glass all got piled outside the door. Djoss watched the pile grow. He blushed, but he said nothing.

When the door closed, and the tub was pumped full of cold water, Djoss ducked underneath the surface and held his breath as long as he could. When he couldn't breathe anymore he tried to stay down, beneath the surface. His lungs blossomed with burning. His heartbeat quickened.

He came up for air, and Jona was there. The door was open behind him.

"Trying to drown, huh?" he said.

"No," said Djoss, "Just trying to get clean. You must have really been rich to get a fountain in all the rooms."

"My dad lost it all in the war, with his neck. We're lucky just to have the house," said Jona. "There's only a couple rooms where the pumps still work, anyhow. Rachel loves you and I don't. I think you're too far gone for anybody. Want me to just give you a few coins and leave you in a hookah den for a while? I would do that, if it was best for Rachel. Is that what's best for Rachel?"

Djoss said nothing.

"What's best for Rachel?" said Jona. "Me? I don't care if you walk away and fade away into whatever burns you up."

Djoss spoke softly. "She wants to stay with me not you," he said. "I want to do better for her. I can stop if we get out of town, get away from the stuff for good."

Jona squinted. "Is that what's best for her?"

Djoss shrugged. "Only the Gods know, and they'd probably argue about it."

"Right," said Jona. "Erin, Imam, Senta koans like Rachel's spells, and the Nameless dancing in the dark with demons. Not a one has anything to do with you or me or Rachel. We're just doing our best. Sucking on a hookah is a dead man's game, Djoss. Once you start, you're a dead man walking bleeding out slowly. The water in the tub is stained pink from you bleeding out."

Djoss creased his eyebrows. Then, after a deep breath, "Thank you for your hospitality," he said. "May I please bathe in peace?"

"Yeah, I guess," said Jona. "You're a giant to her. The way she describes you it's some kind of giant. Look at you, now."

Jona shook his head and stepped out into the hall. He waited, and wondered if he shouldn't just throw a bunch of money at him and kick him out into the street. He wondered if Rachel would stay if he did that.

He just wanted Rachel to stay.

***

When Djoss got out of the bath and dressed in his same, dirty clothes, Jona led Djoss downstairs, to the basement. Between the empty buckets and empty boxes and ruined remains of all the things that weren't worth selling, two stone columns rose up from the floor. Chains with heavy iron clasps lay rusty on the floor. They seemed to be more rust than metal now, sitting in the mud.

"These used to be my da's before he died," said Jona. "You know how it is with some of us. It touches us all a little different. Night terrors. I don't think Rachel has them. I'm lucky I don't have to sleep, so I don't really know what it's like. We had to chain my da down, though. He'd sleepwalk sometimes."

On the other side of the stone columns, ancient armor, a shield and a nobleman's mace rested against clay bricks. With all the sweat and blood in the metal from Jona's father, it could not be sold off safely.

Jona clapped his hands, and rubbed them together industriously. "You know what we gotta do," he said.

Djoss frowned. "Does Rachel know?"

Jona placed his heavy hand upon Djoss' back. It was like palming a boulder there was still so much knotted muscle there. "She doesn't know like I do. You'd gnaw your hands off to get one little puff when the urge comes. I have to chain you by the throat like a dog."

"I won't gnaw my hands off."

"You would," said Jona. "And you know you would when the hunger strikes real bad in a day or so."

Jona pushed Djoss forward. Djoss frowned and turned back to throw a punch.

Jona grabbed the fist in the air and placed Djoss' own blade at Djoss' throat. "I'm trying to help you," said Jona. "I don't have to do this. If you're here, you're chained. You know the feeling you get when you can't get enough of it."

Djoss calmed. He stepped back to the wall. Jona's knife stayed on Djoss' throat. "Pick up the chains and latch your neck. I've got the padlocks in my pocket."

Djoss leaned away from the dagger. He picked up the old chains from the mud floor. Each side had half the chain.

"When Da used this damn thing, he'd wear chains on his arms, too. We buried him in those chains. We didn't know what his body would do. Wizards steal the bones of demons. I've seen things built with bones. Horrible stuff. You have no idea what it's like to be a monster in your own home, to be used like one. You don't know anything about us."

Jona attached a padlock to each side of the latch. It fit around Djoss' neck with an inch to spare. Jona's father was a large man, before he died.

"What will you do tonight?" said Djoss.

"I don't sleep," Jona said, "I never sleep. I was born with wings, but my Ma cut them off of me before anyone could see them. Tonight, I'll be finding you a way out of this town, like Rachel wants. If you're smarter than I think you are, you'll leave her free and easy and never look back."

***

Jona left Djoss there, tied up like a monster with the heavy chain around his neck. Djoss watched the light fade in the closing door. He sat down in the mud and the darkness. He reached with his hands against the walls. He felt only darkness. He pressed against the chains around his neck. He reached into the night. He felt nothing. He reached harder and harder until the chains choked him. He sat down, on the ground. He reached through the darkness for the bolts on the stone. He found them. He clutched the bolts with both hands. He listened in the darkness for any sound at all. The house was too large. He couldn't hear anything. They probably couldn't hear him on these old chains.

These chains were strong enough for most pinkers, but they weren't strong enough for Djoss. Jona wasn't the first king's man surprised by this old, hard strength.

Upstairs, Jona and Rachel sat in the kitchen. Rachel was cooking something. She didn't really know how to cook what was in this kitchen, but at least if she was moving pots and fire she wasn't forced to really talk to Jona about the important things. Instead, she could ask him where something was. She could describe it with her hands. "It's a pot with a shape like this on the bottom, about this wide?"

"It's in the third cupboard."

"It's flat and has a crank on it to smash the wheat flat," she said, holding her palm down and her fingers straight, "Real flat."

"It's in the drawer next to the stove. Do you need matches?"

Rachel shrugged. She flicked her finger at the kindling, and little drops of fire like drops of water splashed over the bark and coal. The stove sputtered a moment, and then it crackled.

"When does your mother come home?"

"Soon," he said, "She'll hate that you cooked."

"What will you tell her about me?"

"The truth. She'll understand. You couldn't turn to a temple for help, could you? Just because our blood is wicked, we don't necessarily have to be. She knows that."

"Still," she said, "what about Djoss?"

"He's sleeping," said Jona

Rachel sighed. "Why is he asleep?" she asked.

"I don't know," said Jona, "He got out of the bath and fell asleep in a spare room. I say let him sleep. We're going to have a long night. I'll take him to some friends of mine. I'll stay with him and make sure he doesn't do anything stupid. He saves up enough, with you two sleeping here, and then you hire passage on a ship and sail off into the sun. My mother might have something for you around the house, but we won't be able to pay you ourselves. If that's what you want, anyway. If you want to try something else, I'm up for it."

"No," she said. She waved her hands over what she was cooking, "That's fine, Jona. Thank you." She opened a drawer, and rummaged through them. "I had a knife. I know I had a knife. It was the only one I had."

"It's out," said Jona. He pointed right in front of her.

"Oh."

***

Djoss had broken the chains. Of course he broke the chains. They were old and rusty and he was still not so far gone that he had lost all his strength.

Jona imagined, from what he had found afterwards, that Djoss found the stairs. He climbed carefully. The basement door wasn't locked. He slipped into the lower hallway. This part of the house was full of servant's rooms. They were all empty, and caked in dust. Old trinkets that no one would buy gathered dust on the shelves. A dusty teddy bear. A broken clock. Lost books. Things that weren't worth selling. They sat on the floor like dead prisoners.

Djoss opened doors down the hall until he found the stairs. He climbed up to the next floor. This was the main hall. He knew where he was now, and he knew he couldn't get out the door without passing too close to Jona and Rachel whom he heard still in the kitchen. He went up another floor, and then another. He climbed all five flights to the roof. He climbed out. The afternoon sun was high and hot. Flecks of humidity licked his skin. On the roof, the house laundry dried in rows of sunlight like limp, wet rags. No wind blew them.

Djoss looked down at his filthy clothes. He stripped off his shirt, and pulled one of Jona's uniforms from the line. It was a tight fit, and the seams screamed, but the uniform held together enough.

Djoss didn't know where to go from here. He sat in a corner of the roof, behind the doorway. He frowned.

***

"Do you think he's hungry?" she said, stirring.

"Him?" said Jona. He reached around Rachel to pull out two bowls. "I think he's snoring like a baby."

Rachel turned. She looked up at Jona, his arms spread around her with the bowls. "Did you tie him down?"

"The door's locked and there's no window," said Jona, "He's going nowhere."

She leaned into him. "I hate that we do that. I hate it. He's been good for days. Let me untie him."

"We can't leave him alone if he isn't tied up."

"Then I'll sit with him. I want to be with him right now. Where is he?"

"Let him sleep."

"Why are you being like this?"

"Just sit down," said Jona. He wrapped his arms around her,

with the bowls in his hands, "Eat."

"He's my brother, Jona," she said, "Don't you understand that?"

"No," he said. "I wish I did. Bloody Elishta, I wish I understood this. I don't know what you think will happen next. We'll try your way, and get you out of town, okay?"

***

Djoss snatched at the ropes from the laundry. He didn't bother pulling the laundry loose. He untied them all from the stones. He left them lashed in on the side near an alley. He looked over the edge. He looked at his ropes. He figured it was still going to be a good drop to the ground. He tugged off all the laundry. He put them in a big pile near the edge, where he planned to jump. He dropped them in one big lump over the edge. He grabbed the rope. He spun it around in his hand, so the many threads wrapped all over each other and then around his waist.

He took a running start. He jumped. The ropes caught at the second story. He slammed into the wall. The wind rushed out of his lungs like his body was on fire. He crumpled to the ground, into the pile of laundry.

I'm sure he knew that Rachel would come looking for him. When that happened, he wanted to have it all back—all the money he had spent, and all the futures he had lost. He swore to himself he wouldn't touch the weed again. He was going to be strong, like he had always been. This was his chance to earn it all back.

***

Jona had turned around for a moment. He was scrubbing a dish clean. He pumped the water out from the line to the canal. He scraped the steel pots clean of rice with a pumice stone. He talked to her, she was sitting behind him at the table, and she wasn't say-ing a word. "My mother never told me what to do if I ever met anyone like me," he said. "She never really believed I would meet anyone like me. I think she thought I was the only one in the world. Whenever I asked her what to do if I found another like me, she just said nothing to it. She'd just act like she didn't hear me ask her that, or something. I don't know what it means. I don't know what to make of any of this. We make people sick, but they don't make us sick. They don't make demons sick, either, I think. If they do, how would we know? Where are we supposed to go to find out how we are the way we are? Maybe Lord Sabachthani knows about us, but if we tell him it's our death, right? Maybe we stick together and we find more people like us. We find out what they know. Maybe we can make our own way underground and see Elishta's Nameless for ourselves, or we find people who know about it and find out what they know. Maybe someday we get enough people like us, we split off and make our own place, our own district, our own city. Bloody Elishta, a whole city. Maybe someday we can be together, you and me, and have a family, and nobody cares if the kid has wings or scales or big, sharp teeth like a lizard, because it's still just a kid, right?" He stopped scrubbing with his stone. He pumped some fresh water into the pot. He rested his arms on the side of the sink. "Rachel, I wish we could be a family…" he turned around to look her in the face.

She was gone.

A candle burned on the table. The flame flickered in slight winds from invisible places in the stale room. The clay white wax curved gracefully over the puckered, melting lips.

***

I do not know her path through the Joni house. I do not know whether she found the basement where her brother had broken through the old chains. I do not know if she found the roof where the laundry lines fluttered down the side of the building like banners.

Ragpickers had snatched the cloth on the lines close to ground. Industrious boys piled crates along the side of the house and climbed up the ropes, jamming feet between bricks, and pulling at the bits of uniform and bedsheets and women's working dresses. Jona's appearance scared them all overboard, like sailors jumping ship.

Jona looked over the edge of the roof. He pulled the laundry lines back to the roof, shaking off the boys that clung too long to the lines.

He threw the clothes on the roof, and went back inside. He sat alone in a dark room until his mother came home.

He thought and thought, and nothing made sense, and none of it was going to make sense, but he kept thinking. Pretty soon, he stopped thinking and just felt that feeling that comes to young men, when nothing turned out like they planned, and she's gone.

There is a wailing that came next, a gnashing of teeth, and waiting for daylight on the roof of the house, where the stars and the moon occasionally showed themselves past the clouds and lamplight.

CHAPTER II

I do not know all that we must know to see inside of Djoss'
mind. Once they left Jona's house, I lost his memory of
them, and the shape of their lives stumbled in his own tu-
multuous emotions. I do my best to piece together the things I
heard from the street, and from what is remembered in Jona's
skull, and what I can taste in the air as a certainty of systems and
mud and blood. The rumor and innuendo Jona collected may be
inaccurate. I have been unable to locate corroborating evidence
among the official records. I asked around with my husband. We
bribed the street boys with food and coin. We learned everything
we could and sifted at as best as we could.

They who build the cities—they who work every day and
whose children work and have more children—lead lives as silent as shadows. When the sun sets for them, it's like they never
existed at all, and all of these children and grandchildren and
buildings and streets appeared out of thin air. There was a sea of
warm bodies rising up, lifting kings and merchant lords like ship
captains.

They who live beneath the builders of cities are shadows of
shadows.

There is no sign of the life of death Djoss led hidden in any of
the corners inside of Jona's memories, or the rumors of the street
boys that had long forgotten their fallen kings.

Here is what I think, and probably what you think. He punched and fought his way into a room with hookahs. He did this after passing through all the places he knew with illegal coins, muscling and beating and maiming until he had it all. Full of himself, full of the awesome power of taking all that he wanted from the night, he could not contain his greed. The pipes called to him. The sweet stain of smoke pulled him back to death. At first, he thought he would just steal the weed and sell it somewhere, a symbolic gesture of power over the monster that ruled him. Then, it was in his hands, and he was alone, and no one was going to stop him. Rachel wasn't there to stop him. The bouncers were bleeding on the ground. The night was empty for him, and it was all for him.

He was smart enough to take it all somewhere else before he smoked it, or else the night would have found him long before Lady Sabachthani would bother with the hunt.

Here is also what I think: Lady Sabachthani wanted to kill Djoss because it would drive Rachel away from Dogsland. She was very interested in all the demon stained. Sabachthani wanted Jona to do it, because it would tear Rachel away from his heart forever.

A message came for Jona.

Rachel's story fades from us.

There are things we know.

There are things we almost know.

The words flood the street outside our window. Jona's memories sweep through the public houses and temples, where all secrets come to light. It is impossible now for my husband and me outside, with the Sabachthani family back on their heels. We stay hidden in our Temple, back in the record rooms, away from the eyes of even our own men and women, waiting for the rage to rise up into a boil.

We do not have very much to do.

There is some certainty in her heart from what she told to Jona, and what truth was hidden in the cloth upon her back and her voice's different way of pronouncing the same words as everyone else.

My husband doesn't think it is worth the time to construct this life, but Jona loves her, and he imagined it all from her words. It was a dream of her life, that led her to his lonely, empty, dirty, little room.

Write it down. Write it all down. If it will get the ghost to settle in your heart while we wait for word from the Anchorite.

CHAPTER 12

The more I see into Jona's memories, the more I see the older fragments of the mind. Are they dreams? Are they real? I don't know.

Jona and Rachel spoke of their youth sometimes.

My husband and I have made a detailed study of everything we could pull from Jona's brain. We arranged the details of Rachel's past as best we could.

All these things that Jona remembered from different conversations merged into clear fragments of Rachel's youth in my mind like Erin's form of dreamcasting, with no koans to meditate upon like the Senta, just with our knowledge in the service of Erin, our senses of animal and man. Also, my best imagination, and little else. I write it down to soothe the ghost in me, but I know it cannot be true.

Also, it gives us, my brothers and sisters, a point of beginning for our hunts into the gap where the doppelgänger crawled out from the crust of the earth, from Elishta.

***

Rachel, when she was just a little girl, saw her father at the edge of the dock, sitting on a crate. No ships came or went today. The ducks swam beneath the harbor. The birds sniffed through the filth for the fish that searched for food among the filth. Every little piece of filth rolled from the alleys into the harbor water.

And the man—what parts of him that were man—held a loaf of bread up to his ear. He leaned against it like he was listening.

Rachel knew that something was slipping out of the ear and reaching inside of the crusty shell for all the soft bits inside. She hadn't ever really seen the thing. She knew that she was not allowed to talk about it, even if she was alone with Djoss or her mother.

When the insides of the bread were all devoured and only the shell remained, the man would eat that as if he were just a normal man.

Rachel didn't know, yet, what that meant. She was still too young to understand that her father was not like other fathers.

Rachel's mother led Rachel and Djoss to a blackberry bush so they could eat and catch their breath.

Djoss cut a long branch off with his knife. He held it up in the air like a fisherman's line. He walked into the shade of a poplar tree. He started eating all of the blackberries. The branch was covered in tiny thorns.

Rachel reached for a single blackberry like her mother, but Rachel stopped when she saw the tiny thorns.

"It'll bite me," she said.

Her mother smiled patiently. "Just be careful, Rachel," she said.

Rachel put her hands on her hips. "No," she said, "They bite."

Her mother picked a ripe blackberry from the top. She brushed off the seed dust. She held it out for Rachel.

Rachel crossed her arms. "No," she said.

Her mother ate the blackberry. She chewed it. She smiled. "See?" she said, "Tasty. They don't bite. Look at your brother."

Rachel looked over at her brother. He started at one end of his thorny vine and worked his way to the other. His lips were purple from the berry juice.

Rachel frowned. "If they bite me, I'll scream."

Her mother plucked another blackberry from the top, heavy with juice and dark, dark purple. Rachel closed her eyes. She opened her mouth. She reached out with her tongue for the berry.

Her mother smacked her daughter's head. "Hey, close that mouth!" she said, sternly, "Never let your tongue show like that!"

Rachel rubbed her head. Her mouth jammed into a pout. "It bit me," she said. She took the blackberry from her mother's hand, and squashed it into her mother's dress.

"Rachel!" said her mother, "No! That's a bad girl!"

Rachel stormed off to the shade where her brother had already eaten halfway down his long vine.

"I'm hot," said Rachel, "and I'm hungry."

Her mother was still scraping blackberry out of the ruined suede skirt of her dress. "Rachel, all we have are blackberries. Share with your brother."

Djoss smiled at his sister, and his teeth were all purple. He chewed one with his mouth open.

"They look like bugs," she said.

Djoss smashed a blackberry into his sister's hair.

Rachel rubbed at it, screaming and jumping. It felt like a fat, dead bug.

Djoss laughed at her. "Serves you right," he said.

Rachel stood up and started to jump up and down.

"I can't deal with you monsters!" said her mother, "I just can't!" She pressed her hands into her temples. "Rachel, you have to be quiet now."

Rachel kept jumping and screaming. Her hands smacked at the mess in her hair.

"Rachel!" shouted her mother. Her mother clapped her hands at her daughter. A strong wind blew her back into the grass. Ice clamped over her arms.

Rachel kept screaming.

"Djoss, cover your sister's mouth!" she said, "Hurry!"

Djoss said, "She'll bite me. I'll get sick."

Ice filled her mouth. The cold ran all through her body. Now she wanted to scream from the cold. She gasped for air. She breathed hard from her nose.

"Please, kids," said her mother, "Please be quiet. You know they're looking for us."

Djoss had his knife out. He went back to the blackberries. He cut another vine. "Because Da killed a guy," he said.

"Your father didn't kill anyone," she said, "Don't talk about it in front of your sister. He'll find us as soon as he throws those people off our trail."

"He'll be pissed when he catches up with us. We won't be able to ditch him. I hope they get him," said Djoss. He bent the empty vine like a rope so he could lash long blackberry canes together. "I hope they burn him alive."

"Djoss," said the mother, "Don't say that in front of your sister."

"We should leave him," said Djoss, "We should head south, back to the village."

"Djoss, you have to protect your sister," she said, "No matter what, you have to protect her. You know what would happen to all of us if he's taken alive?"

Her mother walked over to Rachel. Rachel was crying, hard. The cold ball of ice in her mouth hurt so much. Her mother placed a hand over her mouth. The ice dissipated into the air. Her mother kept her hand over Rachel's mouth.

"Are you going to scream, little one?" said Rachel's mother.

Rachel shook her head.

Her mother removed her hand from Rachel's mouth. She brushed at Rachel's tears. "I'm sorry," she said.

"I hate you, Mommy" said Rachel.

Her mother didn't look away. Her breath moved in and out. She kept brushing away her daughter's tears as if the little girl hadn't said anything. Djoss had gathered a large stack of blackberry stems by now, on his shoulder.

"We need to move," said Djoss, "They probably heard her screaming."

Rachel's mother nodded. "I wonder, little one," said Rachel's mother, "why you scream so much. Didn't you ever hear about the princess that screamed and flailed so much she accidentally swallowed her own hair and then she was bald and her handsome Prince wouldn't marry her anymore?"

The ice at Rachel's wrists and legs melted away. Somewhere in the thicket hills, a dog bayed. Then it stopped like it was stopped suddenly mid-bark. Rachel didn't know what was happening.

"Carry me, Mommy," she said. Rachel held out her arms.

Rachel's mother picked her up. "All right, little one," said Rachel's mother. She moved Rachel up to her shoulders. Rachel curled into her mother's head, holding on with her hands. "Hold on tight, now," said Rachel's mother, "We need to move very fast while we still have daylight."

Rachel buried her face in her mother's hair. Her senses filled with the sweaty road dust, with the woman's true scent underneath.

Later on, Rachel dreamed of the scent. She didn't always recognize it right away, but the smell lingered at the edge of her consciousness until it hit her in a burst. Then, when she remembered the smell, the dream faded, and the smell faded, and all that was left was a hollow feeling.

And she'd tell Jona about it, sometimes.

***

Rachel's father was tall, like Djoss. Both men's shoulders filled shirts like meat in a sack. His dark, terrible eyes weren't terrible, yet. They were warm, kind eyes. He spent his days unloading ships, and his nights with his wife and son. They traveled with the seasons over the oceans to follow the prevailing winds. Better winds, more ships with cargo to unload.

Between him and the fortune-telling of his wife, money was enough. Their boy was growing up like his father, with the same huge smile, and tiny, intense eyes in a huge head.

In autumn, the winds favored the fjords.

(Another reason my husband does not suspect the Rejk fjords is how bitter cold it is in Rejk, and none would dip their head in the water unnecessarily. My husband thinks they must have been wandering the Okena.)

"What you need to do is," I can hear the man's voice in Jona's imagination. He sounds like Nicola Calipari. He looks down at his daughter with such soft eyes. "What you need to do is, get some sleep. We've got a long walk in the morning to the wheat fields. Harvest season's here. Good money if we can get there in time."

He's taking off his boots. His boots were the most expensive thing he owned. They were brown leather, worn in thick creases where they bent. They smelled like mud. They felt just as hard as a dog's padded paws. His feet emerged from the shoe, as tough as the shoe-leather. He rubbed one foot.

"Were you listening?" he said.

He put that foot down. He picked up the other foot, and rubbed it.

Rachel was listening. She curled up into a ball in her bedroll.

She felt her father's heavy hand on her foot. "Little one," he said, "You should keep your boots on in case someone discovers us sleeping here. Where are the boots I made you?"

He pulled a blanket over her foot. She could feel her father watching her sleeping. She pretended to be asleep.

"You're such a beautiful thing," he whispered, "Where's your brother?"

Rachel shivered, pulling herself tighter into a ball. She pressed her eyes closed, hard.

"I asked you a question," he said. He thumped her leg. "Hey, where's your brother?"

Her mother spoke. "The last I saw of him he was out with his friends. Leave him be. The little ruffian's going to make more tonight than we did all day."

"I'm going out, too," he said. He reached for his boots. His joints crackled.

Rachel's mother reached out to him. She touched his skin and rubbed it. She didn't want the man to find her son. She sang to him, "Aren't you tired after your long day?"

"No," he said. He stood up. Every bone in his body popped and groaned. He didn't seem to mind the painful sounds.

***

Rachel's mother placed a hand on her daughter's head. Her other hand pointed at a stevedore. Men milled about the deck, and men milled about the dock, but Rachel's mother had been pointing at precisely that stevedore. "Rachel, go over to that man over there and tell him that his wife knows," said Rachel's mother.

The stevedore wasn't particularly tall, but his neck was as thick as a tree. He had a sour face, bent all crooked, like he had spent so much time in his life angry that he couldn't untwist what he had spent so much time doing. The stevedore stacked boxes onto the pallet that a crane would lift into a ship's hold.

Rachel didn't want to go over to the man.

"It's okay, little one," said Rachel's mother, "He's harmless. I'll watch and make sure he doesn't hurt you."

Rachel carefully stepped over to the man. She tapped the man's knee.

He looked down. He had angry eyebrows, like two caterpillars trying to push the skin between together. "What?" he grumbled.

Rachel took a step back. She looked over her shoulder at her mother. Rachel's mother smiled serenely and gestured for her daughter to go ahead.

The man crossed his arms. "What is it, kid?"

Rachel crossed her own arms. "Hey," she said, "My mommy wants me to tell you something."

"Yeah?"

"She says to tell you that she knows something."

"Well, little one, you tell her to leave me alone," he said, "I'm working."

Rachel shrugged. "Well, that's what my mommy says to tell you. She says that she knows something about you," said Rachel, "Your wife knows it, too."

"Huh," said the stevedore. He bent down on one knee. He looked Rachel in the eye. "Your mother, she's a Senta?"

Rachel nodded.

The man looked past Rachel's shoulders at the woman across the dock. He fumbled into his pocket for some coins. "Give your Ma this," he said. He pressed coins into Rachel's hands. "Tell her 'Thanks'."

The man stood up. He went back to work.

Rachel walked back to her mother, staring at the coins. Rachel handed the coins up to her mother. "He gave me this," she said.

"Good job!" said the Senta. She slipped the coins into her pocket.

"Why'd he do that?" said Rachel.

Rachel's mother smirked mysteriously. She looked back at the man working. "I saw that he had a wedding ring in his nose. That's where the wives mark their husbands up here. A man like that always keeps secrets from his wife. And, their wives always know the secrets, too."

"What secret?"

"Any secret at all," said the Senta, "Remember that trick, Rachel, and you can make a few coins doing something besides begging. Did you see how mean he looked?"

"He was scary."

"Well, when you see a scary man and he's married, he's keeping something from his wife. And, she knows about it. You pass on this simple truth, and he will be grateful. He will give you coins. But, only stop a scary man if he is working. Never stop a man who is doing nothing at all. Nothing is scarier than a scary man with nothing to keep his hands busy."

***

Djoss jumped into a ring of boys. Two boys in the center whacked at each other with long sticks. Djoss grabbed both of the sticks at the ends. He smashed the two boys together on the ends of their sticks. He tore the sticks from their hands. He swung the sticks around heroically. "A guilder for the boy that can beat me!" he shouted, "One whole guilder!"

A cheer among the boys and a challenger jumped down. Djoss tossed the stick at the boy. Djoss was younger, but he was about the same size. The boy spun his stick elegantly in the air, showing-off for his friends. Djoss ground his knuckles into the wood like a bull stomping before a charge. Then, he charged.

The other boy jumped sideways. Djoss managed to jam the tip of his stick onto the boy's boot. The boy's legs spread. His hands thrust out to catch his fall.

Djoss smashed the boy's stick hard. The boy dropped it.

"Ha!" said Djoss.

The boys were cheering.

Rachel sat on a fence near the boys. She watched her brother, watched the boys cheering him on.

Her mother had told both of the children to stay there and read from their books. Djoss had handed his book to Rachel, and had jumped down to play with the boys.

Rachel opened the book he had given to her. She ran her eyes lazily down the words of the Senta koans, meditating only slightly in the noise and boredom.

A princess was born blind. The king, her father, didn't want his daughter to know that she was missing out on the beautiful world. He instructed all his servants to cover their own eyes, and never mention to the beloved child that she had no sight.

The princess grew up beautiful despite her blindness. She married a handsome prince from a distant land that did not know she was blind.

He told her that she looked beautiful.

She thought he had hiccupped. She pounded his back as if he had hiccupped.

He laughed and loved her all the more for it.

She never understood what he meant when he recited poems that compared her beauty to purple petals of an orchid. She called them nonsense words. He laughed at that, too.

He never understood why she did not concern herself with make-up and decorations and continually bumped into things when she walked alone.

For her part, she never strayed from her beloved with the vanities of the kings, for she could not see to bother with handsome courtiers and innuendo in a glance.

In the end, they lived happily ever after.

The cheers subsided. Djoss collected coins from losers, bowing gracefully to each of his vanquished foes. After he got the last coin from the last boy, he declared that he was going to buy a sack of apples to share with them all, for being such gracious losers.

He told Rachel to stay there.

Rachel frowned. She told her brother that they were supposed to wait here and read.

Djoss rolled his eyes. He disappeared around the corner with the pack of boys, his new friends.

***

Djoss kept the stick with him for days. If he saw his father getting too close to him, he'd smack the man over the head, hard. Rachel's father hissed and kicked at Djoss. Djoss ran off, jabbing at his father's legs.

Her mother covered Rachel's eyes. "Don't look, little one," she said, "Don't look."

All the guilders for the winner.

***

The family slept at the edge of the village, in a poplar grove. The huge poplars, with their branches pointing to the sky like a bunch of scared pine trees, barely broke the wind off the mountains.

Her father was asleep. He was lying on his side. His head rested on a balled up wad of old cloth. One hand draped over Rachel's mother's stomach like he was holding down the red X right where the two lines crossed.

Djoss wasn't asleep. Neither was the sun. Djoss sat next to his father's head. He waved at Rachel. "Come here," he whispered, "Don't wake them."

Rachel crawled over on her hands and knees.

Djoss pointed into the man's ear.

"Look," whispered Djoss. He pointed into the man's ear.

Rachel leaned over, but her shadow fell over the ear and she couldn't see anything. Djoss nudged her out of the way of the sun, so the light could fall into her father's ear.

She blinked. The insect edge of something like a centipede's head was down there, looking up at them both, with sharp, tiny mandibles.

"It's asleep," said Djoss, "It's not Dad, but it's controlling him. That's what Ma says. She says it's your father, but not mine."

"It's gross," whispered Rachel, "What is it?"

Djoss frowned. He took his sister's hand. "Come on," he said, "Let's go into town and see if we can get something to eat. You can play a trick and then we'll get some money and we'll find something to eat."

Rachel let her brother lead her away into the village. They walked down a hill to a small fishing village. The town had more taverns than shops, and most of the men spent their days at sea hauling fish in nets to another town on an island over the horizon.

They walked down a hill, and onto the dirt avenue between the buildings. Women waiting for the return of their men swept out the old bones and scales from their plank floors. They looked at the two children walking hand-in-hand to the marketplace, where women had clumps of fish, seafruits, and gathered mushrooms.

Djoss asked the mushroom vendor about the different kind of mushrooms in the mountains.

The old woman smiled. "I know my mushrooms, dear," she said, "None of mine are bad. I picked them all yesterday."

"How do you know a good mushroom from a bad one?" said Djoss.

"None of mine are the bad."

"Don't even got a single coin," said Djoss, "I just want to know how you know the difference."

"If you aren't buying, best move along, dear," said the old lady. She smiled. She pulled her baskets back from the two children. "I don't mean to be rude about it," she said.

Djoss looked around the marketplace. This early, the shopkeepers had barely all arrived, much less customers.

Rachel reached for a mushroom. "I think this one's sour," she said, "I can tell."

The old woman smacked Rachel's hand. "How dare you say such a thing, dear! My mushrooms are all clean! I've been picking mushrooms for nigh on thirty years and not once has a body gone down from my mushrooms! Get on out of here with your awful accusations!"

Another woman, selling strawberries, laughed. "I wouldn't be so quick to dismiss the girl. Her ma's that Senta. Mayhap she knows something you don't."

"Hush up, Kari!" shouted the old woman, "You'll be poxing me!"

The strawberry woman, Kari, held up two plump, ripe strawberries. "You two, kids. I'll give you these free if you promise to leave us be."

Rachel immediately grabbed the strawberries. She shoved one into her mouth whole. Djoss had to force Rachel's hand open to acquire the other strawberry for himself. Red juice smeared her lips and her fingers. She licked at her hands.

Djoss led Rachel into the mountains.

"I've got an idea," he said, "We've got to find some mushrooms."

Rachel was still licking her fingers, though most of the strawberry flavor was gone. "What for?" she said.

"We're gonna find out which ones make someone sick," he said.

"Why?"

"You'll see," said Djoss.

"Why, Djoss?"

"Hush," said Djoss.

Djoss led his sister out of town. He avoided the hill where their parents were probably still sleeping, in the poplar grove. They walked up a dry streambed. Tiny frogs leaped away from them like grasshoppers. Rachel tried to catch one. Djoss grabbed her hand and tugged her up the hill.

"Come on," he said, "We're doing something important."

He led her into the shaded forest.

"We're looking for mushrooms," he said, "Any kind of mushroom. When you see one, give it to me, okay?"

"Okay," she said.

The forests smelled like cool rot. Red cedar trees smothered in moss sank in the weight of the rot in the air. The roots eventually let go. The trees collapsed into more rot. Two children strolled over the huddled mass of ruin upon ruin like flies landing briefly upon a battle in progress, unaware of the mass dying all around.

Djoss reached into a fallen stump, and he pulled out two different kinds of mushrooms.

"Here, hold these in your skirt," he said, "but don't eat them. They're probably poisonous."

Rachel gathered her skirt up in her hands so she could hold the mushrooms. She sniffed the air over her skirt. She curled her nose. "They're going to make my dress stinky," she said.

Djoss grunted. "Rachel, you already smell awful," he said.

He led her deeper into the woods. "We're following the stream so we can find our way back," he said.

Djoss climbed between roots and ferns searching for mushrooms.

Some were brown, some black, some spotted, and some covered in yellow flecks, as diverse as bugs under stones.

When Djoss and Rachel had found a few dozen different kinds of mushroom, he led her back to the stream, and back to the village marketplace.

"Don't drop anything," he said, to his sister.

Djoss went up to the mushroom lady. She frowned. "Didn't we tell you kids to leave?" she said, "Go on, then. Scat."

Djoss grabbed a mushroom from Rachel's dress. He held it up in the air for the woman to see. "I'm going to eat this mushroom," he said.

"Don't be a fool, boy. Look, some of the mushrooms out there might really harm you. Don't be eating things you don't know is safe."

Djoss shoved the mushroom in his mouth. He started to chew. He smiled with chunks of mushroom squishing between his teeth. The mushroom lady didn't seem to mind.

Djoss reached for another mushroom. "That first one tasted

squishy," he said. He held up the next mushroom. "This one looks better."

The mushroom lady spit to protect herself from evil. She took the mushroom from Djoss' hand. "Fine," she said, "You want to know bad enough you'll eat bad mushrooms to find out? Show me what you got."

Djoss opened Rachel's skirt. Fungus spilled from her dress and bounced in the dirt.

"If you touched any of these," said the lady, "you be sure to wash them hands of yours off in the salt sea. Some of this stuff be nasty, nasty." She took a long stick and speared three of the mushrooms. "Those three can make a fellow real sick. Real sick. Mayhap kill. They'd kill you if you ate them, easy. The one you ate will be making you pretty sick later, but it won't kill you. Nobody to blame but yourself, you foolish brat." She kicked the rest of the mushrooms on the ground into the street, and away from her little stand. "I ain't telling you which ones of those are good and tasty. I don't want you kids going after them and selling them, too. Strictly business, mind you. But, I don't want you getting sick."

The mushroom woman tossed the mushrooms on the stick off into the piles of trash around the marketplace.

Djoss was sick for a few days. His mother stayed with him, and left only to bring him food. Rachel told about the mushrooms, but her mother didn't punish Djoss for it. Djoss was very sick.

When Djoss got better, Rachel's mother went back to the village, to cast fortunes for coins. It wasn't a very large village. When the village ran out of fortunes, and out of things to move, the family would move on to a new village.

***

Djoss' father lounged in the grove, sleeping off alcohol with his huge arm resting over Rachel's back. She had closed her eyes. She had curled up tight. She didn't want his hand on her back. She wanted to pull away from him—to run away from him.

She heard Djoss. He said, "Hey," and he seemed to trudge up to the poplar grove. The hand moved off her back. She didn't open her eyes right away. Instead, she listened to the sound of eating, but it wasn't normal eating. Her father had something pressed against his ear, and the thing inside of his head was eating something from the inside out. That's how he ate.

"This tastes like shit," he said.

Djoss snorted. "You don't like it, you go get something for yourself."

"Where's your ma?" He's talking and he's eating at the same time. Rachel can hear the chewing, smacking noises of eating, and she can hear them speaking like they're not eating anything. She's afraid to open her eyes because she's afraid she'll see the creature darting from the ear, its black, centipede body wiggling in and out of the man's head like a bug tongue.

"I asked you a question," said her father.

Djoss didn't say anything.

Rachel heard her father standing up. "Whatever you got, you eat it. It's awful."

"You know that'll just make me sick," said Djoss.

"I'll make you eat something else and it'll make you sick, too," said her father.

"No," said Djoss, "And back to Elishta with you."

She heard the sound of hands striking skin, hard. A body tumbled to the ground. The body rolled towards her, and then she heard the body cursing and it wasn't Djoss, or her father, really. She heard the sound of vomiting, but it wasn't human vomiting, and it was muffled. That was her father. Her brother had knocked her father down in one strike.

She opened her eyes.

"What the hell did you feed me?" said her father. Golden bile spilled from his ears, into the tree. The fluids smoldered in the wood. That poplar was dead, now. Brown death rolled up from the roots to the branches. The poplars had always had their branches up in surrender, and now they were going to die from the ankles up from the demon stain.

Her father's eyes rolled in his head.

Djoss had a quarterstaff in his hands. He stepped on his father's back to hold the older man down.

"Rachel, get out of the way," he said.

Rachel didn't move.

Djoss swung the stick hard, directly onto the man's skull. The first strike drew blood. The fourth scraped skin away. The fifth cracked bone.

Through the miasma of blood and tissue, a long, slender insect unrolled out of the crevice like a living chain, wriggling in its own toxic vomit. The thing had tiny insect eyes. It looked directly at Rachel.

"Rachel, get out of the way!" shouted Djoss. He kicked his sister away from the long centipede crawling out of her father's cracked skull.

The poplar tree and the grass seemed to burn in the blood spurting out of the body.

Djoss' stick descended upon the narrow demon. Djoss cracked the creature's chitinous back. The red blood that leaked out of the long demon looked human. Every little drop seemed to kill the grass.

When the beast stopped wriggling. Djoss tossed the staff onto the beast. The staff had been badly burned where blood had struck it. Bits of wood burned away in the acid. The staff was only half as long as it was.

Djoss stepped back from his handiwork in the poisoned grass. "You all right, Rachel?" Djoss said. He started coughing. He choked up something and spat it out. Blood. His eyes had turned red, all bloodshot and weeping blood.

"What did you do?" she said. She wasn't crying, yet. She looked at the broken skull and the dead black centipede.

Djoss kept coughing. He clutched at his own stomach. His skin was green. He was dying with all the plants. The poplars groaned and cracked in death. A brown wave of dying grass like the essence poured from some invisible decanter in the clouds, splashing all around them.

Djoss touched Rachel's arm. "You can tell Mom when we find her," he said, "We have to find Mom."

Rachel touched her face. She was crying, now. The tears burned. When they touched her dress, they burned the cloth.

"Elishta! You're crying! Stop crying!"

"I can't," she said. She brushed at her own tears. The sleeve of her dress burned where she wiped.

Djoss picked Rachel up, and slung her violently over his shoulder. He staggered to the water down the hill and along the beach beside the village.

Behind them the poplar tree, where her father had died, had collapsed into a dead heap and the grove around the tree was dying. The poplars' bark dropped away like peeling wallpaper. The branches wilted. The trunks popped and groaned. The weight of the branches falling swung the trees around until they cracked entirely, tumbling down.

Rachel was still crying. She felt bruises rising in her stomach from her brother's sharp shoulder bouncing into her. Every leaping step hurt her more until she was screaming.

When he reached the fjord, he threw her into the cold water, clothes and all. He jumped in after her, letting the blood seep out from him and his own sickness.

"Stop crying, Rachel!" he shouted.

Rachel couldn't stop. She cupped water in her hands to splash the tears away from her face. She tried to say something, but she couldn't speak.

Djoss turned around and looked up at the hill. Some men from the village had climbed the hill with axes to investigate the fallen trees, perhaps collect wood. The man looked down at the dead body of man and the dead demon beside the body. The man looked surprised.

Rachel kept crying. Djoss jumped into the water. He grabbed his sister again, and carried her under his arm like a bag floating in the water. He ran down the beach, away from the village. He stopped long enough to puke blood. He collapsed three times. Rachel helped him up, out of the waist-deep water. She was able to walk now. She had his arm around her shoulders, and she was holding him up, in the water. He was terribly heavy. He told Rachel that he couldn't see anymore.

Then, when they had gone a way through the water, and he was having too much trouble walking to walk through the water, the two turned up the beach and into the low salt flat marsh grasses at the edge of the woods.

She put him down against a tree. He rested his hands on his knees. He gasped for air. "She'll find us," he said.

Rachel curled into a ball and turned away from her brother.

"I need you to wait here," he said, "Can you wait right here and be very quiet?"

Rachel didn't say anything. She was clenched up tight on the ground. She let her tears smolder on the mossy ground below her face.

"Rachel!" said Djoss, "Are you listening to me?"

She didn't respond.

"Just stay here!" he said.

And he stood up and ran off again, looking for his mother in the village.

Rachel didn't move.

"We have to get up," he said. He fumbled at his belt for tiny bottles of clear liquid (holy water, I suspect or alcohol) to pour into his eyes.

"Where's Ma?" she whimpered.

"I'm going to smear mud on our faces so people won't recognize us, okay? Then, we're going to go into the village and we're going to see if we can find Ma, okay?"

"I want Mommy."

"Rachel, I need you to stand up, okay?"

"Okay."

Rachel stood up. She let her brother cover her in his shirt on top of her old clothes, leaving him naked to the waist. She let her brother smear mud all over her face. She let him take her hand. She smeared mud all over him, too, his strong shoulders and back.

They walked along the beach to the village. He had to stop three times. He said that he was sick. He said he was going to be sick a long time, maybe forever. He said he would need Rachel to steal holy things for him, to help him get better. She didn't say anything to him.

They arrived in time to watch their mother burned alive in the village square, screaming in pain and agony in a voice that didn't sound like Rachel's mother at all. The waves of death from the demon's body spilled an announcement to all who could watch the falling trees. The body was recognized by its clothes, and the wife was called for by a crowd of village men and women all of them angry and sickening.

In less then a hour everything had changed in the village. Everyone was sick. Everyone was angry. The wife of the beast—a Senta gypsy—had brought this death into the village, and she had to burn for it. She didn't know she needed to escape until she was surrounded by the villagers looking for her.

Either that, or she knew from the beginning that Djoss was going to kill the demon, and that she would face death for being with the demon for so long.

Every dead mother is a mystery. She is a ghost that haunts dreams, with her scorched face and screaming.

This is no mystery: Djoss pulled his sister into the woods above the fjord. He placed his hands over her eyes, but she had already seen.

That night, he watched his sister by moonlight. Her pale moon face was like a blank piece of paper. Dirt and mud and grime all over it like words that had been rubbed while wet, and smeared. When the ink mess dried, it was a girl's dark lips, a girl's dark eyebrows, a girl's dark mouth, and a sheen of mud across her moon face.

He watched her because he couldn't sleep. He was vomiting blood, and seeing visions of a darker world in his high fever.

(She told Jona about this, about when her father died, and her mother died, and her brother almost died in bits and pieces I've been pulling out of Jona's twisted memories and she talked about what her brother felt that night, looking at her, and I can feel him in the corners of the memories, a boy acting like a man and alone with this strange, deformed child sleeping in the moonlight, connected to him by half of his own blood.)

***

Djoss was sick a long time. Rachel was not. Rachel never talked to Jona about how her brother conquered the demon stain. I suspect he had learned things from his mother to survive the pollution he had lived with most of his life.

Holy water retains the divine dweomer even when it is stolen. Imam and Erin still spare mercy for the thieves.

***

My husband and I have spent a long time discussing exactly where the doppelgänger emerged from the bottom of a canyon. We do not know if the man was alone, or if he was with his family when it occurred. We have narrowed the world down a little, in hopes that you may find the gap in the crust, oh my brothers and sisters in Erin.

In a mountain range in the far north, near the Okena, water leaps from a crevice in a granite mountain, and lands in a pool of sandstone. The water carves the sandstone down and down into the pool. Further down, the pool becomes a river littered with chunks of granite that dig into softer sandstone.

This has carved a canyon. When the mountain snows melt, the water fills into the thousands of passageways in the soft sandstone. When the summer sun is high, the river is a trickle of rocks that a child could cross alone.

And there, says my husband, a committed demon could push through the soft sandstones, and the mud. The veins of Elishta could erode open, and ooze their putrid acids into the river. Narrow demons, like doppelgängers, could squeeze through the small holes in the ground.

I disagree. I think the cliff is against the ocean. I suspect that the twisting fjords by the Rejk tribes in the far north, and their various cliffs and gaps in the geology are probably the source. Near the port of Nolika, where Nolanders come from, countless fjords reach into the land like fingers. Over time, a small vein of Elishta could have been pried open by the waves.

I have written these lines on this page with my own prejudice.

A porter—Rachel's father was mostly a porter—would probably work near the ocean. Oceans have more ships than mountain ranges. Ocean ships meant more work for porters and stevedores. Sweaty summer work meant strong men might dive into the water at high tide to cool off.

CHAPTER 13

Jona was alone down in a dive bar out on the other side of the Pens. The place stank of dead animals.

The living animals smelled worse. I remember this place. The last time we were here, Geek was eating eggs, and Tripoli and Jaime were still alive.

The other people there were mostly desperates stumbling in a haze. The killers came after a hard day's slaughter to pretend like they were normal folk a while and they had blood all over their arms and they kept slapping each other on their backs with their big, bloody overalls and the only music was a round or two of song that the killers kept singing because they sang all day while they worked while they were shoving cattle and goats and pigs up and down the killing floor, all terrified. And pinkers were there—were everywhere—slipping unsteady hands into anything that might hold a coin to feed the hookah. No one slipped a finger in Jona's pockets. Jona was there alone, and he had a good two arm-lengths all around him; only the stink dared to touch this scowling king's man.

That's where Jona was, and he was doing everything he could to blur. He didn't want to be anywhere, or be anyone. The black pit in his gut was so strong that it felt like everything inside of him had shriveled up into a poison so toxic that his very breath could kill a man.

He wondered if he drank enough, if he could fall asleep, and have a proper nightmare. He'd never been able to drink himself unconscious and tonight was the night to really try for it.

Then, he wondered if he could kill someone, just to kill them.

Then—right then—a narrow-faced lad that was a little too clear-eyed to fit in this particular location slipped into the empty space of Jona's black mood.

Jona turned and looked that narrow fellow in the face.

The fellow held up a green feather.

Jona scowled. He snatched the feather. "Good," he said. "Very good."

He tried to stand up straight. The narrow-faced lad noticed that Jona wasn't steady on his feet. The lad wrapped an arm around Jona to help him stand.

"Need help, king's man?"

"I need you not to touch me."

The narrow-faced lad smiled, politely. He stepped back from Jona enough to bow his head and shoulders a little. Then, the lad was gone. "I hear this one's special just for you," said the boy. "I hear some rich lady paid a fortune."

Jona slipped the feather into his pocket and stumbled into the street. The Night King had work for this killer tonight.

Jona went to the toy shop, with a smile on his face that would make a corpse shiver.

***

"What did they do?" said Jona. He didn't have a smile on his face anymore, and he had sobered up fast when the fear jumped into his blood. He thought about what lady might pay a fortune for this.

"I don't care what they did," said the toymaker. "I only care what you'll do to them. I care what you did the other day. I saw your report. Pathetic. You have a lot to earn back for our good graces. Now you do what you do for us, loyal and no more stupid questions. We've got them sighted in the room. That Senta is enough to spook a fellow ain't got the hard guts like you do. You've dropped Sentas like nothing. Demon blood spooks Sentas, too. The big fellow shouldn't be too tough. He's cheese-for-brains. The Senta is a hard scrapper, though, been setting fires and casting ice, and fast with it. Probably need to drop her first, and quick. The big fellow, you're supposed to cut off all his fingers one at a time. Then, cut off his feet. Then toss him into a river and let the sharks finish him off. Bring the Senta body back here, though. You're supposed to strangle her, and not spill any of her blood. Just bring her back here, whole."

Jona's hands shook. "What did they do?" he said.

The toymaker shrugged. "I have no bloody clue, nor do I ever want one."

"Who else knows about the mark?" said Jona.

"Night King says drop someone, we do it."

Jona looked around the room. The toymaker sat at a table. It was only a table. There were no signs of strings or traps or hidden surprises.

"The Night King is telling me to drop someone," he said. "That's exactly what she's doing."

The toymaker reached under his shirt.

Jona was faster. Jona was stronger. Jona was a king's man all day and a killer in his sleepless nights and he lived for bats and teeth. The toymaker only had a small knife and the poison on the tip was not enough to take down a demon child whose very blood was the same kind of poison.

Afterwards, Jona poured all the alcohol and kerosene he could find in this shop all over the corpse. He struck a match. He stayed long enough to make sure the fire caught the wooden furniture and boxes.

Jona slipped out the back and ran.

***

The signpost had a picture of a woman standing next to her severed head. Disorganized, infectious music tumbled from the windows. Bouncers tossed drunken men into the streets, where the men could fight each other away from the mugs and tables.

Women who had only just begun to work for the night told filthy jokes arm in arm with filthy men, all of them laughing and laughing and drinking on their side of the tavern.

The bartender was a stocky midget with the top of his thumbs severed. He walked barefoot across the bar to serve drinks. The mugs were as dirty as the bar.

Jona snapped his fingers at the midget walking up and down the bar. The midget had only half his thumbs. The single joint wasn't enough to grab anything too hard, but he was nimble enough.

The midget shouted over the crowd. "What you drinking, king's man?"

Jona grabbed the midget by the leg and picked him up like a flailing fish. Jona carried the midget outside so fast, the drunks couldn't raise up a shout in protest that their bartender was gone. Bouncers looked up and down at the uniform. Jona, with his free hand, pulled out his bell in his lapel pocket. "I won't be long," said Jona. "I only need one thing from him, and then he's back with you free and clear."

The midget hadn't said a word. He kicked and struggled, but he struck air, and Jona was too strong to let go.

Jona pulled his bell out in full and held it up like he was about to strike the midget with it. "You run, and I ring the bells on your little tavern, and all your customers and bouncers wake up in the tank, and all your liquor'll be confiscated by the king and anything you don't want found out is your neck. I'm only after one thing, and then you'll never see me again."

"I got no business with the king's dogs!" said the midget, cowering on the ground. His tone of voice was not as brave as his words.

"I want a helmet," said Jona, "just like the one you gave a fellow name of Salvatore Fidelio."

"Don't know about that."

"Yeah?" Jona struck the midget over the head with the bell. It made a limp ringing sound, but the midget's head muffled the ring enough, for now. "Listen, you tossing maggot. I'll roll you into the river if you lie to me like that again. I know Salvatore Fidelio got his helmet from you. A particular kind of helmet that was, and a fellow could really go places with it on his head. All I want is the helmet. You give me that, and I'm gone like a ghost and nothing but the bruise to remember me by."

The midget scowled. He pointed at the back door. "I had one, but I don't have one anymore. I sold the only one to Salvatore, and he never came back."

"Where'd you get it?"

A bouncer came around the corner. He wasn't the biggest fellow in the Pens, but he was big enough. He had his hands up. "Hey, king's man!" he shouted. "All you want is the helmet, and then you leave my man alone?"

"Right."

The bouncer pulled one out from his cloak. "So, let my boy go."

Jona put the bell back in his pocket. He held out his hands. "Toss it to me."

The helmet shone like a mirror when the streetlight caught it, flying. Jona snatched it one-handed. He didn't pause to bow. He popped it on his head, and left fast. He dropped into the same old sewer grate that Salvatore had shown him, straight to the Island, and Lady Sabachthani.

The huge guardians of demon bone and metal let him pass just as they let Aggie pass. He walked in the front door, and watched for dogs in the darkness. He kept to shadows and climbed an arbor to the roof.

He waited in the dark, staring at the horizon.

Every night was a long night. Every single one was longer than the last. This one was the longest, yet.

The rain came, and he got wet in the rain. It was a terrible rain, that made everything so slick. He clung to the slats and pressed himself into them and waited for daybreak. There was no sunrise with all the clouds. When the sun came, it pushed through clouds, and the fields around the estate were all covered in mud.

***

She had, in her hands, a single dog silent and still as a statue, though alive. She sat in a chair upon a balcony, away from the workers of the yard. She could look down and observe if she wanted to do so, but she did not. She sat far from the edge, holding a parasol up against the hot night air and threat of rain. The season of parties had passed, and all had been here, at her house. The rains returned to wash the streets clean and the grasses that had been danced to mud disintegrated in the damp into a swamp. Mosquitos and flies swarmed among the workers. None rose up to the high balcony, where lemony grasses and bits of rotting bone lined the edge. Jona knew the bones were from dogs. He recognized the skulls and paws. He had seen dead dogs enough before to know their bones.

"You can come down from the roof if you like," she said. "I won't kill you, yet. Killing me won't save that whore's maid. It won't save your mother, either."

Jona and Lady Sabachthani locked eyes. He climbed down to the balcony carefully, half-expecting to be stabbed on the way down.

"You've found the shipment of the demon weed from my lands. What matter is it to me? You will not be arresting me, or stopping me. You knew that already, though. Is your curiosity satisfied? What do you want? Tell me why you who are nothing but the scum of my boots when I walk in the Pens, why I should not kill you and your mother and everyone you love?"

"I've been thinking about things. You're the Night King," he said. "You want to be the day king, right? You want to be both."

"I want to marry the king of the daylight. Imam's stars and Erin's moon are nothing to the sun that burns them all away. I am the sun, rising from the cool night. I am the fire of the hills burning the daylight clean. Together the king of the city and I will bring a peace to this city. Every criminal answers to the king, and every king's man answers to the king. Every citizen pays taxes to the king, whether their income was legal or not. This is my vision of the future, Lord Joni. There will always be crime. When criminals answer to the king that terrifies them, their sins will be contained. They will be placed away from the good people of the street who choose not to see it much."

"Does your father know?"

"He taught me everything I know."

"Ever been up to the red valley? The place he opened up to Elishta where souls are trapped?"

"No. I don't leave the city. I have too much to do to take a holiday."

"Well, I've never been, but Calipari's seen it. He says it's awful."

"It is. It is a terrible thing, and hopefully we will never need to do such a terrible summoning again."

"Elishta is your sun. That's your sun rising up, burning everything. Polluting dogs with it. Eating everything up, soul first."

"Dogs have no souls. You've been making trouble, Lord Joni. Do I anger you so much? Have I hurt you so very much?"

"I don't know what to say," said Lord Joni. He looked up. He looked right at her. "I just wanted to know where it came from. You know nothing will come of it. I can write all the reports in the world, push people and break 'em and nothing will touch you. It's just… We know it's there, every day. Where does it come from? What is it? That's all it was."

"Jona, there is a woman dancing beside your old friend, Salvatore, late into the night. You know where she lives, do you not? I want you to bring her to me gracefully. Do not disturb her husband. Do not disturb Salvatore about it. Just bring her here."

"Why?"

"Because it will answer your question."

"I don't want to help you, anymore. It's time for you to start helping me."

"It would be very easy to destroy you," she said. "You should know why you are still alive. It's time for you to see what your real choices are."

"Salvatore is a monster."

"So are you. Bring me Mishaela, Lord Joni. Do it now."

"I am a monster. She's already floating in the bay. She's dead. I killed her and dropped her in the water. You were going to use her like you did Aggie, only worse."

She petted the dog gently. "You're lying," she said.

"I'll kill her before I bring her to you."

"Well, that leaves us in an awkward position. I don't have room for disobedient monsters."

Jona had enough of her games and intrigue. He had had enough. Here was the Night King, alone and unarmed. Here she was, and she had made him do such terrible things. He had his hands around her throat before he could think. He picked her up. She stared at him, coldly. She stood with his grip. He lifted her up to the edge of the balcony. The men from below shouted and waved their arms. Some of them were already running up. He realized he could kill her so easily. She was staring at him with a fury that would not end. She was so angry. She was trembling like a bird or a leaf. Her skin went pale, and her eyes were so angry.

Then, he saw her eyes surrender. He saw the fear come into her face. He saw it, and this was the first time he had ever seen her. It was the first time he had ever seen her for who she was, what she was. He saw her life before him, and the shape of it, like something from a dreamcast. He knew her. He looked in her face and saw her. He felt something killers aren't supposed to feel. He let her go.

She sat down. She rubbed her neck where it was already bruising. The men from the yard were there, shouting, but she waved them away. She said she was fine. She coughed. Everything was fine.

"Everything's going to be fine," said Jona. "If I was going to kill her I'd have done it."

She coughed and threw the dog on the ground, kicked it. She sat down so angrily, and looked up. The dog was mute, without a tongue to bark, and it gurgled a whimper at the balcony door.

"What do you want, Jona? What could you possibly want? I gave you everything! I gave you everything and you threw it in my face!"

He shrugged. "You never really asked me what I wanted," he said. "And when I told you, you didn't like the answer."

"Where is your whore's maid, anyway? Who even cares what they did to my men?"

"She's leaving town. She would if you let her. Her and her brother just want to leave town. They're never coming back, not when you got so much demon weed pouring out of the dogs' backs."

"No."

"I'm not leaving. I'm staying. My mother's here. My life is here. I want to help her, though. I want to help her leave. I want her to be safe. You know, I bet nobody ever asked you what you wanted and meant it. I bet your whole life nobody ever looked you in the face honest-like, and said something to you they really meant, and asked what you really wanted."

"Lord Joni, you ask too much. For what you've done to me you'll be dead before you ever see your mother's face again."

"I just saw you for what you are, exactly as you are. I saw you dying. I saw you facing death. I know everything about you. I'm asking you now, what it is you want. Don't be ashamed to be yourself. I'm worse. I was born worse. I never sleep. I never dream. I never face the demon in me. I don't regret. It's like I can't."

"Would you be the king of the day, to rule the streets and the stars and moon over this city? Will you let them crown you and let me rule here, as I see fit?"

Jona shrugged. "Why do you want to rule, anyhow? What's the point of power?"

"Power means I can... I don't know, Lord Joni. I guess it doesn't matter. I don't even know if I really want it. But, someone has to have it, and I don't want anyone else to have dominion over me. I hate the idea of someone ruling me."

"I hate that, too."

"With you beside me, we would build a city like no other, and push our power out into the world. The day and the night together, imagine it? Two worlds living together in harmony, hidden from each other always, but together."

"Elishta, too. You want demon children here?"

"I do," she said. "There's a power in your bloodline. It's a power I want for my own children, as long as I can protect them. I want children with power, Jona. Your long nights are so powerful."

"Mishaela goes free. She's not touched."

"Salvatore must live, too."

"And Rachel?"

"Everyone lives that can be spared, Jona. She will be free to go. I'll hire her and her brother for a caravan. There is room in the world for a little poison. It is a fire that rises up from the depths, and burns the sky clean."

"What's next for us, then?"

"You will need to be an officer before we can wed, and you'll need a little glory in your pocket before the king dies so the union makes sense to my rivals. Things will be arranged. Wait for my message, and obey it when it comes."

"All right" he said.

"Kiss me, Jona. Kiss me and be my beloved."

They were alone on the balcony. The men of the yard had left by her command. Jona hesitated, and she looked up at him, expectantly.

He bent over and kissed her. He did it so fast that it was awkward. The white sheen of her make-up marked him. He felt the powder on his lips and it disgusted him but he held his feelings back from his face enough that she didn't seem to notice.

"I'm going," he said.

"You'd better. My father will send someone to kill you if you don't after your little display."

"Okay," he said.

She probably wasn't lying.

"Go now. My people will be in touch."

"Everyone lives," he said.

"Everyone," she said. She nodded. "I have only ever wanted to kill the sinners that deserved to die, Jona. Criminals would hang if they were caught, and float if they were not. I am not so evil. Everyone lives that can be spared."

"Okay," he said.

He left the way he came. Maids backed away from him in fear. The Seneschal hid from him, behind a locked door. Jona wanted to hit someone, and he could have hit the Seneschal. He could have hit anyone. No one came close. He was in the street outside the grounds before he knew what to do with the odd feeling inside of him.

He was on the ferry back to the mainland before he knew.

Then, he was home, alone in the dark, staring at the ceiling, and waiting for daylight.

He still didn't know what the feeling inside of him was. He would never know. He knew that it didn't feel good, whatever it was.

***

Djoss Nolander? I heard about that giant. I heard he had six fingers on each hand and six toes on each foot and he was the biggest tosser in the Pens. I heard one time he grabbed this nobleman by the neck and squeezed so hard the noble's head busted open like when you squeeze a sausage too hard.

Naw, that didn't happen, tosser. Nothing about that's true. Djoss had six fingers on one hand, though. That's the truth. He was always sucking on the pinks until he thought nobody could stop him on account of how big he was. He busted into this dive and started throwing fists like everybody should listen to him. They get him calmed down, and you know what that pink bull does? He starts throwing fists again over nothing. Some folk are like that when their head's cheese. Think they got arms like Imam and they need to roll the world.

He may have done that once, but lots of fellows did that. That's nothing. I heard Djoss busted this toy shop up bad looking for something to steal and he found all these pinks. Pinkers steal pinks. Then the toymaker gets all crazy over it, and tries to kill Djoss. Djoss throws the fellow over a table, out a window, over a crate, and the toy fellow lands on a cart in the middle of the street. Cart driver thinks he's under attack, and he's no fellow worth a thing to a thing so he just bolts like a greased pig. Djoss comes out with all the pinks and sees this cart sitting there with the toy fellow in back. Djoss takes it for a ride. But, he's cheese-for-brains so he can't steer and the horses take him on the delivery route, and he's stealing the whole way and smoking his pink pipe the whole way and by the last stop he just falls over on his face in someone's house because he's cheese-for-brains. Toy fellow fronting for the pinks wakes up and sees the cart full of things worth stealing and rides off like nothing happened. Made more money than he lost from all the stuff Djoss stole in the cart.

Naw, naw! That didn't happen at all. Not to Djoss, anyway. That was a different fellow and I know the toy fellow was a tabor man so I'd know if it was Djoss. That was that guy with six fingers!

Djoss was the guy with six fingers!

Djoss didn't have six fingers.

What do you know? Nothing.

I know lots, mudskipper. Lots more than you. I remember Djoss, too, I do. He didn't have six nothing. He just had really big hands. He went to Erin's temple every single day because he drank their holy water and not one of the priests dared stop him. I heard he got in trouble with the Night King on account of his sister.

He didn't have a sister, tosser.

Bloody Elishta, he had a sister. I remember. I met her, once. Ugly as sin, with mudskippers to spare. Sparrow was her name. Anyhow, his sister gets all mixed up over some blood monkey, and Djoss don't like it. He starts throwing this monkey around until the monkey's hurt bad. But blood monkeys don't scare easy, you know. The monkey comes back on Djoss hard, but Djoss gets the jump on him because his sister warned him. Then Djoss strips the fellow naked and throws him out a window. After that, Djoss can't go out unless someone finds him. His sister, she gets locked up somewhere and Djoss can't find her. Next thing you know, he's running around quiet-like looking for his sister. I don't know if they caught him or not, but if he crossed the Night King like I heard he did over his sister and some monkey, the monkey's dead on account of how someone got the drop on him, and the sister's dead on account of how she messed up a good monkey, and the brother's dead because of everything he did over just how his sister was giving herself away in the street and that's not any monkey's fault. Monkey's taking advantage of what's available to him, you know what I mean? Anyhow, that's what I heard.

There's no Night King and you know it.

What do you know? You only just got here. I bet you never knew Djoss at all.

I heard Djoss was last seen alive with this Senta. Senta's screaming and screaming at him, but he acts like he don't hear. She says all kinds of stuff about how he's going to get himself killed if he doesn't give up the pinks, but he don't listen to her. He just keeps walking. Then he tells the Senta to toss off. She was messing with the fellow's push, you know? So this Senta conjures up all this ice and it surrounds big Djoss like a prison. Why in bloody Elishta some Senta taken a personal interest in some tossing pinker is too big for my head. Anyhow, Djoss pushes and he pushes on the ice and then he cracks it loose. He tells the Senta to toss off. She doesn't listen. She keeps yelling at him. Then the Senta makes this wall of fire all around Djoss, and he doesn't care. He jumps through it. Then, this Senta brings down a storm. And bloody Elishta, this storm is like the Breaking all over again.

You don't even know what the Breaking is.

I don't know why he got a mark on him over a Senta, but I heard it was because of a Senta. Those bloody gypsies are nothing but trouble.

Do, too. It's a big, tossing storm. Let me tell the story. These foundations cracking all over the Pens because they're all flooding out from this storm. And she's screaming about how lightning's coming for Djoss if he doesn't turn home. And he doesn't listen. He keeps going to the pits. Lightning strikes him right on his head. He gets blasted into the air three blocks away, big explosion and all that stuff. He gets up like nothing happened, dusts himself off and goes down into a pit. Never comes out. I hear he kept climbing down and climbing down and the Senta opened up the earth so he would keep climbing down to get to his pinks and he just keeps going. Then, he just keeps going until he's down in Elishta and baatezus eat him up. That hole's why we got so much demon fever. It's coming up from the hole that Senta made in the ground to swallow that pinker.

That didn't happen.

Did, too!

Look, we know Djoss is dead because he crossed the Night King and he ain't around anymore. It's that simple. Happens all the time. How he crossed the Night King, I don't exactly know. Lots of ways to do that. But, you know the thing I heard was like everybody been saying.

Fellow was a pinker, and he roughed up the wrong fellow when his head was all cheese. There was a woman involved, and I know that, too. That's the way it is, you know? Anyway, you gonna give us apples or aren't you? We're hungry. We told you everything we know and you said you'd give us apples.

CHAPTER 14

What is the difference between a palace and a prison? That is what I think when I see it. It's a huge building, far from the nobleman's Island, deep in the heart of the city, where the city's oldest huts were consumed by the courtyards and fields and walls.

There were enough windows to make a glass smith very rich if a strong-enough storm blew through. They were colored, too, and spotted with jewels. If we were closer, we could make out the images they contained, and decipher the symbols. None of that mattered, though. The king was not permitted so close to the windows that people could see, and people were not permitted so close when there were enemies in the world that could strike down a king.

The matron herself rode in with us. The Anchorite had not left her order's walls since she was sequestered there, but she told us, in her letter, that her duties were clear, and she would help us because though we were incorrect in our faith, we were never known to be dishonest in our old alliances. She did not speak to us when her carriage arrived to take us in, nor did we speak with her. She smiled to herself and looked at the city outside the carriage windows. She did not speak.

When the guards came, she held out her hand through the glass, with her insignia on her finger. The men seemed to shiver.

They backed away and waved us through, shouting at each other to let us pass.

"Did you know I am the cousin to the king?" she said.

I shook my head.

"I am. It is how I could maintain such a place of honor, and never marry a man against my will. Imam has been good to his servant. I have had such a good life."

We said nothing.

"Aggie was such a bad girl. She was a thief. She was disobedient. She refused to submit no matter how many beatings we gave her. She never cowed to the rod. A spirited girl. If we could only have gotten her through. She could have walked away from us if she had just been stronger. I pray Imam took her soul to rest. I pray every day since your awful letters came."

"We told you the truth, as I saw it in the mind of a demon child."

"I know," she said. She scratched her chin. "I am grateful to know the truth. Despite our squabbles, I am very glad you came here. We pray and pray and... I don't even recognize this city anymore. I don't even know where I am and I'm only a few miles from my place of birth."

"You should get out more," said my husband. "There are sins in this city that cannot be washed clean with prayer."

She looked up at him. "Prayer is a greater power, you old wolf. Let's not discuss theology. I left my convent for your sake. How could I remain there, when Aggie was burned alive and this hand signed her death warrant?" It was the hand with the royal ring. She held it up in wonder. "I came here, to my cousin, to stay. That's how you're getting in to see him, by the way. Don't think anyone else has enough power against Sabachthani, even with your seditious letters."

"We are grateful for your aid," I said. "Ignore my husband. He has spent too long as a wolf to appreciate the delicacy of the human heart. Our seditious letters are being copied every day, by every one. They are spread like fireseeds upon the city. Everyone will know the truth about their city. Everyone will know the truth about Sabachthani's unholy deeds."

"Knowing the truth doesn't mean anyone will do anything about it."

My husband grunted. "You should have more faith in the darkness of men. The wolves of the city will rip her apart. They will riot at her gate, and she has no more guardians to frighten the mob."

The carriage stopped. The old woman rose up and pushed her way out of the carriage by herself, without aid. She walked easily into the door to the inner palace. There, another carriage waited for us, open to the air, that would lead us through the interior gardens.

At the center of the gardens, there was a fenced off house, with a locked gate. The guards there stood at attention. The abbess' ring appeared again and they backed away.

"I am expected," she said. "Come with me, then, Walkers."

Inside, the cherry trees were in blossom, though it was not the season for such things. They smelled too sweet. Their color was too purple. The grass was thick and lush. It burned beneath my feet. I felt it burning. My husband was tense. He felt it, too.

The king sat, staring confused and befuddled by a butterfly that had landed on his tea cup. He held up the cup and looked at the butterfly. He saw us. He put the cup down and sneered at us. "Who are you?" he said.

The abbess held out her hand. "You don't remember your dear cousin?"

"No."

"Well, I am your dear cousin. I have brought some friends with me to visit."

"Have you seen my sons? No one will tell me where they are. Are we winning the war?"

"You have won all the wars, old warrior," I said. I plucked a seashell from a crevice in a tree. The salt smell filled the air beneath the too-sweet flowers. I slipped it into a pouch at my waist.

My husband plucked handkerchiefs and necklaces from the king's body. "Do not struggle, now."

"Hands off! I'm the king! Robbing me is death!"

"I am here to help you, old man. Your possessions shall remain with you, always."

"Liar!"

My husband was far stronger than anyone the king had known in life. My husband peeled away all the shells and bones and diamonds from far below the earth where they were hidden in the king's clothes. I entered the house, spreading my seeds.

The abbess sat down across from her cousin. "I have brought you something to drink. Do you remember the apples at my mother's estate? We used to sneak them before they were ripe. We ate them tart and bitter and dared each other to finish the apples we had taken."

"What is this man doing to me? What are you doing?"

He started coughing. He started coughing and coughing.

My husband lit a match and held it up to the flowers. They took to the fire as if the tree was long dead kindling, and not fresh wood in bloom.

The king was coughing. The guards at the gate were quick to jump through with arabesque blades drawn. My husband threw the wolfskin over his back and howled. This sent them jumping back, afraid. He growled at them. *It is holy work we do!*

The men ran.

The abbess took her cousin's old hand. He was coughing and gasping. She held out a small bottle of cider. "This cider comes from the trees of that orchard, when we were young. Take a drink, old friend."

He smacked her hand away. He stood up and looked at the fire spreading through the flowers. He ran towards the gate. The abbess walked after him.

In the little house, I spread fireseeds. I spread coal. The fire from the yard would make it here on its own.

The old man couldn't run. He could barely walk. He fell over outside with his guards. The abbess strolled out ahead waving her hands to the guards.

"Take him somewhere safe," she said. "I will be there shortly to check on him. The fire was no accident, but it is not a crime. We meant no harm to the king. We did no harm. He is merely frightened by our help. The assassins that ruled here, the Sabachthani clan—they are no more in power. They are criminals who were poisoning the king with demon power. Don't you see the flame?"

Was she believed or was my husband's wolf-ish countenance so terrifying? There had to be faithful of Erin among the soldiers here. There had to be men who knew exactly what we were. The guards dragged away the king, while my husband howled to the wolves beside her.

I came out. The shell was still in my pouch. It was the same sorcery Sabachthani used to extend his own life.

"Our old kingdom," she said. "Enough is enough. How long will he live without such demonology?"

"Not long," I said. "Scrub his walls clean. Keep out all visitors. Accept no gifts. Hold matches to everything to see if they burn."

She nodded. She pointed. The king was coughing and coughing. Blood was falling from his mouth. The guards were frightened. One was running for aid.

"That might be it. You had better go," she said. "You can run faster than that guard? You'll need to."

We pulled the wolfskins over our backs. We bolted past the guard. We leapt over walls and charged through gates like monsters. We ran to the walls, and ran to the woods, and ran to the edge of the kingdom of the dogs.

Let the fires come. Let the retribution happen. Let Ela Sabachthani's head replace Aggie's on the spikes of the wall. Let her house and all its sins burn to the ground and beyond, and remain as dead as the red valley of the north.

The dogs will come for dogs. King's men will ring bells by the will of the king, Elitrean the mourning lord, who lost his son to demonology. Sabachthani would find no safe passage, no safe harbor. Every sanctuary was known to the king's men. Every place she could hide and muster escape was known. Her father would not be able to save her, or himself.

Everyone dies.

The fires of the island came, next. Once begun along the grasses, there was no stopping it. We did not bother attacking the house directly. She would be too strong there. We set fires. We set fires in the trees and grasses and ferries and docking stations. We ran and set fires. The guard had been pulled away. Eritrean had seen to that.

For three days the fire burned.

Eritrean's men, with the king's men, hunted down and slew anyone they thought might have been of Sabachthani. Been home to the sleeping dog.

It happened all over the city. It was news all over the city.

It was such a simple thing to do.

Jona knew enough to tear it all down, and he didn't even know what to do with it.

The paper was enough. I wrote it all down. I handed what I knew from the mind of Jona.

We returned to the city one last time, to seek out Salvatore who had no one to keep him from us anymore. We sought out the empty sanctuary of the damned near the Pens district that had been a sanctuary for Salvatore before. We slipped into the darkness of the abandoned brewery, never removing our wolfskin cloaks for a moment. We hid in the shadows there.

Dog came back. He was still alive. He stumbled into the ruin. He was shaking. His sweat was pink. His eyes were bloodshot. He opened his mouth and howled and howled but it was only a whisper's breath. I barked at him. I jumped and snarled to keep him back. He was crying blood, shaking his head. He was mouthing something, but I didn't know what. His tongue had been cut so deep. However this was done, it was done that they had reached deep into his jaws with a hook and ripped his tongue from the back of his throat. He stank of blood from his failing skin and pores. He stank of dirt and filth and blood and death and the slow rot that comes to anyone who spends so much time in this mud. He was crying. He was in withdrawal. He had gone days without any weed, and it had driven him insane.

I pulled the wolfskin from my back. I touched his skull. I said, "You poor man." I let him hold onto me. I let him scream and wail and clutch at me. My husband watched the doors for signs of anyone following after him, but no one came. The rain was too strong. It drowned out everything. Dog had come here to get out of the rain. He knew he could be dry a while here, even in such pink agony.

He fell asleep in our pile of blankets and rags. We left him there.

We left him the matches.

We left.

Do you know where we can find a demon child?

No. You?

No. Shall we hunt again? Have we healed enough of this place?

We must see the estate first. I want to see the estate, what's left of them all once the decree goes out.

***

The rubble had only smoldered when the fire came. It would be a long time before anyone came back here. The fires we had started with Jona's memories written down were not put out by anyone by the king's command. They had spread, drawn to the center of the demon stain in the estate of Sabachthani. The house was destroyed. The willows were standing sticks of ash still smoldering. Rubble and bones floated in the lake burning, still.

We remained as wolves. We remained alert. We did not need to warn each other that this could be a terrible trap.

We sniffed the ground for any remnant of the stain. It was still everywhere, worse than the red valley. Salvatore's smell was everywhere, too. We trailed it through the trees, around the lake, through what used to be hedges and fields, and out into the city.

He might have been coming into the estate. He might have been leaving the estate. Either way, we followed what we could to the edge of the ferry where his scent grew thin from all the ash and smoke that blew and fell, and the people running over the ground.

Remain as wolves. Run through the streets in the night to all corners of the huge wall. Howl in the dark and call to him. Call out to every dog that remembers in their blood the singing of the wolves. Call out his name. Cry out with me.

Cry out, husband.

Cry out with me.

Salvatore must die.

CHAPTER 15

Caravans traveled along different roads. They clung closer to the waters to trade for fish from the boys that lived near the shore in the spiraling shantytowns. These young dervishes of mud jump to the roadside with their hands waving overhead. They held them up and shouted for the caravan driver. The driver kept fishhooks in a small sack. He traded two hooks for each good fish.

Past the merging rivers, the pebbled shoreline grows a rocky shell. Young oyster divers leap nude into the surf to gather supper to feed the fullers in the wool factory who stripped lanolin from the sheets of wool in ammoniac tents.

The end of winter, the sheep faced their fate in the mouth of the shears. The wool, too rich in oily lanolin to roll into decent yarn, has to dance with the fullers.

The liver and ammonia stink of weeks-old urine hung in the air. The caravan driver burned pine cones in a bucket, and he held it up in the air. They cracked and snapped in the heat, but they burned the edge of the smell out of the air.

Djoss asked him why he moved this way.

The caravan driver said that raiders kept away from the fullers, on account of the stink. Further north, past the city, nothing mattered.

North and north for weeks, and then they turned east.

And that is where my husband and I encountered the caravan, at the edge of the fullers, with the stink of the demon in his cart, where Rachel rode. He told us of his escape from a raider camp, and how lucky he was for the porter's Senta sister.

***

Another koan felt in the slanting light of an empty room. Rachel's voice echoed in Jona's mind.

A Senta student asked the master if the prayers of the faithful reached the ears of the Gods. The master snorted at his student. *Of course not. The prayers need only reach the ears of the one praying.*

Jona stared at Rachel's naked neck. He hoped his prayers reached his father's soul, in the bowels of Elishta. Then, he pushed the hope aside.

Rachel wondered aloud if her prayers aimed to the nameless, unseen deities that had fallen from the clouds ignored, and fallen into the unholy pits of the planet. Her hand reached up to the ceiling and down in an arc like a meteor.

If so, she whispered, *I pray that all of the Nameless demons kill themselves and leave your children alone. We want no part of your selfish ways.*

CHAPTER 16

Jona, long before he was the last of the Joni and had a name all his own, knew nothing of the war. He knew a war was happening, and that was all he knew of it. He did not know what it was. The only servants in the house were women, or old, crippled men. All the strong men were off fighting.

His father said that Jona might have to fight in the war, someday, if it kept on like this. A city to the north sent wave after wave of troops south into Dogsland's countryside. Dogsland sent wave after wave back north.

Lord Joni kept a large garden for the women that worked on the estate. He let them grow anything they wanted, and keep anything they grew.

Jona liked to sneak out of his room at night—he never slept—and raid the garden. A big, yellow dog chained up and mean got rid of rabbits in the night. Baiting the dog was better than the garden. Jona slipped out of his room, climbed down a trellis, and ran over the lawn to the dog near the fence.

Jona untied the dog's leash and let the animal run free through the grounds. Jona ran with the dog for a while, but the dog wasn't chasing anything. The dog stopped to sniff hard at the ground, and leave a trail of dog's water behind him.

Even against the walls that kept the city out, Jona's grandmother had planted vines with big, fat leaves that made it look like the woods never ended at all. Jona and the dog ran along the fence together.

Owls kept counsel among the leaves of a fat ash tree, gossiping like women. The dog came here to sniff through the owl pellets. Jona heard the dog crunching on hairy rodent bones.

Jona wanted to climb the tree to touch an owl. He grabbed a low branch. He pulled himself up and wedged his boot against another tree next to him. He had to use his hands to feel for new black branches against a black sky full of clouds.

He got up high enough to scare the owls to the higher branches. He stopped because his hands rubbed raw on the bark. He straddled a branch, resting his left foot against another branch for leverage.

A wind swam through the branches. A sea storm was coming. Jona stayed where he was, waiting for the rain to come. He looked up at the dark sky, watching the city lights bounce off the boiling night clouds.

He listened for the sounds of the dog down below. He looked down at the black ground. He couldn't even see shadows.

Thunder rolled in.

Then, lightning.

In the flash, a naked man covered in blood.

Jona froze.

Thunder.

Lightning again, and this time, Jona saw his father's face, all twisted up like a ghoul, and the man's face covered with dog blood, and the dog hanging limp from the nude man's mouth.

Jona clawed higher up the tree. His hands didn't bleed, but they felt like they might bleed.

Thunder again.

The rain fell hard. Jona clung to his tree all night, terrified. He only came down for breakfast when he heard his mother calling him.

Was this a dream, a piece of a dream, or a memory?

I don't know. The man was arrested, and hung high like a criminal.

His wealth was lost at sea. Lands were lost. A mother remained, with a boy, and she had to send her son to temple school like a beggar.

***

There's another dream I have at night.

Jona and the kitchen girls climbed up the ladders cutting oranges off the branches. They're all giggling and giggling. One of the girls—the one with freckles and a club foot—cuts into the orange in her hand with the knife. She bites into the flesh. The chef down below screams at the girl. The girl waves her hand at the woman. She hands the orange—her face all sticky—to the girl on the ladder near her. That girl takes a bite. She hands the orange to Jona.

The chef is screaming now, all red in the face. She calls the children filthy thieves. Filthy dogs. Filthy, filthy dog thieves.

Jona hands the orange back to the girl with the freckles, and she has orange all over her face, and everyone has orange on their face and no one is working.

And another girl cuts into another orange, and the children pass the oranges around.

Then, Lady Joni has run out into the grove, and she's screaming, too, and all the girls are listening now. They climb down the ladders, hanging their heads. They don't look well. Lady Sabachthani tells the chef to take all the girls into the kitchen for a good whipping.

Jona comes down, and then his mother has him by the lapel of his little white suit—all stained with orange juice. She drags him up to his bedroom, and locks him in. She tells her son, curtly, that he is never, ever to share food with anyone.

Jona spends three days in his bedroom, with only his mother visiting him. She tells her son that he is different, and he can't share food with anyone else.

When he's finally released, she tells everyone that her son recovered from the illness. The girl with the club foot and freckles had died. The rest of the girls were sick and under Lady Joni's personal care.

Jona looked down at where he had been so happy picking oranges, and the orange trees were gone. Lady Joni had them torn away for making her son sick.

"But I wasn't sick, Ma," said Jona.

"Hush," she said, "Don't call your mother a liar. You were sick. You're lucky you didn't die."

And Jona didn't understand.

***

The boy at night, waiting for the world to wake up, used up candles that his father had bought on the black market—candles were rationed—and burned black-market coal. Coal was also rationed. The boy read books, but he hated them. He played with blocks, building night cities full of people that never slept, and books became the large foundations of castles, or the high city walls with paper flags in the wind. Boys and girls wandered in the dark, and shared songs and dancing and the best games. And down this avenue the parents waltzed in grand balls.

Tiny cities spread across his floor in the flickering light. At the end of the night, the boy tipped over the largest palace—where his mother and his father lived—and the tumbling towers—a different architecture each evening—ruined all the buildings below like a volcano.

Then, Jona kicked his way through the streets, humming lullabyes to everyone because now was time for bed, but not for him.

He had other games, too, but they were normal enough. Imaginary monsters must be vanquished. Balls must be thrown and bounced. Pranks will be played upon the sleepers. Jona spent entirely too much time by himself, for a boy, when no one watched him in the long night hours.

***

Jona's name was not Jona, yet. His father had named him Tintaba. His mother called him Little Taba. His father called him Young Lord Joni. The children in the house called him Taba. The staff in the house called him Lord Tintaba Joni.

The visitors that came for his father called Jona "Lord Tintaba Joni". Three men, each wearing a king's man's uniform and each far beyond their fighting years. One man used his sword like a cane. He held the pommel and leaned into it. His knee wouldn't bend. This limping man hailed the boy. "Lord Tintaba Joni, lord of these lands, please give the king your precious time."

Jona frowned. He walked right up to the man with the sword like a cane. "Who are you?" he said.

The three men did their best to bow to the young lord. The gesture took them effort. One man made sounds as if he was lifting a heavy load. The one with the sword for a cane had to balance precariously on the tip of the sword's pommel on the ground. The third was merely very stiff, and struggled to force his stiff body low enough to qualify for a bow.

"Lord Joni," said the stiff one, "We are the King's Guards, and we have come looking for your father. Can you direct us to him?"

"I don't know where he is," said Lord Tintaba Jona, "What do you need him for?"

"We wish to discuss very dull, boring, unexciting things, my Lord," said the man with the sword like a cane, "If you'd like we can talk about them with you. You seem like a mature young man, who can handle boring, dull, unexciting conversations."

"I'll go see if I can find my father," said Jona, "Wait here."

"Gladly, my Lord," said the tall, stiff man.

Jona ran up the stairs to the top floor. His father liked the top floor—even though it was the hottest floor in the summer—and pushed papers around a desk near the south wall.

Jona knocked. His father's voice called out for a few more moments.

Jona leaned against the wall across from the door. "Father, some men are here to see you. They're dressed the same."

"Oh? How many are there?" asked Lord Joni.

"Three," said Jona, "And they're wearing the same clothes."

"They're king's men, Lord Joni. They are here to arrest me." The old Lord opened the door.

"What does that mean, father?" said Jona. He stood up from the wall. He looked up at his father.

Lord Joni smiled. One hand clutched the doorknob. The other hand, hanging at his side, trembled. The man was pale. "They're going to take me to speak with the king, Lord Joni, and I will be going away for a while. Please, don't worry," he said.

"I'm not worried, father," said Jona, "They're old."

"Old, you say? Undoubtedly any young king's men would be assigned to the army for now. Did you know there's a war on?"

"Of course, father."

"Do you know what that means, Lord Joni?"

"It means that there are only women and old men everywhere. All the men are off in the woods or at sea because the king says so."

"All except me and few others like me," said Lord Joni, "Unfortunately, fighting in this stupid war may be the best I can hope for now. I was allowed to remain here instead of fighting because of the ships. Do you know how our family earned money?"

"No," said Jona.

The father took his son's shoulders and led him into the study. Mounds of paper burned in a trash bin. Heaps and heaps awaited the fire, upon the desk.

Old Lord Joni led his son past the burning papers to the open window. Smoke from the fire leaked into the sea air. The sea breeze carried the smoke into the city beyond the garden. He picked up his son so the boy could see the ocean in the distance. "We owned ships," said Lord Joni, "They used to be some of the best ships in the world. Now, they are all at the bottom of the sea."

"Ships don't belong on the bottom of the ocean," said Jona, "That doesn't make any sense. Ships sail on top of the water, father."

"Of course, they're supposed to stay on top of the water," said the old Lord. Tears welled up at the corner of his eyes. "Unfortunately for us, our ships were sunk at sea. Every man on board was killed. Every pebble of coal was lost, and now the king is very upset with me. Swords and arrowheads cannot be made without coal. Armies cannot fight without weapons. This was a terrible blow against Dogsland. And, because they are my ships, I must bear responsibility for them."

Jona looked up, and tears burned at his father's collar, melting the edges of his fine shirt. The man cursed. He abandoned his son in the window and leaned over the fire in the trash bin. Each tear that fell flashed like a firecracker in the fire.

"Father?" said Jona. Jona reached up and touched his father's belt. "Don't cry, father."

The man breathed hard. He choked down his tears. He placed his hand on his son's head. "We may hate the king, but he is the king and we must respect him no matter what. Do not hate these men that came for me, son," said Lord Joni, "Are you listening to me, Lord Joni?"

"I am," said Jona, "Don't be sad."

"Where is your mother?"

"I don't know."

"Go find your mother. She will already know. Just find her, and stay with her. You're going to have to take care of her while I'm gone, Lord Joni. The household and everyone in it depends on you, now."

"I've always been the man of the house," said Jona.

"Good boy," he said, "That's my brave young man. Before you go find your mother, make sure all these papers are burned. Do you see all of these papers?"

"I do, father."

"Burn them all. Let no one enter this room until all this paper is burned, not even your mother."

Jona watched his father stroll out the door. He thought about how scared his father looked, with shaking hands. The door closed too loudly. Jona sat at his father's chair behind the desk. The chair was far larger than Jona was. Jona clutched at his stomach, and rocked a little. He watched the fire burn. Eventually, he stood up, and tossed more papers into the flame.

Dinner had been such a habit, that it wasn't until the table had an absence that young Jona remembered anything.

Servants were missing. Food was a thin soup, with barely any meat and fewer vegetables. The house was still full of fine furniture. The lands hadn't been sold, yet.

And his mother leaned over her soup, and she had her head in her hands, and she wept unabashed.

Jona watched her, confused. All he had asked her was when his father was coming home and now she was crying.

That sick feeling in his stomach came back. He didn't feel like eating his soup. He pushed his bowl across the table.

Jona's mother, through her tears, collected her breath long enough to speak. "Jona," she said, "Eat your soup." The last word trailed off into her sobs.

Jona pulled his soup back over, and picked up his spoon.

"I don't like it," he said. He took a bite of it. His eyebrows crossed. He wondered why he had to eat bad soup and how come his father wasn't here, and why his father had taken all the servants with him.

Eventually, his mother said, "I don't like it, either, Jona."

"Who's Jona?" he said.

"You are now, little one."

"I'm Lord Joni. I'm the man of the house until father comes back, so I'm Lord Joni."

"I know, my Lord," she said, sadly. "You are also no longer my little Taba. Now, you are the man of the house, and your new name will be Jona Lord Joni, for you have no father to give you a name. You have only a title. Your father is already home. He is dead, and we buried him very quietly under the house. We couldn't risk a funeral."

"I don't understand."

"I like your new name. It is a strong name for a strong boy. Have you finished your soup?"

"No. Can I have dessert?"

"No dessert tonight, Jona. If you're done, help me with the dishes."

Jona picked up his bowl of awful soup and threw it across the room. The bowl shattered into tiny pieces and the soup splattered like red paint.

His mother said nothing.

If she had had any tears left in her, I imagine she would have cried again.

Jona stomped off towards his room. He slammed the door to the dining hall, the door to the stairs, and the door to the hall. In his room, he left the door open. He wanted to wait for someone to come by so they could hear him when he slammed it shut.

No one came all night.

***

A father is not remembered in a picture, or a voice. He's remembered in a smell, and a way of moving. This man, Jona's father, Lord Severa Joni, smelled like flecks of iron, rich garlic butter, and ink stains on his fingers and sleeves like a printer. His face, like Jona's, was narrow and firm and tended towards sour scowls. His hair was red as strawberries—Jona had inherited his mother's plain black hair—which he often tossed about with his hand. Lord Joni rarely stepped into the yard. When he did, he was walking towards his carriage, and holding a parasol over his head to keep the sun off his brow.

I see an image of the man, in Jona's memory, the only time Jona saw him and it stuck. Lord Severa Jona has one boot on the carriage step. He hands the parasol to his servant. Lord Severa turns back once to look at his house.

Jona catches his father's eye from a second story window. Jona waves. His father clenches his jaw. Then, as if catching his bad behavior and correcting himself, the father smiles. He lifts one hand up in a wave. He gets into the carriage with the three old king's men and he's gone forever.

CHAPTER 17

W̶e climbed over the rubble that used to be his home. We dove into the sewers after him, smelling his stain in the ground. We ran through the dark.

He was here. He had to be here. There was nowhere else to run with Sabachthani burned to ash except into the ground, into the inns of the city, or into the streets. He had no safe harbor, now. He had no known place to hide. Eritrean was looking for him. There were king's men at all harbors. Erin's faithful swarmed the hills, howling wolves, packs of wolves that never bothered to pull the skin of man across their beautiful, terrible bodies—claw and tooth and strength of the wild beasts.

The dogs of the city know that we hunt. They that remember the woods in the their blood howl back to us. They howl when they smell the demon stink on their streets and alleys.

Howl, dogs. We howl back, and we run.

The streets are clean enough of the stain that we can find him.

The fires have burned enough down that we can find him. He has no harbor here.

Cry out for us, dogs. This is your city, dogs, where you piss your boundary lines and claim all buildings and streets. You would have his stain removed.

They cry back.

We all hunt.

***

Jona spent weeks alone after Rachel left. He drifted listlessly in and out of alcohol. He showed up for duty his uniform torn and wrinkled and the undershirt showing through the places where the old uniform had burned through. Calipari sent him home, and docked his pay. Jona needed new uniforms soon, but his mother couldn't make them fast enough.

Jona didn't care.

Jona spent his nights drinking and avoiding his mother. For weeks, he showed up for work a little drunk, and sobered up slowly in the daylight until night came and he drank again.

In the daylight, Jona sank like his father's burning ships. Calipari wrote a letter to the lieutenant requesting a change of duties for his troublesome corporal gone to pieces over a woman. Sergeant Calipari was concerned that after he retired, Corporal Lord Joni would be put under a new sergeant that didn't know how to keep Lord Joni in line. The lieutenant wrote back word that Jona was going to be the new sergeant, and probably an officer soon after if his friends in the nobility had anything to say about it, and it didn't matter what happened in the Pens to anybody as long as whatever happened stayed there, and the meat kept coming through.

Calipari waited two weeks out until the end of his assignment, watching Jona show up dirty and drunk, and the other king's men avoiding him.

Nothing mattered in the Pens.

Calipari asked for an early out of the desk job, and a chance to travel to his promised ground. His request was accepted. To his surprise, he was assigned Corporal Jona Lord Joni to go with him, for the inspection tour of the northern guard towers. The lieutenant suggested it would be a chance for Calipari to clean up and train the next boy in the Pens.

Calipari thought nothing of it, then, and just wanted to drag Jona away from the drinking halls a while and help him clear his head.

As far as Calipari knew, Jona had never had a girl before, so he had never lost one before. It takes a few to learn how to lose one.

Jona died on this journey. We found his skull where he fell. Calipari drove a sword through his chest where Rachel destroyed him.

***

There are two nations on this isthmus. We have spoken long of Dogsland. North of Dogsland, past a series of fat hills that stretches one bumpy finger into the sea, there exists another sea power. I call it Northland, for it is north of Dogsland, though this, too, is not the real name. Let them not burn our woods over mere words in a scroll.

To talk of Northland is to talk of Lord Sabachthani. Lord Sabachthani stood on the hills that border the two lands, and sacrificed to the demons of Elishta. In one particular valley, the two main land armies smashed together. The king commanded Lord Sabachthani to win the field with his magic, no matter the cost. Sabachthani called upon his demon lords.

Purple smoke followed a powerful wind into the valley, and this presence ignited in the blood-stained grass with a purple flame. No flesh or fragment of grass burned in the flame. The souls inside the flesh burned, and the force of life in all the grass. Each body that fell dead below the thrust of sword stood up again, and turned their weapons upon the living.

Everything the fire touched was blighted. The armies of the dead marched along the red valley, guarding their red valley until their bodies and bones rotted into dust.

The fighting stopped. Neither nation had the land army to

overcome the city walls after this. The merchant companies forged expensive alliances with both nations, and commerce continued. Guard towers line the hillsides, each with a signal fire in view of another tower. The people grow up, marry, give birth, work, and die in this state of endless hostility as if they live in peace.

Because the guard towers were built by the king, city guards manage the towers, not the army.

And every year, Northland gave some soldiers the clothes of raiders, to wear in Dogsland's hillsides. They hassles merchants until the army chases them back north of the valley. Dogsland did the same in return, out on the waters, blockading and stealing and sinking ships under no city's flag or port of call as if it is not done by Dogsland.

And my husband and I watched these raiders from the shadows. We cleaned up the broken camp to help the wild places thrive again where they've been trampled and burned. We bury the dead. We planted new trees.

***

Nicola Calipari's apartment hall was cramped with destitute beggars. Jona crawled over the stink and the human waste with his hands on his pant legs. He pulled the cuffs up out of the worst of the stink. Beggars saw his uniform and pulled away from him. Jona could have arrested the lot of them for trespassing.

Jona reached the door where Nicola Calipari was still sleeping. He knocked politely. He knocked again, a little louder.

A muffled voice from behind the door muttered something unclean. Jona jiggled the doorknob, and recognized the kind of lock. Jona slipped a dagger in the gap between the door and the wall. He wiggled the blade back and forth to coax the bolt out of the wall. Less then a minute, and Jona had the door open.

There wasn't any sunlight in the cheap flat. The only light came from the hallway beyond the gaps between door and wall. Jona flipped a match from his pocket. He lit it, and held it up while his eyes adjusted.

Two full chamber pots sat at the foot of the bed, covered in black flies. Clothes were strewn across the furniture. A single candle sat on a nightstand next to the bed. Jona carefully picked his way across the floor to the nightstand. He lit the candle with his match.

"Sergeant Calipari?" he said.

The man in the bed snored, lightly.

Jona pushed at his arm. "Sergeant Calipari?"

Nicola rolled over and moaned. "Mm... You got the wrong room."

"I have the right room, Nic. You awake?"

"Oh," he said.

"You were late for muster. Captain sent me here. It's mid-morning. We've got to hit the road."

"That's nice. I'm almost through with all this pomp and circumstance. Bloody Elishta but I'm done with all that."

"You get your supplies together?"

"My what?"

"We'll be on the road for three weeks. Did you get food, Corporal?"

"Was I supposed to?."

"I figured you wouldn't. A little hunger is good for you."

"You ever leave the city before, Lord Joni?"

"Who would do a fool thing like that?"

"Place is a pit. I'm glad to be rid of it."

"You still drunk?" Jona leaned over and sniffed. Calipari stank of piss gin.

"It's nice out past the wall, Corporal. Gets your head clean when there isn't anything but fresh air and the sun and the birds. These days I wake up in the Pens, I feel like my bones are put together wrong."

Sergeant Calipari stepped up from bed, and he was already in his uniform. He had slept in it. He pulled his boots on over bare feet and grabbed his cloak and belt from the night table, which was almost the only furniture here. "You hungry?"

"I ate. I thought we'd be at the wall by now."

"I'm starving. Let's go get something to eat before we go. "You're acting like you already quit. You going to make me do all the work?"

"That's the idea, Lord Joni. You're still the king's man. I'm just biding one last trip. I'll get something on the way. We'll be at the Owl and the Ass by midnight, if we leave right away. The other sergeants hate it, but I like it. I met Franka on this detail. It gets me out of the Pens."

"How long will it take? It's already mid-morning."

"It's going to take a week to make the first post. An hour now and then won't bother the king's biscuits."

"It's your call Sergeant."

"Are you still drunk, too, Jona?"

"No," he said. It was mostly a lie.

Calipari was up and ready, and leading the way out the door. He locked it behind him.

"Because the one thing about this detail is I don't want you puking on my stuff. Get your head cleaned out, you know?"

"Are you going to talk this much on the road? Because I'll be drinking more if I have to put up with that."

"Bloody Elishta, Corporal, but life kicks you in the teeth."

***

Sergeant Calipari stopped at a fruit vendor and bought seventeen apples. The vendor piled them into a cloth sack. Jona carried sixteen, and Calipari chewed on one slowly while they walked to the main station for the cart.

Calipari didn't talk. He just ate. Jona carried the apples.

When they arrived at the station, Calipari tossed his apple core at the man at the door.

"Hey," said Calipari, "spread the word to the towers for my girl Franka, at the Owl and the Ass. I'll be by and by come midnight easy."

The guard nodded, and tossed the apple core back at Sergeant Calipari, who let it fall at his feet. "Don't forget your apple, Sergeant."

Inside, the captain didn't look up from the desk.

"When are you retiring, Nic?" he said.

"Soon, sir."

"You won't if you keep showing up late. I'll give you so many demerits, you'll spend the rest of your life scrubbing pots in the bowels of the training ground and your city land will be assigned to some crazy buck private who won't last twenty years to claim it."

"Sorry, Captain. I was getting supplies for the trip for us both. Didn't Corporal Lord Joni tell you?"

"Is that true, Corporal?"

"My fault for not saying anything, sir."

"Corporal, you're a disgrace to your noble blood. Sergeant?"

"Yes, Captain?"

"Close the door."

"Aye, sir."

"The courts were busy last week. They gave me more things than I can handle. I'm sending you out with a full load to restock the outposts. All these sharp things are no longer a threat in the alleys, and they got you a cart for once, so be grateful. Your boys rang some good bells, and lots of teeth showed up in the trash. Lord Joni's got a knack for turning out trouble. When you reach the dead valley, open this envelope. Can you read, Sergeant? You aren't one of the desk sergeants who foists all his work on the scriverners?"

"I can read, Captain. You know that. I'm the best desk sergeant you ever had."

"Well, go out a ways, and then read this message. It came straight from Sabachthani. Lord Joni's got quite a career sponsor. You hear that, Corporal?"

"Sir?" said Jona. "I don't know a thing about it."

"Right. Don't linger with your wife, Sergeant. You'll be sick of her soon enough."

"We ain't married yet, Sir."

"More reason not to linger on the king's business. Get out there, gentlemen."

"Sir," the two Pens' guards said, in unison.

"Wait," said the captain. He eyed Jona up and down and curled his lip. He didn't like what he saw. "I just wanted to get a good look at you before you go. Bloody Elishta, but I don't see anything worth the trouble. You the one found our troublesome boy lying at a hookah in the night?"

"Yes, sir."

"Well, that's good enough for me, and Lady Sabachthani says you're her friend. You're alive, too. A lot of the boys in the Pens don't last. Still, you don't look like you're worth much to me, Corporal. I don't care who your friends are if you don't work hard and keep your head clean. You hear me, Lord Joni?"

"No, I don't," he said. "I don't have to put up with you going on like that, pushing me around. You don't know a thing about walking where the Joni estates used to be all orange orchards, and now it's all meat. You've never set foot in the Pens. You never jumped into a sewer line below the abattoir. You've never rang the bells for the hookah dens and the men that keep the pinks hot. I've never seen you at Lady Ela's parties, either, invited or not. What do you know about the city, Captain? Paper. Nothing but paper. Can you read? Can you walk home at night without a beggar dying at your door? Let's go Sergeant."

The captain said nothing.

Outside, Sergeant Calipari whistled.

"What, Nic?"

"Nothing," he said.

"It's a nobility thing, Nic. I'm noble. He's not."

"He's still the captain."

"I obey the king."

"So do I," said Calipari.

"Also, I'm going to fire him soon. If I got friends, then I got friends, and I can do something good with them. The captain's no better than a scrivener private."

Calipari nodded. "He's got friends, too, Jona. Everyone has friends. I hope you remember that."

The captain of the guard had said nothing about this, to us. I assume it was because he was angry he couldn't whip the corporal for it when Sabachthani had him in her fold.

(Sabachthani is gone now, and the captain remains.)

***

The donkey was tall and bumpy. The little spots of spine stuck out in his back. One look and both men knew no one was riding on top of the animal. The cart was full of steel weapons in piles beneath burlap. A few bits of armor hid inside of a smaller sack.

"Decent armor. We hardly ever get armor from the streets. Must have been a privateer in the shipyard getting rolled."

Calipari reached inside, and wrapped his palm around a helmet. He pulled it out.

"This one's still shiny. Looks brand new." He popped it on his head. "How does it look?" He turned over to Jona.

"It looks like it's going to be hot when the sun starts coming down. Another rainstorm is coming tonight. It looks like it'll rust."

Nicola laughed. "You're a real happy fellow, you know that?" he said, "Franka likes it when I come in with all this shiny stuff on."

"Guess it's better than seeing your face," said Jona, smirking.

"Keep it up, Corporal, and you'll be walking next to the cart," he said, "I'll drive the donkey since I know the way. You watch the stuff."

Jona stretched. "With both eyes open," he said. He didn't mean it. He hopped up into the cart. He sat down next to the bags of weaponry, and rested his elbows on his knees.

Calipari climbed up to the front of the cart. He grabbed the reigns. "When we turn west, on the way back, I'll show you my parcel of land. I figure we rush through the mission, and swing west to check my land. I need to spend a little time on the roof. Raining like this, and I haven't been over to put more slats down. I've gotten the left side of it, but the right is still a mess. Franka has some things for it at the tavern. Hammers and nails and stuff. Lucky you," he said, laughing, "you won't have to carry anything this time unless the donkey dies."

***

They rode the cart to the wall. It took all day. Jona sat on one side of the cart, and he watched the sun fall down over the rooftops, into the slanting shadows of crowded alleys. He wondered when the alleys became more crowded than the streets. People needed places to live that weren't alleys. Beggars needed work. When he became king, he'd try and get Ela to do something.

The guard at the gates told Nicola that Franka heard he was coming.

The night beyond the city walls was as dark as the sewers. It was darker, with no lamplight to drown out the stars and the moon. The clouds only made it darker. The humidity was terrible. It was still hot enough to melt conversation even an hour after sunset, but the breeze was clean and the sounds of the singing insects and frogs held none of the ominous echoes of wind and storms.

It wasn't going to rain, yet. The sky was just going to sit there and wait. Jona shoved the gear around so he could lie down on his back, sweating. He used the sack of armor like a metal pillow. He wondered how many nights he could lie like this before his sweat burned the cloth and damaged the wood. It wouldn't take long, in this heat.

He kept his eyes open. He looked up at the stars. He couldn't remember the last time he had seen so many stars. From where he was lying, he could see the helmet, still on Sergeant Calipari's head, bobbing back and forth with the motion of the cart. In the near perfect darkness broken only by a small lamp hovering out above the donkey hanging off a branch Calipari had cut from a tree, the helmet was an absence of stars, luminous in the moonlight. It was like a ghost's head hovering atop a shadow. The animal was exhausted and kept trying to stop and kick. Calipari whipped it hard, and often, to keep it going. He cursed at it. He made no friend that night.

"You going to sleep on me?" said Calipari.

"I'm trying to," replied Jona.

"Well, don't expect me to wake you at the tavern," said Calipari, "If you want to sleep in a bed, you have to be awake."

"I'll keep that in mind."

Jona looked up at the stars, and wondered what they were. Religions had answers, but there was never an answer that satisfied Jona when his own existence was an abomination to the religions. He didn't feel like an abomination. He just felt lonely. Also, the hard road and the grumpy mule made the journey rough, and soon his back hurt on all that armor. He hopped out of the cart to walk off the jostling in his body.

Behind him, he saw the city wall like a cliff, with the torches burning high on crenelated heights. His father's skull might be up at the top, somewhere.

He tried not to think of his father, but the night was so empty and there was nothing else to do but think.

***

They reached the first tavern soon enough. Franka stood in the dark. She was a tall woman in dirty white with a long shadow in torchlight. She stood beneath the sign of a huge Owl carrying a rich man in its claws by the exposed backside. Jona strained his neck and squinted to see her better. Her voice was all he had. Her voice was high, and carried a sharp edge to it. This woman had the voice of a woman weary of speaking to men that wanted something.

"Is that you, Nic?"

"'Tis, my love."

"What took you so long? Heard from the wall that you'd be here an ages ago, and I been out here all night and now it's almost morning."

The cart came to a halt in the tavern's muddy yard. Already, sleep had claimed whatever drunks were inside. A few slept in heaps beneath the eaves where the rain might not wake them.

Nicola stood up with his dark cape flowing, his hand on the pommel of his sword, and the ridiculous helmet reflecting the torchlight where it wasn't covered in rust. He was a tall man on the cart, and he frowned down at her. "You waited for us all night? That's foolish, Franka, and you know it. Stay in out of the damp! You'll catch fever over nothing!"

Franka touched his leg. She held out her other arm to help him down from the cart. "Well you should have thought of that taking your time. You know I wait up for you when you're coming."

"If I'm late, go to bed, love."

"Shut up and get over here, already. I'm not tromping through mud for you."

"Aye," he said. He swooped down from the cart and did his best dashing walk in uniform across the muddy yard. She held her arms out for him. They embraced.

She rapped her knuckles on his headgear. "Nice helmet," she said, "Is it new?"

"No."

"I don't kiss helmets. Might cut myself."

Jona cocked his head. Franka was much taller than Nicola. It looked strange to see her leaning over him, and him straining up. It reminded Jona of a mother with a child, but the kiss was all wrong for that. Jona looked away.

The sergeant turned towards his corporal one last time that night. "Take care of the brute," said Nicola, "We leave in the morning, soon as we can stand up. There's probably a room for you somewhere, but it ain't with me." He threw the helmet at Jona.

Jona caught it in mid-air. It was still warm from the sergeant's skull, and had a misty patina of sweat. Jona tossed it back on the cart where it clanged.

The sergeant and his lady disappeared into the building.

Jona looked around, and didn't see a stable. He walked around the building. It was solid stone bricks along each side, mortared together with good plaster. The front was logs in lumps like an old cabin, as if the stones had collapsed on one side and been replaced.

Jona unhitched the mule from the cart. The worn out animal immediately kicked and snorted and stepped towards a trough of water near the hitching post. Jona slipped a rope from the cart, from the lip of the sacks. He tied it to the mule's neck. When the mule was done drinking, Jona pulled the stubborn animal into the stable. The warm stink of fresh manure was as deep as the darkness. A single sliver of moonlight crept through a crack in the roof and reflected on the murky metal of the shovel. Jona stood in the doorway, waiting for his eyes to adjust.

"Hello?" he said.

He heard horses breathing. Somewhere, a mouse scurried

through the hay.

"Is anyone here?" he said, again. Jona's eyes adjusted to the dark. He fumbled for a match. The innkeeper would kick any fellow out for lighting a match around all that hay, but Jona needed the light.

He looked up into a white face. Both men froze, hands on hilts.

"Are you my new boy?" said Jona.

Salvatore whispered, "Only if you're the blood monkey I'm following."

"Aye," said Jona, "How've you been, Salvatore?"

"Fine, I guess," he said. He folded his arms in the dark. Jona suspected he was fingering his blackjack inside his sleeve.

"Do you know me? Do you know my name?"

"It'll come to me," said Salvatore.

"I'm Corporal Jona Lord Joni," replied Jona, "You got a message for me?"

"I do," said Salvatore. He handed a small sheet of paper over to Jona. Jona pocketed it. "How's your girl Mishaela?"

"She's gone," he said. "I think her husband found out."

"They're just gone?"

"Yeah," he said. "Listen, I don't remember so good. I mean, I'm not good for remembering things. So, don't get mad if you have to tell me twice."

"What do you remember?"

"I think… That's all I really want to say about that."

"Aggie. Do you remember that?"

"It sounds familiar."

Jona didn't allow himself to draw back his fist. He just threw it up hard and fast, right into Salvatore's neck. Jona punched him in the throat hard enough to knock Salvatore over. Salvatore looked up, furious.

"Every time you forget something important, I'm going to hit you like that. Can you remember that?"

Salvatore had his blackjack out and took a swing, but Jona was ready for it, and dodged it. He grabbed Salvatore's shirt with his free hand and threw him hard into the hay. The match burned up to his thumb and singed him. Jona pinched it out and tossed the dead match into the mud in the yard.

The animals were restless; Salvatore held still. Salvatore had to breathe hard with the wind struck out of him like that.

"Don't think it's personal when it's not," said Jona. "You're going to remember things. I don't have time for people who forget important things."

"I'll have you killed if you touch me again."

"No, you won't," said Jona. "You don't know anything about this, and you'd forget even if you knew. You stay close, Salvatore. You stay close and wait for me to make the move. Have you got the uniform already?"

"Fellow brings it for me in the morning."

"If he doesn't show up, you can always win one in a card game. The kids in these towers got nothing but cards to pass the time. They love a new challenger now and then. They don't know when to stop."

"Fellow'll come," said Salvatore.

Jona bedded down his mule. He lingered in the dark with Salvatore, fingering the mule's ratty mane. "Hey, Salvatore," said Jona.

"I got nothing to say to you, king's man."

"Right," said Jona. He walked out from the stables. He looked over his shoulder at the shadow in the dark. He touched the note in his pocket, and wondered if he'd get the chance to kill Salvatore before the tasks were through.

Jona resolved to kill Salvatore as soon as he was done with him. He wondered if that wasn't the reason Lady Ela Sabachthani had sent Salvatore along. That, or she was trying to help him forget his girl, too. It was easier for Salvatore.

There was a hole in Jona's stomach that knotted up like a black hand holding him hard.

Even now, his skull cries out her name into the dark.

***

The sleepers slept. The night was clean. Jona crept in through the main hall and into a different hall up the stairs. He followed his ears to Franka's room, where the two betrothed rustled in the darkness. He slipped open the door a crack, silently. He looked down on the two of them together, their bodies moving in unison.

Jona heard footsteps in the hall.

He looked, turning his blade in the night. He saw a child in a shadow.

"Go to sleep," said Jona, "It's too late for you to be up."

The kid's shadow backed into a room.

Jona found an empty room. He played cards until the maid came with soft feet to clear chamber pots before morning light. He threw a few coins at the girl's feet. "Sometimes night maids like to earn a little extra," he said.

The girl nodded. She picked up the coins. She peeled off her dress like a dirty washcloth. Her bones protruded at odd angles from her papery skin. Her eyes were black in the darkness of morning twilight.

He looked over the body in the moonlight. "Keep it," he said. "That's enough."

She seemed offended and confused, but she didn't say anything.

"Wait," said Jona. "Franka ever do this?"

She shook her head, *no*. Then, without touching anything or cleaning in the room, she was gone with her clothes into the hall. Afterwards, Jona sprawled naked in an empty bed. He closed his eyes as if he could sleep. He thought to himself that Rachel was sleeping somewhere, surrounded by men who would kill her if they saw her real skin. He stood up and started to pace.

In the city, he could do something to fill his mind. He could find a game of cards and bully the men into handing over all they had. He could find another woman, prettier, and he wouldn't make her sick, but maybe he'd talk to her in a bustling room for a while or have tea with a phony and let everyone lie to each other. He could dance. He could drink. He could find some gangers and knock some teeth.

Out here, all he could do was wait in the darkness and hope it wouldn't rain. When it rained, on the road, he and Nicola crawled under the cart, and waited it out. If the wheels got stuck in mud, they used the worthless weapons to dig and wedge the wheel free. It rained a little every day. When it wasn't raining, there was a haze of damp and bugs that bit at them.

"You want to live out here?" said Jona.

"You smell that air? Smell like animal shit to you?"

"No," said Jona.

"Well, there you go. Anybody try to grind you today?"

"Just you," said Jona.

"I didn't do a thing, Lord Joni. I'm telling you, this is the dream. Land of my own, and a way out of the Pens. The air is so clean I could drink it in a glass."

At all the taverns along the way, when they could sleep in one out of the rain instead of huddling beneath the cart, Jona sat down on the edge of the bed again and waited. He looked over at the useless bed. Somewhere in the night, Rachel might not have a roof over her.

The first guard post was one day's journey past Franka's tavern, but from the top of the tower, the walls of Dogsland were still in view as large as mountains. Sergeant Calipari inspected the place quickly. The boys inside, both young privates, saluted sharply. They had kept their log in order, and smiled at the weapons, even if the equipment was rusty confiscated scrap from hookah dens. Sergeant Calipari adjusted this and that for the sake of adjusting this or that, and within an hour, the inspection tour was on the road again to the next tower and they didn't even stop for a meal.

Calipari wanted to get to his land. They ate hardtack and the apples that hadn't rotted.

The second one had half the wall blown apart and left where it had fallen. The men there slept in tents and wondered when their time would come to return to the city. In the report, Calipari wrote down the damage to the guard tower, and said this had been reported since the war, when a falling war machine had shattered the wall like a catapult blow, but it had come from their own broken siege device. The tower had never been repaired. They traveled farther, until the farms thinned out and the roads were just fallow fields and woods.

These men knew each other too well. They spoke so little to each other. They had nothing to say. Sergeant Calipari was supposed to be training his replacement, and he had given up on the Pens.

(Jona lay back in the cart at night and stared at the naked sky, with his beloved in his eyes among the stars. When they stopped for the night he shuffled off to empty his body of water, and saw his shadow there, following.)

Up the roads north, across two fords, and through the farms and pastures, the cart moved on. Farmers' children walked to the edge of the fence, and waved at the men in uniforms passing through. Nicola pushed Jona from the cart towards one of the women. Jona stumbled against the fence where this beautiful girl in green and brown linen placed her baskets on the ground beside her garden.

"Hello, king's man," she said, looking away and locking her hands together in front of her dress.

"Say hello, Corporal!" shouted Calipari.

Jona bowed gracefully to the woman, as if he were at a ball. "Hello," he said, "my name is Jona Lord Joni, corporal of the City Guard."

"My name is Flower," she said.

"A pleasure," said Jona, rising from his bow.

She eyed him with a raised eyebrow. "Are you really a lord?" she said.

"Yes," said Jona. "Are you really a flower?"

"I've never met a lord before."

"If you'll please pardon me, I have to get back to work. We have to keep the roads safe, and inspect the guard posts. We'll be back this way again soon."

"Are you really a lord?" she said, and then, louder to Sergeant Calipari's back, "Hey, is he really a lord?"

"He sure is," shouted the sergeant from the cart, "He already attends balls with the king, himself."

Jona ran to catch up to the cart. He shoved a fist into Nicola's back. Nicola fell forward. He kept on the cart by pushing against the donkey's backside.

Calipari laughed and laughed, anyway, and Jona never laughed. He never did anything but skulk and wait.

They passed soldiers on the road, out patrolling the highways for the king. The army kept the woods and roads. The king's personal guard kept the towers and the farmlands. Out a few days, the distinction was meaningless. They were men in uniform that saluted each other as they passed. Some of the older men recognized Calipari and shouted at him, and he shouted back.

The worst thing, for Jona, was how there was nothing to do for days but walk or ride or whip the mule. He didn't even know a song to sing to distract himself.

***

At the next guard post, Calipari shook hands with a fellow he had known for years, a sergeant past the last months of service. He spent his days in the guard post waiting for his replacement to arrive from the city, and slept nights in a farmhouse on a ridge where he already had his first crop of wine grapes growing. The old sergeant and Nicola traded war stories for two drunken days.

Jona had to take the old sergeant's shift on the top of the tower, looking up to the top of the far hill, looking for fire. The other guard was a private that had racked up demerits in a fist fight with an officer. The officer used to be a plain corporal, and the fight occurred before the private knew about the promotion. The captain would've arrested the private for striking an officer if it hadn't been for the rank mixup. Instead, the private will spend the rest of his career at this empty station, watching for fire, and keeping his own kindling dry in all the wet rain, with no hope of a decent parcel or of a fleur, or of anything but this.

The private didn't like to talk much. That was fine with Jona. Jona and the spurned private sat on the guard post, listening to the two sergeants singing old songs and pissing all over the broken furniture in heaps beside the tower and shoving each other.

The sun set beside them all. Jona and the private of the tower stared north, to the top of this hill covered in pine. The blue sky misted in orange and purple. Evening twilight, and the two men sat there, looking up to this spot on the hill in the distance until it became a silhouette of a tower rising over the trees, like a giant land creature with four fat legs and a jagged back. Ahead was the last tower, at the edge of the woods that Dogsland called her own. Beyond that tower was a red valley that took so long to heal, and beyond that terrible boundary was a new city's lands. Jona knew that an army was coming to that tower, and he looked out ahead to the watch tower's horizon, seeking out the lines of smoke. There were none.

"Have you ever lit the fire?" said Jona, to the private.

"Aye," he said. "Once it dries off a bit, the raiders come. Only getting too wet for an invasion. Can't march horses in mud. Can't do anything with the mud."

"It's not raining tonight."

"It will," he said. "You wait. There's already clouds for it from the west. It'll be a hard one, too. Ocean's over that way, I hear, and it always sends the worst this time of year."

After nightfall, the spurned private lit a pipe. He puffed away quietly. It smelled so peaceful. Then, it smelled of rain. The heavy rain fell hard, flooding the roads for a day. There was nothing to do but wait and watch the hills for the warning fire.

Even in the worst of the storm, birdsongs drifted away to the cadences of bugs. And owls in their trees gently cooed their territory in the dark. And wolves far away howled to the waxing moon, my husband and I and our pack were smelling something wrong traveling the woods, but we did not know it yet and our place in Jona's death had not begun.

Jona took a deep breath in the dark, while the private fell asleep beside him. He closed his eyes. He held real still, smelling rain and the sweet damp of the pine forest hills.

He wondered if this was like dreaming.

Tomorrow was another day. Calipari rested in the back of the cart with a damp cloth over his eyes. Jona drove the mule.

They kept a pile of paper in a heavy leather sack to keep the rain out of it. They kept a series of reports about their inspections. Calipari filled them out before they left each station. They were destined for a room of files where they would be skimmed quickly by a clerk and filed away.

Calipari shoved coins in Jona's pockets. Calipari had led them off the path to this barn on a little milk farm.

Jona stumbled into the dark. He had a flask in his hand. He hadn't tasted a drop. He listened to an old horse breathing heavily in a stall. The stench of cows and horses and pigs was everywhere, but Jona could only sense the old horse wheezing.

An oil lamp crept out of the darkness. The dim light spilled across an anonymous woman. She pressed one finger to her lips.

Jona closed his eyes. He held the flask out to her. She took it. Jona turned away from her. He took off his cloak. He spread the cloak over a low pile of hay and told her just to hold him a while, and do nothing.

"I just want to hold you a while, until you fall asleep. Okay?"

She shrugged. "I could do more."

"I know, and you'd be good, too. But, I can't right now. I don't want it. I just want to hold you and watch you fall asleep. Can we do that?"

She shrugged. Pressed into her, it was all wrong. She smelled like the animals and a little bit like spoiled milk. She felt wrong, too, with too-soft flesh and bones pushing uncomfortably. She snored when she slept. He thought she was faking to get rid of him, and he was fine with that. He left the cloak and the money. It was drizzling outside, and he pulled his collar up. He walked back to where Nicola was asleep under the cart.

Salvatore was wandering these hills, following in Jona's footsteps.

He wondered if Salvatore had some trick to keep the girls from throwing up and trembling all pale and terrible as if they were giving birth to their own death.

CHAPTER 18

I know this scent.

My husband stops before I do. He smelled it first. He bristles.

Underground, then. There's a sewer grate that's thrown aside, and it connects to many dry lines. As long as it doesn't rain too hard, he would be safe below ground, for now.

Not for long.

***

Salvatore and Jona checked in with each other in the dark.

Salvatore waited, leaning into a tree. He had a brand new guard uniform on, with the rank of private, and who knows how it got there from the city, but there it was.

"Have you found out where we'll need to do this?"

Salvatore shrugged. "I've been making the signal, but no one's come out of the woods yet. I don't know where they're crossing the valley or if they're going around. Horses fight to go around. I can see their camp fire smoke. They don't care much for who sees them. No one thinks they're coming in the rain storms."

"I'm getting tired of waiting. We're half the day from the last watch tower. We'll settle things before they get here. If they're coming, they're coming."

"Want me to bring you the message and tag along?"

"Sure. After this, what's your plan?"

"After this?"

"Yeah, we do this job, and then what do you do?"

"I go back to Dogsland. My contacts there let me do what I like. What else should I do?"

"I don't know. Maybe you could try to... you know, figure out what happened to you. See if you can find your history somewhere. Go east. You look like an easterner. You've got the nose for it."

"No, thanks."

"Well, I heard when this is over, I'm going to get married to a rich woman."

"Do you love her?"

"You care about that?"

"I was married once, I think."

"Did you like being married?"

"I don't know. I'd do it again if I could find the right girl, which I guess means I liked it. I don't know if I have kids or not. I don't think I do. I don't remember any. You going to have kids?"

"Maybe," said Jona, "Maybe, someday. I'd better head back."

"Bye."

"Hey, whatever you do, don't kill Nicola. The guy I'm riding with? Don't kill him, okay?"

"Oh, I'm no blood monkey," said Salvatore, "I don't kill people."

"Right," said Jona, "Right, I forgot. Well tell the others not to kill him for me, okay? He's mine. I want him."

Jona didn't want Nicola to die when the time came. Jona didn't want anyone to get hurt, but he knew blood was going to spill soon.

The last tower on the northern edge was the end of the way things were, for him. After that, he'd be a decorated officer, field commissioned, and marrying the future queen.

(Of course, he died in these woods.

He saw Rachel again before he died.)

***

We found the lair at last in the labyrinth of sewers underground. It was the same hammock, attached to a wall, replaced when it wore through from the acid sweating from his skin in this hot, damp tunnel. He had stale food hanging from bags in the ceiling, rigged to keep the rats out. He had lived like this before. He had tools for the job of living in sewers.

We disturbed nothing. We slipped into the darkness and into a dark corner that was free of his scent. He would return home. We would hear him.

We held very still.

Below the street, the muffled echoes of the city came down to us through the stones and the mud. It dripped like the water through the grates, and empty chamber pots and trash, that were the muted remains of a life, poured into the earth. Do you see the end of Salvatore's life in all this noise? Do you hear it? I'm writing in the dark, and waiting. It's hard to write, but I can see enough in the streetlight. I have the ink under my wolfskin cloak and the paper. I write, and I wait.

I can only imagine what he is feeling, now, so separated from the patterns of his life, with no one to guide him. He's adrift, and hiding.

I can only dream of his life as Jona knew it.

I can write it down.

Wait, I hear him coming here to hide. I know it is him because Jona recognizes the sound of his footsteps inside of me.

It's him.

CHAPTER 19

Calipari and Jona returned to the road. Calipari drove the cart during the day. Jona drove it into the night.

When the whip would no longer move the cart an inch, it was time for them to stop. The driver unhooked the donkey, and let the animal wander off into the woods. If it was after dark, Jona followed with the lamp held over his head. When Killer realized he was lost, Jona dragged the animal back to the cart where Calipari was sleeping like nothing had happened at all. Then Jona fed the animal hay and oats from the back of the cart, which usually woke up Calipari. Calipari was sleeping on the back.

The first night on the road, Jona was driving the cart and Calipari was sleeping on some hay piled in back like a bed.

Salvatore stood in the road in front of the mule. The lamp illuminated his boots first. They were shiny as patent leather. The mud hadn't seemed to touch them at all. Jona saw his hands held up in the dark. Jona nodded at him. Salvatore had an envelope in his hands, too, with the official seal of the king. A forgery, of course, but a good one.

Salvatore walked around the mule. He handed the note to Jona. Jona pointed at Calipari. Salvatore nodded. Jona turned to his partner. "Hey, Nic, wake up. Hey, Sergeant?"

Sergeant Calipari bolted up fast, his hand on his sword. "What?"

he said, "Why'd we stop? It isn't my turn, is it?"

Salvatore bowed. "Rush message from the captain himself, for Sergeant Nicola Calipari and Corporal Jona Lord Joni. That you two?"

Calipari frowned. "What?" he snorted. He pointed at Salvatore in a muddy uniform. "Who in Elishta are you?"

"Private Salvatore Fidelio, Sergeant," said Salvatore.

"Fidelio? Never heard of you."

"Never heard of you either," said Salvatore, "Are you the sergeant on patrol, inspecting watch towers?"

"I am," said Calipari. Calipari adjusted his clothes until his twisted-up cloak and the clumps of mud and hay fell away to reveal his sergeant's rank.

"Message from the captain, sir."

Calipari snatched the letter. He looked over at Salvatore. "How'd you get it out here?"

"I walked straight from the city."

"We had a cart and a mule."

"I had no reason to stop and inspect a watch tower if you weren't in it. I moved fast. Took long enough to catch you anyhow, all this way."

"So, that's it then. Off you go."

"I'm supposed to come with you."

"What? Why? Does the captain want me to send him a response? Captains don't ask sergeants for a response. I can't believe he wrote me a note at all!"

"I'm just doing what I'm told."

Jona laughed. "Good morning, Sergeant," he said, "Waking up in a cart is worse than a two-day piss gin banger."

"I don't need this, Corporal," said Nicola. "I don't need messages from the captain. I don't. Bloody Elishta, but I don't..."

Calipari tore open the envelope. He read the message. His brow furrowed. "Straight from the man to me, and sealed. Toss me to the Nameless. Roll me into the bay."

The more he read, the more his brow furrowed.

"We got a bad bird, Jona, singing for the wrong city."

"A bad bird? Who?"

"I don't know. It's one of the fellows at the next station. We find the bird. We do him in fast and send our boy... Whatever his name is, here, to replace the dead bird. I know this corporal up at that station. He's been here forever. I don't know who they got him with this time."

"You think it's the corporal?"

"What's that guy's name... Kapelli? Matteli? He's useless. He got corporal in the war and a few medals because he got out alive, and he hasn't done anything since but wait for land." Calipari turned to Salvatore. "What's your name, Private?"

"I'm Private Salvatore Fidelio," said Salvatore. Then, as a mumbled afterthought from his thief slouch, "Sir." He looked like a man in a costume. Jona wondered how Calipari couldn't see right through the dirty disguise. Maybe he did, but it was a letter from the captain in his hand that had him thinking he was part of something bigger than he wanted on his last patrol before his parcel.

"Right, Fidelio," said Nicola. "I don't know you and me and the corporal go way back, so you hang back and wait for us to finish our investigation. You don't talk to anyone, got it?"

"Sir," said Fideli.

"How long ago you finish training, Fidelio?"

"I'm new."

"You ever kill anybody?"

"No, sir."

"You got green all over yourself. I can see it from here. Stay out of the way. This is a bad business. I'll handle the execution myself. Finishing the business like this. That's me. Blood had to be my way out from the Pens."

Jona smacked the reins, and the donkey kicked into life again. Jona looked over his shoulder at the two men in the cart. "Hey,

Nic," said Jona, "you gonna let me have a piece of him, too? I'm so bored, I'd break them both just to pass the time."

Calipari said nothing. He re-read the note in his hand. He put it in his lapel pocket. He grabbed a stone from his pocket. He hocked a fat ball of spit onto it. He dragged his sword across the stone.

Jona waited, and when nothing happened, he kicked the reins. The donkey started to walk again.

Salvatore did his best to lie down and sleep with the mule cart bouncing around the road.

Calipari was an old hand at sharpening his sword in a cart. Not once did his hands slip in a bumpy rut.

***

Howl with us, dogs, for the victory of Erin.

My husband is very sick.

He said he would not die for me.

I knew it was a lie.

We are human, still. We wear the skin of the wolf, but it is not who we are.

In the darkness of the sewers Salvatore came. He carried bread and stolen jewelry. He had no fear in his eye, and did not know to be afraid. How could he remember fear of death? How could he even remember he was alive if he could not remember his benefactors?

He came into the darkness, then. We swept over one side and then another in the sewer to surround him before he knew we were there.

"Please," he said.

He's mine.

No, he can see you. Let me.

"Please, I want to live."

I want to kill him.

That's Jona. That's not you.

He must die.

"Please, I don't... I don't know what you are... Big dogs... Elishta... But your eyes..."

My husband pulled the wolfskin from his back and stood tall. He lit a match and threw it onto the ground, where the sweat and urine of the demon caught the flame like lamp oil, burning against Salvatore's skin and clothes.

Salvatore backed up, smacking at the flame, then he saw me behind him. He jumped ahead.

My husband opened his arms. "Come here," he said. "Everything will be all right. Everything is fine, now."

Salvatore stepped towards him, while I howled and swiped. I missed. He dodged me.

Don't talk to him!

"She won't hurt you," he said. "She's just angry, but it will pass. I have come to help you, friend."

Salvatore stepped towards my husband.

"Look out," he said. He grabbed Salvatore and pulled him from me. I was pouncing and snapping.

Salvatore was so scared of me that he did not see the blade enter his back from my husband's hand. I saw him take the blade. I saw his gasp and shock.

"Please, no..."

"It's done," said my husband. The blood poured out over his hand. I felt its power, and my eyes watered and my throat closed up in pain.

"Please, I want to live!"

"Hush, now," said my husband, holding the knife. He eased Salvatore down. "This isn't your fault. You did nothing wrong. I'm sorry for you."

The blood was all over his arm, eating up his clothes and burning his skin.

"I don't want to die," he said. His voice was weak and pinched.

"Everyone must die," said my husband. His throat was closing up. Blood was coming out of his eyes and he fell beside Salvatore. "Everyone dies," he said.

Salvatore whimpered and started to cry. Then, he stopped crying.

My husband held his clean hand up to me. "Stay back," he said. "Get the fireseeds."

It was the last thing he said before he vomited blood.

The fire from the ground stain was touched by the blood. It spread.

No time.

I bit into my husband's boot. I dragged him over the dirty rocks and mud. The fire caught the body, then, and dug into the blood. The noxious smoke filled the little hall, and stained a black, thick stain that would last a thousand years upon those rocks.

My husband knew I would drive my teeth into the demon child's throat. He knew I would taste the blood.

He knew me.

He had turned Salvatore's body away from me. He had pulled him back from my claws and teeth. He had taken the blood upon himself, instead.

I did not die for you. Don't write that. I'm still alive.

You could have died.

I didn't. I'm just very sick. We both could have died and we didn't. I will heal. Nicola Calipari has healed. He took Jona's blood upon his face and neck and went without your care for weeks.

We are men, more than we are wolves, my love. Jona was not as close to the source as Salvatore. At least, we don't know how close he was to the source of the stain. You love me and sacrificed yourself, as Jona did. We serve the world of men as no true wolf could. We are Walkers not wolves. We stand on two legs and walk these lands as man and wife. You are my husband, and my beloved. I would die for you, old wolf...

Don't.

Just as you nearly did for me.

I am a wolf that wears the skin of men. That is all.

He rolled over. The wolfskin was pulled across his back, and he turned from me, with his ears twitching.

***

The guard tower at the edge of the dead valley used to be the altar of arcane mysteries that Sabachthani used to cast his wicked magic. The giant bowl of mortal blood was covered in sticks and doused in kerosene. Soldiers had hammered a rough roof to guide the rain away from the pile unless a hard wind blew. The lord that owned this particular hillside preferred to keep his grape vines on the other side of another hill. He didn't like to risk poisoning his wine so close to the dead valley. On a windy day, the red dirt soared up the side of the hills leaving a small trail of dead and dying plants.

When the rain came—and a little rain came every day—the poisoned earth leaked into the groundwater, and flowed into the ocean.

My husband and I had spent countless weeks experimenting with methods to break the spell without ingesting the dust ourselves.

We still seek our solution to this day.

***

When the three men got to the final tower, Jona gestured at Salvatore to wait outside. Sergeant Calipari opened the door as if he owned the place. He stomped inside, and coughed at the stink of two men living in close quarters. Piles of animal bones rotted in a heap in the corner with the husks of vegetables and broken dishes. The two men had their cots on the other side.

A table had a deck of cards abandoned mid-game. One of the chairs was broken, and someone had shoved it under the table.

Someone was sleeping in his cot. Someone else was undoubtedly up on the top level, staring out across the red valley, and watching for fires from the other towers.

Jona found a lamp next to the barrels of kerosene against the far wall. He dug around for a new match, and after he lit the match, Sergeant Calipari had already pulled out the broken chair. He was trying to fix it so someone could sit down in the chair. The seat had cracked in half, and one of the supports had been completely ripped out. Calipari rolled his eyes. He threw the broken chair in the corner with the remains of food.

The sleeping fellow rolled around from the wall.

"Who's there?" he said.

"Your vigilance is an inspiration," said Calipari.

"Nicola Calipari, that you again so soon?"

"Hello, Corporal."

"Haven't seen you in a long while."

"It's been a year. I get stuck with this detail because no one thinks the Pens needs a sergeant for long."

"Well, inspect away. Try not to be too loud. I'm trying to sleep. I have to take night watch tonight."

"Get out of bed you lazy oaf. I want you to meet someone."

"I'll meet him later."

"Get up! You're about to meet Lord Joni."

"Who? A lord?" said the sleeping sergeant. He rolled back around. He sat up, rubbing his eyes. He had a wide face, and a neck creased with fat. He had the kind of puffy features that push up against the seams of his loosely-buttoned uniform as if it had never fit. "Did you bring me some kind of joke?"

"No," said Calipari, "I told you. I brought Lord Joni."

Jona bowed gracefully. "Corporal Lord Joni at your disposal, sir."

"A corporal? A lord? I'm going back to sleep, Nic. Make your-selves at home."

"At least introduce yourself first."

"Howdy, Corporal Lord Whatsit. I'm Corporal Belari."

"Come on, that's not all of it. How many medals did you win in the war?" said Calipari.

"Seven," said Belari, "but I don't win medals anymore. I just watch the hills and wait for something to happen. When it does, I light the torch for the soldiers to come and stay out of the fight-ing. Me and Nic fought together, you know, way back when. How many medals you win, Nic?"

"I didn't win medals," said Nic, "you know that. I was just a kid. Kids don't win medals. Mostly kids were fodder at the front of the line."

Belari laughed from his chest like he was wheezing. "I forgot," he said.

"I run the Pens Station now. My girl and me are getting mar-ried, and got ourselves a nice farm southeast of here already. How come you ain't out, yet?"

"I stayed in the army too long." He rolled up. "You bring me anything good?"

"I got something for you. Your partner up on the roof. What's his story?"

"Him? Terrible card player. Terrible temper, too. He broke the chair. Private Ginoa. He's been here about six months."

Jona glanced over at Nicola and nodded at him. "I'll go up and say hello," said Jona. He tested the ladder before he started to climb it. He adjusted his cloak and his sword. The wood bent and groaned beneath his boots. The wood stank like it was rotten and needed to be replaced.

On the roof, Jona opened the trapdoor. He looked around for Private Ginoa. The private had his back to the trapdoor and didn't turn around.

Jona snorted. "Aren't you going to say hello?"

Ginoa glanced over his shoulder. "I'm on duty," he said, "What're you here for?"

"Inspection."

"You need anything from me?"

"No."

"Good."

Jona nodded. He walked the perimeter of the roof. He looked down at Salvatore, waiting below with the mule. He nodded at him.

Jona pulled a knife from his boot. Private Gino turned at the sound of the sheath.

Jona shoved his knife into a chunk of wood. "Checking for water," he said, "You keep these dry?"

Private Ginoa turned back to the hills. "No, the fat one does that." Ginoa yawned. "You bring us anything?"

Jona stepped up behind Ginoa. "No," he said, "You like it here?"

Ginoa scoffed. "What do you think," he said, "but I sit a bit and maybe I get to do something else later. Better than scriveners or stock boys, right?"

"I was a scrivener. I never sat a watch tower or walked the roads before," said Jona. "You're right about it being better out here than scrivening. It's easier work." Jona pointed out at the dead valley. "That's a strange thing to see," he said. Ginoa shrugged. He stared across the red sands, with Jona's hand.

"As long as nobody's crossing it..." he said. "They come once a year, and we light the torch and we make a break for it. My partner does it every year. Says he has a great hiding spot on a hill below one of the bluffs."

"What bluff?" said Jona. "Can we see it from here?"

He turned to point.

Jona's hands left the scenery. He snatched Ginoa's hair. Jona sliced Ginoa's neck as fast as a hawk crashing into a pigeon.

Ginoa breathed in. He clutched at his neck. He held a hand in front of his face, with all his blood. He tried to breathe in again, but he couldn't breath.

Jona slid the knife down Ginoa's back, looking for a crevice in the ribs. Jona pushed the blade into a lung.

It was so quiet now, on that tower.

Ginoa clutched at Jona's leg with one hand. His other flailed in the air. Jona had a strong arm on Ginoa's shoulder. Jona held Ginoa where he was on the roof, bleeding. Ginoa's legs struggled to fall forward, away from the knife.

Jona held on, careful to keep the blood off his uniform.

When Ginoa stopped struggling, Jona gently placed him back on the roof. Jona wiped his hands off on a dirty handkerchief. He tossed the handkerchief into the wind. He signaled down to Salvatore.

Salvatore nodded, and walked to the edge of the cliff. Salvatore waved at the cliffs, and then clamped his hands together over his head. He repeated this until he saw a small cloud of dust on the edge of the red valley.

Jona went back downstairs to Calipari.

Down below he found Calipari standing over the corporal. Jona caught Calipari's eye and pointed at the elderly corporal. Calipari pulled out a sword. He placed it against the corporal's throat.

"You sure?" said Calipari, to Jona.

Corporal Belari leaned back in shock at the naked blade. "What the…?" he said.

Jona sighed. He walked around to stand behind Calipari. He placed a hand on Calipari's shoulder. "No doubt in my mind," he said. "The other fellow was a rookie right off the training ground. You think he has time to build up a network when this fellow sees the raiders come every summer to skirmish a little?"

Calipari frowned. He held the blade up to Belari's throat. "You been betraying the city?"

"What?!" he said.

"Have you?" said Calipari. "Because the captain tells me someone here is betraying the city. Lord Joni, who is a lord and noble-man come to investigate, makes you the birdy to the north."

"It's not me," he said, "It has to be Ginoa."

"Why?" said Calipari.

"Because it's not me!"

"It's him," said Jona, "Private Ginoa don't even know what the word 'birdy' means yet. He's only been in a bit. You're the one been here forever, wondering what to do with yourself when you retire."

"It ain't me."

"I'm with Jona here, Corporal. My gut is telling me it's you. You been a leach on the city for years."

"Prove it."

"Captain's word is all the proof we need. It's either you or… what was the kid's name?"

"Ginoa," said Jona.

"Right," said Calipari, "So did you ever slip anything to any-body? Maybe you look the other way when a fellow crosses the dead valley. Maybe you keep a record of the boys you meet pass-ing through and pass the info along."

Corporal Belari leaned back from the blade. "You already made up your mind? Why don't you push the green boy on the roof a bit? Why don't you give that a shot? I'm going nowhere. Where would I go?"

Jona shrugged. "I know a good boy when I see one. That's what it's like when you're as bad as me. I come up out of the Pens like Nicola, and we're bad men, Corporal. Captain sends us to do bad things."

Calipari pulled his sword back. "I'm already sick of this assign-ment," he said, "so hold still while Jona ties you up. It's time we have a faster conversation."

Jona pulled a rope from the supplies. He wrapped it tight around Belari's arms and chest. He kept wrapping it in one long bind down to the legs against the chair.

Calipari put his sword away.

Jona picked up a hammer from a pile of tools in a sack in the corner. "Which hand you want to start with, Nic?"

Nicola rolled up his sleeves. He looked down at Belari's trembling hands. The man's mouth was clamped shut, whimpering. The sergeant shrugged. "That one ain't shaking so much," he said, pointing at the left.

"Right," said Jona. He swung the hammer hard, smashing Calipari on the back of the head. He did it again, quickly, before Calipari could register the hit.

Calipari fell forward. He blinked in shock. He reached around to his head, his eyes rolling. His knees wobbled. He tried to turn.

Jona hit him again.

"Thank Imam!" said Belari, "Thank you. He's crazy. I'm no bad bird!"

Jona looked down at his friend on the ground. He looked around for more rope. He saw none. Belari had all the rope in the building around his wrists and feet. Jona needed it for Calipari.

Belari still hadn't deduced what was occurring. "I swear to Imam, to Erin, to anybody you want, I'm no bad bard," he said. "Please, believe me," he said.

Jona sighed. He placed a hand on Belari's shoulder. "I believe you," he said.

Jona wrapped his fingers around Belari's throat.

The relief on Belari's face dropped like a waterfall. Jona looked the old man in the face while the air died and the blood stopped and the fear swelled up and burst like a dike leaking tears.

The plan was the guards had to go. They couldn't be trusted. Lady Ela's plan was Jona is the only survivor here among the king's men.

Jona knew the plan. He clenched his jaw. He stared this old, worn-out sack of a man in the face. Jona watched and felt the struggle draining from him.

When Belari was dead, Jona tied up Calipari before he could

wake up, exactly as Belari had been tied up moments ago.

In his head, he wanted to scream.

He felt so numb he couldn't stand it.

Calipari was still alive.

The one thing he wanted in the whole city, and he'd beg his future wife for it, and he'd beg her forever, is that Nicola Calipari must live, and Jona wasn't going to be killing anybody anymore unless they had it coming.

It was something human in him that longed for death.

When the raiders came, from the north, they set up camp around the tower. Calipari was bound and groggy, with blood leaking from his nose.

They were expecting everyone to be dead but Jona and Salvatore. They sneered and pointed.

Jona stepped in front of him.

"No," he said. "No, this one stays alive. He's mine to kill. He's mine. You don't touch him. I'm doing him at my leisure."

"We won't talk around him."

"You'll do what I tell you to do and like it. We're too far in to stop now."

"She said you were more trouble than you're worth."

"You and I both know a desk sergeant from the Pens isn't worth much against the word of Ela Sabachthani. I'll take care of him when I'm good and ready. I thought we could use an extra witness. If he's pliable, he's a reputable enough fellow with lots of friends in the king's men rank and file."

Calipari spit blood out at Jona's feet.

"We talk outside. We don't talk in front of him."

"Fine."

The head of the raiders was called Moose by his men. He didn't look anything like a moose. He was the shortest man in the room. He had a thin body, and his hands weren't particularly rugged. He had tiny spots of ink stains in his hair, behind his right ear, as if he was in the habit of scratching himself with his own quill when he was thinking. He wore the same stiff leather armors as his men, but the only weapon he carried was a small knife, conspicuously plain.

"We have one week until the patrols come this far again," said Moose. "When we return with prisoners, it's important for you to remain inside. If they see you alive, we'll have to kill all of them, and start again. We're in a race against time, here. The army tends to notice two dozen men in the woods taking prisoners for an enemy city."

"The plan seems a little elaborate, doesn't it?" said Jona. "I'm supposed to chase you off in the night, free some prisoners and make a break for it?"

"Some of the prisoners will be us. You'll be safe enough. She doesn't want you scratched."

"What I mean is that it's elaborate. Why not just send me out here and make up a bunch of nonsense and run it through the criers. Nobody'd know the difference."

"The soldiers would know," said Moose. "The soldiers who will be cleaning up this mess will know. As king, you need to think wider than a few narrow streets. We're here to put on a good show. You stay inside with your prize. If you can't turn him, let us know. We'll fix the problem for you if you don't want to get your hands dirty."

"I got my hands dirty already, fellow. I'm so dirty, all the rain in the night won't work. Nothing works. You ever see me coming for you, you're rolling into the water no matter what. I'm rowdy enough to scare the Lady Sabachthani. That's how come she's sweet on me."

"I have heard good things about you," said the man. "We can work with you. We can even trust you a little. That's why I didn't have someone killing your man while we chat. There will be no trouble here. I will not have any trouble. We know what we're doing. The King of the Night is more dangerous than you, even out here on the edge of nowhere. Don't say stupid things where other people can hear you. You stay inside."

"Try not to kill too many people," said Jona.

"What?"

"Be careful, is all I'm saying. You know, so there's plenty of survivors to sing my name on the street."

"It's bloody work we do, and you had better leave us to it. You've got your own unfinished bloody work."

Moose and Jona looked over at the door where Calipari, bound and bloody, waited with death written on his face. Calipari wanted Jona to be dead.

CHAPTER 20

We could piece together the events from the tracks. This hill has this precise curve. Raiders love high ground. They stand there. The road curves below the hill like a stream running around the height. Most travelers are grateful to avoid climbing up the hill.

The horses were grateful for the curve of the road. The guards that walked beside the cart didn't mind much either. There were two guards, and Djoss, which makes one for each cart. The caraven master led the first cart. His son led the second. The third cart was driven by a tired looking old man that whistled when he talked through a gap in his teeth. Rachel hid in the shadows at the back of the last cart. Raiders often liked to come at carts from the rear, take as much as they could carry and run back into the woods. Rachel sat at the last cart, watching the road behind.

The first volley of arrows struck the horses of the first cart. The animal on the hill side screamed. It tried to jump from beneath the yoke, but only managed to push the other horse to the ground.

The arrows of the next volley seemed to descend from the clouds in slow motion. The guards had gazed with open eyes at the raiders. The merchant had maintained his seat and tugged at his reins as if his horses had stumbled in holes.

The second volley struck the driver of the second cart—poor

boy—with two arrows through, one in the face and the other in the arm. He died. (We found him dead in the woods and buried him before we found Jona lying in a bluff. There were others dead from these raiders, and what we didn't bury, the forest took just fine on its own.)

By now, the merchant had come to his senses enough to smack the reigns. One horse tried to run, but the other was jumping and tearing at his yoke, unable to use her front legs at all with arrows in them. The cart flipped, killing her, and the yoke broke free for the horse that had jumped. He bolted, blood down his sides.

One of the guards had decided to run up the hill after the source of the arrows. Djoss jumped behind the second cart, a shield over his head made of the top of a crate. Rachel had poked her head out from the third cart, looking to see what was happening. She jumped out of the cart, and gasped for air, looking around for Djoss.

The third volley struck one guard in the ankle, crippling him.

The merchant, by now had found his legs beneath him, and a spare pickaxe from his cart. He hid behind the toppled cart. He probably screamed something, but we don't see words in the mud.

The fourth volley landed hard across the third cart. The horses were hit, as well, and both of them died very quickly. The man driving this cart made a break for it, away from the hill. A single arrow chased after him, and missed.

Now, the raiders jumped out from behind their hiding places on the hill. They were armed in light leathers, and long pikes. They quickly formed themselves into a line. They charged down the hill at the carts.

Raiders do not traditionally operate with military precision.

Djoss and Rachel ran to each other. Rachel conjured powerful fires and startled the raiders. Djoss deflected one pike with his crate top, and smacked another with his hard fist. Rachel tossed strong winds over the raiders. They fell back, and found themselves buried beneath a wall of ice.

The merchant jumped out swinging his sword. The pikemen stabbed him in both legs. He fell to the ground, and bled out, dead in a few minutes, to be buried with his own son by the roadside.

Rachel ran to Djoss, pulled water vapor from the air, and froze it in a ring of ice.

The raiders watched, amazed. They chipped at the ring with their pikes, hesitating against Senta spells they hadn't seen in times of war. Senta are not warriors this far south.

Djoss frowned at Rachel. He probably told her to kill the raiders. She probably told him she wouldn't kill anyone.

The raiders did not expect much in the way of magic, but they had their answer. When the ice was chipped back, they swore they'd kill Djoss if Rachel didn't come peacefully with anyone else that had, by now, surrendered.

The raiders slaughtered the horses for meat, pulled anything edible from the carts, and anything they happened to want, and then they pushed the carts off the road, and set fire to them. A few ran off into the woods to look for men that had escaped the volleys of arrows.

The raiders numbered at least thirty-two hard-scrabble soldiers. An absurd number for any legitimate raiding party, and the violence made no sense when most would easily just take what they wanted from the carts that were outnumbered and let the people pass on.

The raiders kept their base outside the tower. When the prisoners arrived, they were kept on a rope chain, tied hand and belt and foot, all together.

Rachel had been blindfolded, like everyone else, so she couldn't aim her powers at anyone. She sat sullenly in the mud, waiting for something to happen, bound to the beginning of the rope, against the tower.

CHAPTER 21

"Believe it or not," said Jona, "I saved your life."

Calipari said nothing. He couldn't. His mouth was filled with cloth, and wrapped with rope to hold it in like a horse's bridle.

Jona pulled a bottle of brandy out from a bag the raiders had given him. It was horrible brandy, more rancid water than heat. Jona drank it in little, wincing sips. When he had to relieve himself, he went up top to the signal fire. He'd have to leave it dry, but he wanted to dampen it with the brandy that had passed through him like a flood. He had to piss as best he could in hiding in case someone's blindfold was loose.

He paused when he saw the prisoners bent on their knees in the sun. Wounded bodies wrapped in bandages and ragged clothes and numb faces waited with naked dread beneath the blindfolds torn from dead men's clothes.

Jona was thinking about Sabachthani's promise. She said everyone would live. That's what she had said. As soon as this passed, he wouldn't have to kill again if he didn't want to. But, here he was on the brink of killing again. He looked out at all the people who had survived the killing that had come because of him.

He saw a familiar body at the edge of a chain of prisoners.

Jona looked closer and closer, and the pain swept over him.

The figure of Djoss slept in the sun, tied to a man's corpse.

Djoss leaned over the dead body like a pillow.

The breath flew from Jona's chest. He cursed.

Rachel heard his voice, up against the guard tower where she was bound separated from the rest of the prisoners.

She cocked her head. "Hello?" she said.

Jona cursed again. He scurried back down the ladder, into the darkness of the tower, and Calipari tied to a chair.

These raiders were going to kill most of the people on the chain. Jona wasn't supposed to save all of them. No one would believe a miraculous rescue, only a desperate rescue.

Back in the room with Calipari, Jona paced furiously. Then he looked down at Calipari. Jona pushed Calipari awake. Calipari didn't flinch. He snorted from behind his rags.

Jona thrust his fist into the wall next to Nicola's face. The punch was weak. Jona sat down in a corner. "I know you don't believe me," said Jona, "but I hate this more than you do. I hate it so much. The woman I love could be killed. I don't know what I'm going to do. I don't want to hurt anyone, Nic. I really don't. Sabachthani will be queen. There's nothing we can do to stop it. We just have to stay out of the way, or help it along. I'm helping it along, all right? Bloody Elishta, but Rachel's out there, and they might hurt her. They might take her off somewhere and… Nic, I don't know what to do!"

The sergeant said nothing. He couldn't with the gag.

"Do you think she might foresee her death, and escape somehow? She's Senta, right? She can do that, can't she?"

He mumbled a grunt.

Jona yanked the gag out.

"Nicola, say something. I'm trying to keep everyone alive over here."

"You brought this on yourself, and on me," said Nicola, at last. "I got nothing to say to you, Jona. Corporal Lord Joni, I don't think we have anything to talk about again."

"Nic, I'm trying to save your life, here. I can bribe you. You swear to sing the song we give you, and you retire and take a parcel with all the coin Sabachthani can muster. You and I both know that the Pens was never where anyone cared about anyone. We had to make our own way. My father was killed for treason, his lands taken, and it wasn't true. We have to fight to get along. I had to fight, Nic."

"I got nothing else for you, Jona."

"Lady Sabachthani is the one running all the demon weed. I opened a shipment and saw it with these eyes. Dogs with their tongues cut out, chewing on demon child bones and infected with some kind of vine growing out of their bodies. It's her ship. She wouldn't deny it."

"So what if it is? Arrest her."

"You arrest her."

He snorted. "You dropped good boys like nothing, and you won't drop a bad noblewoman?"

"If I hadn't done it, you'd all be dead."

"This is your grand scheme. You kill king's men right here, and think I'll help you do anything. How many of my good boys have I watched die, huh? I've lost so many boys didn't deserve it in the Pens, and you drop two like nothing."

"I need your help, Nic."

"You will hang," he said. "If I don't kill you first, you'll hang."

Jona paced. "I can offer you money. Be a tavernkeeper, not a farmer. Be anything you want."

Calipari closed his eyes.

"Be a nobleman, for all I care. I can make that happen."

"You just tell Franka how I died, and who did it. You look her in the face and tell her you betrayed me and the king and everything we've lost so many good boys over. How many coffins burning in the bay? How many boys don't come back for morning muster? How many good people hooked into the sewers with no one to claim the corpse? Ain't you seen enough death? I haven't. Not until I see your death. Dropping two good boys like they're animals. I heard things about you, Lord Joni… Terrible things. I didn't think you was so deep in the pinks. I didn't think you was so deep."

Jona sat down. He grabbed at his stomach, feeling it flip and turn.

"I'm not like you, Sergeant. I can't sleep at night. I never could."

The two men sat until nightfall, feeling sick. One more day, then another. Then, when the king's soldiers came calling, Jona would have his great victory.

***

Nightfall, he walked carefully on the balls of his feet through the grass at the edge of the guard tower. He felt the mortar stones scraping away the mud like jagged fingernails.

Rachel was asleep, and the rope around her wrist attached to the wall of the guard tower. The rope along the guard tower extended all the way around, resting in the mud and grass where the building met the dirt.

Jona crept until he saw her. She was on her side in a small patch of grass. Her hands remained bound against the main rope. Her eyes were covered in a cloth torn from the bottom of her own dress. Jona cut her blindfold first, with one swift cut of his knife. Her eyes were half-open. They rolled back in her head like broken marbles. Her mouth hung limp in sleep.

He placed his hand over her mouth. Undoubtedly, the taste of mud filled her dreams. She woke up, gasping for air.

Her eyes focused on Jona's muddy face in the dark.

"Hush…" he whispered.

She nodded. He cut her hands loose from the main rope. He took her hand and led her into the tower.

***

Calipari was drifting in and out of uncomfortable slumber, strapped into his very uncomfortable chair. He told me about it, but he couldn't remember words.

He told me he saw Jona covered in shadows. He saw a woman, wrapped in filthy cloth. He heard voices, murmuring softly as if an invisible wall muffled the sound between them and him.

He couldn't tell me what they said.

I must rely on Jona's memory.

"Jona, I don't know what's happening. What are you doing here?"

"It's complicated. I don't have time. They're going to try to kill you, Rachel. Calipari, too. You're both too dangerous to them."

"Jona, what's happening? What are you doing here?"

"Look, it's complicated. Just give me a minute to get dressed."

Rachel placed a hand on Calipari's cheek. She started to tug at his bonds.

"Don't," said Jona, "Please…" He pulled her hand away from Calipari's bonds.

"Jona," said Rachel, "We have to get Djoss."

"We can't," said Jona, "Look, we just can't. I'm going to have to hide you somewhere. The roof, maybe. When it's all over, I can take you back with me. Just trust me."

"I don't trust you, all right? I can't. Not now." said Rachel, "Please just tell me what's happening."

Jona told her that the men came for him. He told her that all these soldiers running murder through the woods were there so Jona could defeat them, free the hostages, and return to the city a hero.

"That's not very heroic," said Rachel.

Jona pulled his uniform on over his muddy skin. "It's… This is the way it is, okay. You make it sound like I have a choice. I don't. I'm just a pawn. I'm done, though. I'm done with all this. I want to get you out of here. We'll go, you and me. They'll try to kill me for it, but I'm done. Please, will you go with me?"

"Why would they kill you?"

"They'll kill you if I don't hide you."

"What about Djoss?"

"I don't know. I'll try. Look, I just want you to be safe, and to leave with me."

"But Djoss…"

"Please, just come with me. Please, I love you."

"I won't leave Djoss to die. You would ask me to do that… Thank you for saving me. I'll never forget you."

"Please, Rachel…"

"I'm going to save Djoss," said Rachel, "so whatever happens, stay out of my way." Rachel closed her eyes. She took a deep breath. "I'm so scared, Jona."

"Please…" said Jona, "Let me come with you."

"What?" said Rachel.

"I'll leave everything. I'll just leave everything. We'll go out there, and get him and escape together. Please, Rachel, I have to be with you. I love you, and I have to be with you."

"Jona… Oh, Jona…" She centered herself in breathing. Emotion drained away from her face until she was a mask of breathing. Senta fire caught the bonds that bound Calipari. He saw them and held them up to be burned.

"Rachel, please…" Jona had to sit down. He looked at Calipari's bonds burning. He looked at Calipari's killing smile. "Rachel…"

She was already halfway up the ladder. "This is a future that can never be. I cherish the time we had together. I do. I don't understand how you could cause so much pain. Good-bye."

Rachel climbed up to the roof of the guard tower. Behind her, Calipari's bonds burned. The signal fire at the top of the tower caught Senta fires and ignited in the night.

The raiders below, most of them sleeping, did not understand what had just happened. They were asleep, complacent in the plan that was working, and then their dreams filled with the smell of smoke.

Two bandits charged in from the fringe, screaming about the lit signal fire. Eyes looked up. Bandits woke up.

Rachel wrapped winds around her body to soften her jump from the roof. She filled the ropes of the prisoners with fire. People tore at their burning bonds.

Rachel filled the air with fire and ice to catch and stumble the men who would kill in the night. Swords were wrapped in ice. Arrows were blown away. Fire burned at clothes and grasses. Prisoners tore from their bonds with new life and fought back.

The prisoners outnumbered the guards three to one.

Rachel threw tongues of flame in every direction, and cast ice in thick chunks upon weapons and arrows that fell with the weight. She screamed Djoss' name. She ran through the fields of death and flame.

Jona heard the sounds of battle. He grabbed his sword. He shouted at Calipari to help him. He threw a sword at Calipari's lap. He ran his sword down the ropes and sliced them loose.

Calipari roared. He swung his sword at Jona, striking the air only.

Jona threw the door open, his sword in the air. "Help me, Nic! You have to save these people!"

Jona ran after Rachel. He turned his blade to the men that jumped at him. He didn't know if they were prisoner or bandit. He knew they were attacking him. He knew they were in between him and the center of the fire.

Rachel had her arms around her brother. He limped against her, shaking his tight legs loose. He had been bound tight for days, and his muscles weren't working right, yet.

And Jona ran after them. He charged bandit archers with his blade, and they ran in fear of the man that had turned on them too soon. He cut them down, screaming her name. Their arrows would not fall on Rachel's back. The raiders scattered that were left, but Calipari was coming. He was out the door, and staring down Jona, who had betrayed him. He was not fast enough, and it was dark out, and the hills were long.

Rachel was gone as soon as Djoss was on his feet.

"Rachel!" shouted Jona. He leaned into the treeline, where the grassy hillside above the valley faded into wooded bluffs.

She turned once, in the dark, and saw him leaping into the woods. She lifted her hand and a wall of fire rose up from the underbrush.

"Please, Rachel!"

She shouted, "I don't know what you are. I don't know anything about you!"

"Trust me, please!"

She cast wind that pushed his feet out from under him. He fell and banged his jaw on the ground. He bit into his cheek, and felt blood sizzling out into his mouth. He spit and kept after her.

"Please, Rachel, I can't just let you go like this!"

The ice came next, and it swallowed his feet and hands in a weight that pulled him down. He struggled to walk with the ice cracking off his ankles.

"I don't know who I am, Rachel. I don't know what I am. I don't know anything, but I'm so tired, Rachel. Elishta, but I'm so tired."

"Good-bye, king's man," said Djoss.

Jona stumbled forward after her, crawling on his hands and knees. The violence had ended behind him. The raiders had run off into the night. The prisoners were free. The signal fires burned over the hills calling like bells in the city streets for hard men to come. Jona turned to look back at the mess he had made of his life.

His only thought was to leave. He had lived in Dogsland and suffered for it every day of his life. He wanted a new life. He wanted to go somewhere no one knew him, and he could start over brand new, a nobody with nothing to mark him.

He wanted to be born brand new, an infant with no past.

Calipari filled the stars with the darkness of his shadow. He grabbed Jona's throat. The ice that clutched at Jona's hands made it hard to fight back. Calipari punched Jona hard in the face, and held Jona's throat closed.

Jona couldn't bear to fight back.

He tried to tell Nicola that he was leaving, to just let him go, but the fist descended and darkness came. He wasn't dead, yet. He was resting for the first time in his life.

CHAPTER 22

I watched him a long time like that.

Did you pray for him.

I don't think so. I wasn't praying. I was cursing him, a little. I was wishing he was already dead. I was wishing I didn't have to kill him. Mostly, I was watching him unconscious, and telling myself that if he just stopped breathing and didn't wake up that would be for the best. I didn't want him to wake up again, because I didn't want to spill my friend's blood.

Then you were praying, and you didn't know it.

I don't know what prayer is.

A curse is a prayer of hate. A wish is a prayer of hope.

He was my boy. I spent years with him, down in the worst of the Pens. I spent years with him, and he does that. I had so many dead boys. I wish I could kill him again. I wish he was still alive, but not so I can kill him again. I want him to be alive. I wish he hadn't done what he did, and I wish he was alive. Also, I'm glad it was me that killed him, and I wish it wasn't me.

It's all right. You did the right thing. They're hard things to do, but you were right. He betrayed the king, the city, and killed so many good men. Do you know when he started killing for the Night King what he was doing?

No.

She didn't want anyone else to throw a party to compete with hers.

She had her loyal demon child wipe out anyone that accepted another nobleman's money until the merchants and the nobleman figured it out.

He killed a lot of people?

Innocent people. He died, Nicola, and it was right that he died.

Every one of my boys was a little dirty, though. The Pens is dirty. You know, I can't imagine what it's like to wake up and not think about all the terrible things I've seen down there. When I was dying, before you came, I had nightmares.

They're gone now.

***

"What did you see when you were asleep, wicked fiend?" said the sergeant, holding a rusty sword to Jona's chest.

"I think…" said Jona, squinting into the black night above his head. "I think I had my first dream."

"Your first dream?" asked the sergeant.

Jona closed his eyes. "I don't sleep. I never sleep. My blood doesn't let me. My dad was a demon child. My granddad was, too. I am. I don't sleep. I never sleep. I was born with wings my ma cut off. But, I think I was sleeping, just now. I was lying in water. It was so cool. I looked up at the sun and it was hot, but the water was cool. I was just a boy, like I was just a boy again. I was floating in the water. I looked over to the beach and Rachel was waving at me. She was so beautiful there, and she was waving at me. Then she was my mother. Then, she was someone else. I thought… For a little while, I thought it was real. I started to swim to her. Then…"

"Then you woke up?"

"No. Then, there were horses. Thousands of them. Every time the waves broke upon the shore, the white foam was horses. It was so beautiful. I was swimming to shore, and I ended up on a horse's back. We charged up, past Rachel, past the forest, and into the darkness. Into the… Then…. Um… Then…"

"Already, the dream fades."

"I can't… I don't remember. Rachel always remembered her dreams."

"May the Gods absolve me, Lord Joni. You killed innocent men. You caused so much death out here."

"Please don't, Nicola. I'm just going to leave. I'll leave Dogsland, and I'll walk away and I'll never come back."

"No," said Nicola.

The sword pushed through Jona's chest. The blade was cold and hot at once. Jona felt the strange sucking of blood-loss—but painless at first—and also he heard the sucking sounds in his ears, echoing up his bones, like two separate things. Was his body really making these sounds? Was that him? Is that his blood? He looked down on his skin, and saw his hands twisted in pain and shock. He saw the blood pouring all over his chest. He felt his eyes fade to nothing. His eyes fell back into his head, and rolled out of his own wounded neck. His eyes saw a puddle of blood, and red and red and red. Then, a strong wind came and picked up his eyes, lifting them up.

And then Jona saw the whole forest, and the whole city, and everything in the whole world. He was above everything, and it was so beautiful.

It was so beautiful, that he wanted to cry, but he couldn't feel anything to cry with. No skin. No teeth. No tears.

***

Weeks later, my husband and I found this child of a demon— we found his body. He called out to me from Erin's sacred rocks.

Where is my body?

Where is Rachel?

***

And what of Rachel Nolander and her brother, Djoss? They traveled beyond the red valley, but the demon weed ran deep inside of him. He would never truly leave the city. He couldn't. He would come back to the city, seeking it. He would lose his tongue and ears in the night, trying to find it. He would forget himself, and become forgotten in the city.

If Rachel is the person Jona loved, than she would return for her brother. She will be in the city pulling him from the sewer and cleaning his face when he has slept in mud.

We do not search for her there.

The hills call to us.

The forest and swamps and mountains sing night music, where all the creatures of Erin sing as loud as they can their song of joy.

If she is not in the city, she will be found.

That will be enough to quiet the lost soul that haunts me still, and will be with me a long time. Jona, this will have to be enough.

Rest, now, lost child. Find your peace.

***

Calipari's farm was far from a road. My husband and I stopped in at the tavern where Franka used to work, and already they had disappeared into the green hills.

The tavern keeper told us what direction they had taken. He didn't know where it was, exactly. A farmer on his way into the city knew and pointed to familiar landmarks. He told us we could wait for him to finish his business inside the walls and he'd take us on his cart.

We thanked him. We pulled the wolfskin over our backs and

darted into the treeline. We would find the farm ourselves.

We followed bear trails through the marshlands dodging bramble canes and the roots of high sour nut trees that rooted shallow enough to trip a man in the water. We ran into the maple hills above the mud. We howled to the moon, and to our pack, but they were both too far from us to hear.

We missed the wolves of our home.

Through the maple hills and the myrtle marshlands and to the northeast and northeast my husband and I ran, until we came upon a sweaty back digging fence stumps on barren ground. Nicola Calipari didn't have a shovel. He was using a small, flat plank to dig.

He was surprised to see us.

I stood up, a woman. My husband stayed wolf and sniffed the perimeters of the farmland.

"Hello," I said.

He dropped his stick. "You're back, huh? Anything else I can do to help?"

I bowed to him.

"Never thought I'd see you two again," he said, "Still hunting?"

"No," I said, "Salvatore Fidelio is dead. We were unable to find Rachel Nolander."

"Who?"

"If you encounter a woman named Rachel Nolander, tell my husband and I which way she went."

"That's the Senta Jona was with, right?"

"Yes."

"What about Jona's mother?"

"Her head was on the wall when we crossed the gates."

He nodded. "That's it, isn't it? Anything else?"

I looked around his farm. He had a few sticks beginning to look like a fence. He had a plow under a makeshift hut to keep the rain from rusting it. He had a dirty tent where—I assume—Franka kept house. Her son was in a tree, pulling at acorns. He had stopped when he saw us. A man could live a long time on acorns, if he washed away the bitter in the nut.

"You have no animal to pull the plow?" I said.

"Coming soon, if my neighbor is honest." He looked back at the fallow fields. This was a farm before the war, but so many farms in this borderland went abandoned when the armies clashed here. "I've got a wagon coming, too. Wagon has the grain and seed. I bought it all from this fellow Franka knew. Good price." He grimaced. "I think it was a good price. I don't know Bloody Elishta about farming. He's getting it to us soon. He better."

"What will you grow?"

"Some barley, and some beans. Franka wants a separate garden just for vegetables, but we got to get a good cash crop down first. We should get chickens, too."

"A pig might be wiser, for now. Pigs can forage in the hills on their own, and when they are big enough, you can cure the meat to last all through the rains when the fields flood."

"Pigs, huh?"

"Pigs," I said. My husband disappeared around some trees on the land. "You did a great service to Erin when you killed the demon child. Then, you served us again when you wrote your maps and letters for us. The church is grateful. I shall arrange some pigs for you. They will help you through the winter. Collect their dung for the barley fields. Collect your own shit, if you can. You'll need everything you can to feed the fields. Bury everything there."

He scratched his neck. He looked around his farm. "You don't think the wolves'll get to the pigs, do you? I've been hearing wolves all night for weeks."

"We are the only wolves in these hills," I said. "Our brothers and sisters are on a long hunt past the red valley. We howl to them, far away. Your pigs will be safe from us and our kind this winter, at least, if not the next."

He nodded. He looked down at the hole he was digging. He

kicked at the misplaced dirt. He looked over his shoulder at the boy collecting acorns from the tree, who had stopped for us. We still frightened him. He stayed in his tree.

I looked directly in his face. "Are you and Franka married, yet?"

He shrugged. "We're married because we say we're married. Same thing as having someone else say it over our heads, isn't it?"

"Is she here?"

He nodded. "She's asleep. She's been working at night her whole life. She's not used to this farm stuff. We're just not used to it."

"Take me to her," I said.

He nodded. The mud sucked at my feet. Human feet were not padded and wide like wolf feet, and all the weight digs into the sharp heel. The mud grabbed at my feet. I felt clumps of mud leaping up my back when I tugged my feet free.

"Has it been raining?" I asked.

"You can't tell?"

"Farmers speak of rain," I said, "Thus, I ask of rain. It is polite."

"Yeah, it's been raining. Well, I don't know if I'm going to be able to do this," he said. "Franka's in there. She's out hard as a pinker. She won't wake up for me unless I bang a pot over her head, and she's not well enough to work so why bother. I say let her sleep."

I heard my husband's padded feet galloping to us.

I peered into the tent darkness. I lashed the flaps to the side to let light in. She was spread out on a clump of rags on the ground. Her chest rose and fell slowly. Her stomach had swollen since last we had seen her. She would give birth before the end of the season.

I touched around her stomach gently and sniffed at her skin. She was fine. She was with child, and the babe was healthy even if the mother was weak.

"Has her pregnancy been difficult?" I said.

"Like I'd know that," he said.

"So it has been difficult?"

"I guess it has."

I patted her stomach. I touched her cheek. I leaned in close and whispered a blessing into her ear.

Her breath held still. Her eyes opened.

She batted at my hands. "Who the bloody Elishta are you?" she said. She pulled away from me, and grabbed at her muddy blankets.

I smiled. "I saved you from a foul disease, Franka, and I came to check on you and your farmer husband."

"Oh," she said. "I'm sorry I didn't recognize you." She touched my hand. "Oh, please, can you be around when my time comes? There's no woman out here."

"Perhaps," I said. I ran a hand through her hair. "Are we in the wilderness then, with no woman to help you? Where does such a place begin, if not here?"

Where does the wilderness begin? Where does it end? An eternal traveler, I have stood on the high mountains and gazed down at an endless woods like Erin's own gorgeous dress. I have seen the small infections in the emerald horizon, where men have lit campfires eating into the green skirt like moths burping smoke. I have opened a door in the tallest tower of the tallest palace of a gigantic city, and butterflies and roaches and mice and birds and lizards all looked up at me as if humans had no place in their wild home.

I do not know where the true boundaries lie.

I know where I am at peace: when the rain falls on my head and the only boundaries between sky and me are tree leaves or stone escarpments on a rock face. I do not trade for meat or fruit there, I merely take it. I do not tell stories of ancient heroes around a campfire. I am too tired from the hunt. I have no fire because my fur and my pack keep me warm. I spread my paws out across the ground, and I sleep in blessed peace.

I think the wilderness is where things happen and no one writes about them. It is the place where there are no maps, no memorials to heroes, no gravestones, no paper, and no ink.

I have had enough of paper and ink.

My husband and I have done all we can with these demon skulls, and demon stains. We return to the wilderness now.

May the blessings of Erin come upon us all.

***

Once upon a time, Salvatore looked out the hole where he used to have a hallway because he heard all these sounds that woke him up. He peeked his head out to see.

A huge herd of cattle, a hundred head at least, marched down the center of the street in one long blur of brown spots and swaying horns and lowing. Dozens of drovers surrounded the herd. The men swiped listlessly at the cattle with whips. The cattle didn't seem to mind. They walked in that gentle, plodding way that cows always walk until they caught the smell of the abattoir. The aborted canal had changed the path of drovers from the docks. It made noise. It woke him.

In the street, the people stopped to let the cattle pass. They couldn't get across. People who couldn't get across jammed the people who were going up and down the way. Salvatore looked down, and saw Jona in the street. He backed away.

Rachel stopped to kiss Jona on his lips. Her eyes stayed open. Djoss stumbled out of an alley. She saw her brother down the street. She froze.

"What?" said Jona.

Rachel pulled away. She let her hands fall down his arm, down his hands, down his fingers. She let him go. She sighed. She said nothing to Jona.

Her brother's hands had been trembling.

"I have to go," she said.

Jona reached for her. "Go?" he said. She had already moved

on. She didn't look over her shoulder at him. "Go where?" he shouted, "We're going dancing!"

She was already gone, past the crowd bottlenecked around the herd of cattle like water catching in a drain.

THE END

ABOUT THE AUTHOR

J. M. McDermott is the author of six novels and two short story collections, including *Last Dragon*, *Never Knew Another*, *Women and Monsters*, and *Maze*. He holds an MFA from the Stonecoast Program at the University of Southern Maine.